T.J. RYAN

Between the Lines

First edition

ISBN: 9798834251040

Editing by Manda Waller
Cover art by BookCover4u
Proofreading by Oliver Asante, Dale Martin & Julie French

This book was professionally typeset on Reedsy.
Find out more at reedsy.com

For Oliver,
Thank you for being a great friend and confidant.

"Don't you think it's better to be extremely happy for a short while, even if you lose it, than to be just okay for your whole life?"

— Audrey Niffenegger, The Time Traveler's Wife

1

Tessa

I always used to say I was never the type of girl to have casual hook-ups. I couldn't say that any more. How had this happened? No, I knew how this happened – too many multi-coloured shots and the dangerous combination of gorgeous brown eyes and full lips.

So embarrassing.

I took a few moments to stare up at the ceiling. His arm draped lazily over me. I took a peek at him. Yep, still gorgeous. *How do you even look beautiful asleep?* Yes, I'd describe him as beautiful. He was the definition of tall, dark and handsome. His muscular build was ridiculously flawless, his dark skin smooth and unblemished. His lips were slightly parted as he breathed softly.

I knew nothing about him except his name. Jonathan. Not even his surname. My mother would disown me if she knew. Thankfully, my phone was nowhere in sight. I groaned at the thought of the missed calls and texts waiting for me. Nope, that could wait.

As gently as possible, I inched out from under his arm.

I shifted my body to the edge of the bed, easing out from underneath the duvet. He sighed but otherwise remained fast asleep.

Clothes. Where the hell are my clothes?

I practically tiptoed across the unbelievably lovely hotel room. My experience of central London was minimal. My university was the extent of my knowledge. This room, though. Oh, wow. The furniture, sofas, and even the bed were pristine white. The place just breathed money. God, I must stick out in the Mandarin Oriental. I shot a quick look at the humongous bed – Jonathan was still asleep.

I pulled on the crumpled dress from the night before. Red. The irony was not lost on me; scarlet letter may as well have been written over that dress. *No, it's the 21st century, and guys do this all the time.* I hastily dressed as quietly as possible, self-conscious whenever I made a noise louder than a breath. Then I fished out my phone. Ignoring the messages, I deliberately avoided looking at the senders' names as I swiped them aside. I booked an Uber. Only a twenty-seven-minute drive back to Whitmore University. Who would've thought there'd be no traffic in West Minister at this time. The gods must be on my side.

The bed dipped slightly as I pulled on my heels. My heart stopped at the sound of a low groan behind me. Of all the things to wake him. *Please, go back to sleep. Please, please, please.*

He grunted and, with a soft snort, rolled onto his side. He was sleeping like the dead.

"Thank god." I breathed as I finally clipped in the clasp of my heel and gingerly made my way to the door, bag in hand. My stomach dropped when I realised I had no jacket. It would be freezing outside. My eyes fell on his discarded leather jacket on a plush armchair. No, I was not going *Single White Female* – that was the last thing I needed, coming off as a stalker and a weirdo.

Instead, I eased the door open and crept out. My escape victory was short-lived, because I bumped into someone as soon as I turned away from the door. The tallest woman I'd ever seen stood before me; her scowl seemed permanently etched onto her face.

"S-sorry!" I stammered before the giant could even open her mouth. My face burned at the exasperated look on her face. Like she knew exactly what had gone on in the room I'd just sneaked out of.

"Watch where you're going," she barked, her eyes narrowing at me. "Is he awake?"

She was speaking to me like I was his minder. I had no idea how to respond. Who was this anyway? His mother, grandmother? Parole officer? My stomach lurched as I frantically searched my memory for an ankle tag, then I realised how stupid that thought was. There was no tag. Of course there wasn't!

Besides, he had to come from money to afford a room like that. Unless he was in, like, the mafia … Had I just slept with the mafia? I stopped that train of thought in its tracks. My phone beeped – my Uber driver was outside.

"Er, no." I blushed, weaving past her and hobbling to the lift at the end of the corridor.

Fucking heels!

I punched the elevator button, sighing when it opened almost instantly. I rushed inside and resisted the temptation to glance at the door where the giant was watching me leave – judging me with those piercing eyes. I only felt like I could breathe when the doors closed and the lift began descending.

The Uber driver, Aisha, was a few years older than me, pretty without make-up, and her bright pink hijab was the same as her Uber picture. I slid into the backseat, relieved to see the hotel in the rear-view mirror growing smaller a moment later. It had been fun, but this – I couldn't do this again, it was so not me. The knot in my stomach was terrible. Not because of the sex or the guy himself, but I felt like I should be ashamed of myself, like my mother's judgemental eye followed me wherever I went.

To add insult to injury – because I love to torment myself, obviously – I swiped my thumb over my phone screen and checked the mountain of messages. There were a lot of them, mainly Ivy wondering where I was and if I was okay. Except she managed to include several swear words in each message:

IVY: WHERE THE FUCK ARE YOU? DID YOU LEAVE WITH THAT BLOKE???

IVY: Bitch, just let me know you're safe. I don't need details, but do I need to go *John Wick* on your mystery beau?

IVY: FUCK, YOU KNOW WHO THAT GUY IS? ANSWER!

As if I had summoned her, Bloody Mary style, the screen declared Ivy was trying to video call me. Reluctantly, I swiped to answer.

"Hiya," I said, my airy tone doing nothing to improve the scowl on Ivy's face. If that girl wasn't studying to be a playwright, she could easily have been a model. Her dark complexion and box braids always looked perfect; she was easily the most beautiful person I knew.

"Don't you 'hiya' me, Teresa Jane Granger," Ivy said, making me cringe at the use of my full name. "What the hell were you thinking? No call, not even a text. And with him! Christ, after

I'm done killing you, I need details!"

Ironic how the tables had turned. Usually, it was me criticising her for going off with tall, dark and handsome strangers. Something she said caught my attention, though. I frowned.

"What you talking about?" I asked, not getting the look she was giving me. "He's just some guy."

"*Some guy?*" she repeated incredulously, so loud I caught my Uber driver's frown in the mirror. "Babe, you and lover boy are trending on all the socials!"

What? That was ridiculous. I must have said that aloud because the screen suddenly blurred, closely followed by several pings in my messages. I cautiously opened the app, and all the wind was knocked out of me. Captioned over a picture of me and Jonathan No-Surname dancing at whatever club we were in, leaving no room to misinterpret it as friendly, was: ***HOLLYWOOD HEART-THROB JONATHAN ADEOLA SPOTTED WITH MYSTERY GIRL!***

My mouth seemed to have been robbed of its voice, which was a relief because Ivy would only see my gormless face frozen in disbelief if I was back on the video call. Who? What? How? How could I be so, so stupid? I hadn't slept with the mafia; I'd slept with an actual real-life celebrity and had no clue.

"You honestly had no idea who he was?" Ivy asked, seeming to correctly interpret my silence. "He's starring in that film version of those books you loved back in school. Thought you knew. Assumed you planned on fulfilling a role-play fantasy or fetish."

"Eww! No, of course not!" I retorted, whacking my phone back on the call app to glare at her. "I had no idea that was even being made into a film, much less that I'd shagged the lead actor."

That was partly a lie. I knew the film was being made and had made a conscious decision to avoid all news on production or casting. The book-purest in me didn't want to see one of my most beloved reads tarnished in a Hollywood flop. Big mistake there, clearly.

"So, you *did* get to hit that?" Ivy called out that minor detail. My crimson face told her what my voice refused to. "Right, I need proper details after I kill you."

The screen switched to an incoming call. Ivy might have to get in line to murder me, especially if my mother had caught a whiff of what had occurred last night. I groaned to myself, bracing myself for the volcano.

"I got to go. I'm on my way back to campus – promise." I didn't even wait for her response when I switched between calls, putting the phone to my ear. "Hi, Mum!"

"WHY" – her voice shrieked, so much so I had to hold the phone away from my ear, and yet she was still audible – "are you on the front page of every newspaper?! Who is that boy?"

Honestly, I had no idea – yet I would never, ever admit that out loud to her. Instead, I mentally tuned out while she read me the riot act on feminism. I sighed. I was such a disgrace.

2

Jonathan

"Up!"

The cotton landing on my face before I could even let out a groan felt more like a slap. My head ached, and my mouth was dry. Unbelievably dry. I groggily removed what I realised was last night's T-shirt from my face. I cracked one eye open – only to be blinded by sunlight as the last person I wanted to see flung the curtains open.

Mia Robinson surveyed the mess of my hotel room, disdain in her grey eyes as she scanned the empty bottle of complimentary champagne, saw my clothes strewn across the floor like evidence of a crime scene, and seemed to sense adult activities had happened here. She was more like a hybrid of my handler and my mother rather than just an agent.

"Fuck's sake!" I glared up at her and buried my face in the soft pillows, realising with slight surprise that I was in this massive king-size bed alone. I hadn't been last night. My lack of clothes under the duvet confirmed that.

"You do know you have an interview with *Teen Vogue UK* and several other media outlets?" Mia asked tightly, tucking a strand of her blonde hair behind her ear. Funny, I didn't think I'd ever seen her look so disgruntled. If she weren't old enough to be my nan, I might fancy her on a good day. She rarely had one of those.

"That today?" I asked lazily, flopping back on the pillows and stretching. My muscles ached, but I merely forced a yawn. Mia looked like she could spit real fire. Instead of reeling it in, I asked, "Where's that girl? Tanya … no, Tessa?"

"If you're referring to the brunette who made a quick getaway, she left as I was just coming here to get you." Her tone was crisp. Her lips tightened as a cocky grin spread across my face. She knew better than to ask. The truth would most undoubtedly shock her. "Is it too much to ask you to be prepared?"

The edge of disappointment in her voice brought me up short. I had intended on leaving the club early. Honestly. Then I saw I was trending on Twitter. You'd think I'd be used to this, regardless of whether I was in an upcoming film, or whether I was bedding some upcoming actress or actor, which – although I'm not gay – I still found a bit of a stroke to my ego.

But I was instead having my feed bombarded by little keyboard warriors, all of whom were just flat-out racist. I'd been cast in a young adult adaptation of N.K. Yoon's fantasy series, *Awaken – Harry Potter meets Buffy*. It was an okay read and the author herself was more than happy with my casting. Yet we had these idiots who couldn't wrap their heads around a mixed-race actor playing the leading role. They reckoned I should stick to "black roles".

I know it was stupid. Petty even. But I just wanted to get fucked – in more ways than one. I'd achieved that, so what was the big deal?

"I was just having some fun," I mumbled instead, sounding angrier than I felt. "I am allowed."

"You're meant to be promoting a film. At any moment, the way you look or act reflects poorly on the film production. You know this." I did. She had a point, but I wouldn't let her know I agreed with her. "Ten minutes. Get dressed. We'll grab a coffee when we get there and make you somewhat presentable."

Mia marched out of the room, giving me daggers as she slammed the door behind her. My head throbbed in protest. A coffee sounded more appealing.

As I got out of bed, I debated whether I should just wing it and get dressed without showering. Mia would go for my jugular. I looked good – my lean build from my mad gym sessions was paying off, and my fade cut was on point – but even I couldn't strut into an interview smelling of alcohol and sex.

The drive was slow and increasingly uncomfortable, especially with Mia shooting disapproving glances my way. Very slowly but surely, we made our way through London and towards the hotel where several interviews were scheduled for *Awaken*. Doing interviews with my co-star Willow was not something I minded. She was one of the few women with whom I had a healthy platonic relationship – of course, she was a lesbian. She was also a total professional, and I was at my most comfortable, working on set with her.

I needed caffeine, though. I had my head pressed against the cool glass, feeling soothed by the hum of the car, and the chill coming off the window was enough to put me back to sleep. My closed eyelids flashed with the brunette's face. Tessa, that was her name. Tessa. Strange, it was the first time I'd pulled someone who was not looking for an autograph or an Instagram link – she acted like she had no idea who I was. Maybe she didn't?

Not sure how I felt about that. Suppose it was freeing, to be unknown – just for one night. It was just two people, in the moment and having nothing more than fun. Despite that, it was weird that she was the one to duck out … that was usually my routine. I didn't even know her full name. Ironic. I'd got ghosted. Mad how the tables turn.

When we pulled up outside another hotel – which looked so identical to the last one, my hangover-head debated if we had moved at all – Mia went on her typical warpath routine. As soon as we stepped into the reception foyer, a producer who looked more like an intern rushed over. He had red hair and was tall and slim like he'd had a random growth spurt overnight. His eyes widened, flickering over my body.

He was checking me out. If my head wasn't banging, I'd be politer, or flattered even. But right now, I wanted the throbbing between my temples to ease up.

"Oh. Wow. Okay, hi. I'm Freddie. No. Fredric." Freddie backtracked, presumably wanting to sound more mature and professional. He shook our hands, leading us to the elevators. "Willow is already in make-up. Can I get you anything to drink, Jonathan?"

"Something that has no carbs, no sugar and is fat-free," I muttered, wincing as we stepped into the lift. Christ, were the lights always this bright?

"So, water?" Freddie asked, slightly perplexed. Was he being serious? The look he was giving me said pretty plainly that this was someone who didn't joke about a lot. I tried again, forcing my voice to sound anything but exasperated.

"In that case …" I could feel Mia's death-stare burning holes into the back of my head. The lift started its ascent. "Decaf latte, with soy milk."

"No soy milk, I'm afraid. You can have full, semi or skimmed," Freddie gushed, now looking worried as we got out of the lift and headed down another corridor. What the fuck? We were in the heart of London, and they didn't have soy? Were we living in the Dark Ages or some common shit?

"He'll have skimmed! Make mine a black coffee," Mia cut in, perhaps sensing my frustration. She practically shoved me into my dressing room before I could reduce this baby-faced producer to tears.

The interviewers' faces blurred together, all becoming a jumbled heap of generic questions and fan theories. At first, they thought Willow and I were a real-life couple due to our "spellbinding chemistry" on screen. After the assurance that we were just good friends and Willow was part of the LGBTQ community, the angle changed. This film was now promoting *diversity* with its *rich*, *vibrant* and *diverse* cast. No one asked our thoughts on the book, what it was like reading the script for the first time or even about the helpful insights from the author herself.

No, no one wanted anything of substance. They just wanted to hold us up like pretty props to show off. My arse began to ache as I shifted in my chair but the worst of my hangover subsided after several coffees and countless interviews. Willow tucked her long blonde hair behind her ears – the producers had warned her to keep it long in case we got the sequel greenlit – her grim frown looking how my cramped butt felt.

"Think this is the last one," she said, her look of relief mirroring my own. "So, who was the girl you vanished with?"

"No one special," I said truthfully, but she seemed to fill in the blanks with that knowing smirk. I quickly flipped the topic. "Anyway, how are you and your other half?"

"We broke up," Willow said. The slip of her smile made me feel like a right twat. "We wanted different things, I guess."

"Like what?"

"I wanted a commitment, and she wanted to pen the *Chronicles of Vaginas*. She also said she couldn't be with someone who was pursuing their dreams and felt unsupported in trying to figure out hers."

"Fuck, I'm sorry. If it helps, it sounds like you're well rid."

She gave a small smile, not offended, and I left it at that. I gave her a friendly punch on her shoulder – an easy substitute for a hug. Unless they were moaning my name or it had a happy ending, I wasn't really into physical contact. My family weren't big on feelings – the most emotion I'd learned to convey was when I had three cameras pointed at me and a whole cast and crew waiting.

Yet, weirdly, I felt more comfortable around Mia and Willow than I did around anyone – no unrealistic expectations, and they weren't trying to fuck me for celebrity status. Suppose they're the closest to normal relationships I have.

The final interviewer rolled in – literally, this woman was in a wheelchair. She could have been pretty if she didn't have a face that looked like she was sucking on a lemon. Her eyes surveyed me a moment too long as if she was sizing me up.

"Yana Marcus from *Cine-Chat*." She shook our hands before parking in the space where the interviewer chair had sat. Instead of engaging in small talk while the cameras set up, she pored over her notes in silence. Willow and I exchanged a look, neither having the balls to break the silence. This woman had a rough edge about her.

"Right," Yana said as the cameras started rolling again, her painfully tight smile on us. "I'm here with two rising British stars to talk about their upcoming fantasy romance. But first ..." Her eyes zoned in on me, that tight smile growing even tighter. "Jonathan, you've caused quite a stir among our viewers on *Cine-Chat*. Both on and off set. Care to enlighten us on who you were photographed with last night in Soho? A new romance, perhaps?"

This was totally inappropriate. Which I'm sure she knew, by the way her eyes narrowed. She was testing the waters, seeing how far she could push these questions before we – or our management – backed out. Deep breath, I somehow managed to force an easy smile.

"Respectfully, I'd prefer to keep my relationships private," I said, gaining a smile of approval from Willow. "We'd much rather talk about this film, and what a great experience it was working on a project we both loved so much. That's what we're here for, right?"

"Quite," Yana said, annoyance visible behind that pursed grin. "So, what would you say to our viewers who weren't happy with your casting? Kai's ethnicity is never specified on-page. Is this the production to force diversity when no one has asked for it?"

The anger flaring up inside me was inexpressible. Her placid expression said she was honestly expecting an answer. I took a deep breath. Mia looked apprehensive behind a camera operator as I suppressed whatever insult was on the tip of my tongue. This Yana was a fucking bitch, but if I lost it, all anyone would see was an angry black man screaming at a poor defenceless woman in a wheelchair.

Breathe. Breathe, just breathe. Willow's hand rested on my arm, trying to communicate through touch that she had my back in this. I took another breath. Out of the corner of my eye, I saw Mia having heated words with a publicist. I wasn't going to give this interviewer the satisfaction of knowing she'd got to me.

"I think we need to stop thinking that anything other than straight, able-bodied and white is diverse," I said firmly, causing Yana's eyes to widen instead. "I mean, our entire planet is filled with diversity, and we're proud that our film was completely open-minded with who could play these characters right. The director, screenwriter, producers and author saw something in me that was right for the part, and I got to play a character who had layers and was complex. My race wasn't a part of my character's arc, but it was acknowledged by casting my characters' parents as an interracial couple. We need that representation across the board, and anyone who thinks I should stick to 'hood' movies are nothing more than racists."

"Well, that is a strong word," Yana started, but Willow was the one to cut her off this time.

"It's the truth," she said, and something that could be described as affection swelled in my chest for this girl. "Jonathan was perfect for playing Kai, and he was an absolute gentleman to work with. Anyone who thinks he shouldn't have been cast because the author left it up to the reader's imagination what a fictional character looks like, they need to take a look at themselves."

"That so?" Yana asked, training her gaze on Willow, brazen

now. "And what do you say to the argument that only gay actors should play gay roles? Because let me just say, I find that argument highly void if you – a self-proclaimed lesbian actress – can play a heterosexual character without anyone batting an eye. Is that not hypocritical? Or is this another flaw in the woke culture of today?"

Now, there were many ways this could have gone down: Mia could have stepped in and put a stop to it, I could have kept my mouth shut or let Willow answer the question. Instead, I called her out on her bullshit. I told this passive-aggressive homophobic racist exactly what I thought of her, colourful language included. And all caught on camera.

I'd sat through seventeen interviews and had destroyed my career within just one.

3

Tessa

When I was little, I developed the art of being invisible. It helped that I was the middle sibling of a golden retriever brother and a spoiled sister. The quiet child is the easily forgettable one by default. Add that to living in a small Hertfordshire town with little to do, Mum's attention drifting elsewhere during her messy divorce with Dad, and then I was practically a ghost in my own home. While chaos descended upon our lives, no one noticed that I'd spend hours in the cinema or the library – even getting home at an hour most teenagers would be grounded indefinitely for. No one seemed to care when it came to me. Getting into university was my chance to reinvent myself, to be unapologetically myself.

Yet after my first few lectures that day, I wished for nothing but to be invisible again. When someone talks about you and you happen to walk by, it's nothing like how those cheesy American high school movies portray it. No one is openly laughing, pointing fingers, or throwing out the cruellest insults that come to mind. In reality, a stillness falls over the room, and the silence is more telling than anything you might overhear.

Not everyone knew or cared I had bedded an actor known for playing drop-dead heart-throbs on American TV shows. Okay, I googled him – I'll admit that, but only after the silent judging had got the better of me. It was not like the entire university had labelled me a harlot or something. My life was a blip in comparison to the real world. There were just enough stares to make me feel my stomach plummet to the Earth's core.

"Everyone will forget about it in a week," Ivy said rationally as we sat in the library, the scent of her pepperoni pizza intoxicatingly cheesy. My nose wrinkled as I typed my essay on my laptop. She was chewing her food without a second thought for her figure. God, my mother's rant was infecting my mood more than I thought. She would despise my best friend for not only her love of junk food but the fact she burned it off like it was nothing.

"Some won't. Mum thinks I pulled the Women's Rights movement back fifty years." I sighed, but Ivy dismissed that with a wave of her hand. I glanced again at the pizza she was just polishing off. "Where'd you get that?"

"Freebie for people visiting the campus." She shrugged, completely ignoring the fact those pizza samples were meant for visitors only.

"You're already a student here," I countered. "You just deprived a wide-eye wannabe undergraduate of free food."

"And?"

Her indifference made me crack a smile. She genuinely didn't care what anyone thought of her. I wished I had that ability. Instead, I was the girl who deactivated her entire social media presence over some odd glances and some moronic

DMs. I just wanted to forget last night ever happened. Ivy had other ideas. She had been holding off interrogating me after Mum's rant, and she had been battling an internal war with herself all day.

"Okay, fuck it," Ivy said, turning to face me with a determined look. "I wanted to give you time to process or whatever this thing you got going on is, but I can't ignore the fact you boned an actual movie star!"

"You make it sound so sordid." I groaned, wanting the ground to swallow me whole.

"Sordid sex is the best kind of sex!" she proclaimed loudly, oblivious to the incredulous stares from students a few seats away. "Come on, I need the juicy details! Does he look that good out of clothes? Was he any good, or has he got some weird fetishes? Tell me!"

"What is there to say? I mean, it was good—"

"Wait, yes! That's a start!" She beamed, eager for more details. "How good?"

"It was … nice?"

Ivy's face crumpled. She was horrified, like I'd just uttered a disgusting swear word. My face burned as she struggled to find a response to the blandest answer on the planet.

"Tessa, of all the words in the English language to describe sex with a Greek god of a man – you articulate that night of passion as *nice*?" The word seemed to leave a foul taste in her mouth. She cut me off before I could answer. "No, no, no. You need to do better than that; my great-aunt's Kenkey is *nice*!"

How was I supposed to even begin to describe last night? I doubted Ivy would get it. It was great, passionate even. It was just fun too. I'm not sure what I could say other than that. I'd sound like an utter moron if I admitted he was the best I'd

18

had – granted, the competition was slim as he only had one other to compete with. But still … I tried to stop my mind remembering the way his dark eyes drank me in, how his lips trailed over every inch of my skin, and the way his hands—

Ivy clicked her fingers in front of my glazed eyes. Even though she in no way could know precisely what I was thinking, my guilt must have shown on my face.

"He was good, okay?" I mumbled, trying to brush aside my flushed cheeks due to the library heating by taking off my hoodie. "He … knew what he was doing."

"He made you O, didn't he?" Even though my eyes were fixed on my laptop screen, I could feel Ivy's smirk, and I reluctantly muttered the honest answer she was looking for. My voice was so low she leaned in closer. "What?"

"Twice," I said through my teeth. As soon as I met her eyes, the laughter kicked in. Inexplicably, we were cracking up, unable to control ourselves. The ominous feeling that had taken root in my stomach subsided and eased, this childish moment making me feel better than I had in the last six hours. Ivy leaned on my shoulder, gasping as she tried to calm her breathing.

"Okay, was that so hard?" she asked, but that soon triggered another laughing fit as we both clocked the unspoken innuendo at the same time. My ribs were aching, and my mouth felt like the Joker's by the time we controlled ourselves, hiccupping into silence.

"Happy now?" I reluctantly smiled at Ivy's triumphant grin. At least she didn't go *A Clockwork Orange* on me to get this information. Laughing about it like this made it seem like it was a minor thing. Maybe I—

"Tess!" called a sickly-sweet voice that made my skin crawl.

I didn't even have to turn to see who had sauntered over. "Congrats on being an Insta Whore; it's always the quiet ones. Can't believe you bagged Jonathan Adeola."

Kaitlyn Danvers stood behind us. A Regina George knock-off with her blonde extensions and pointedly perfect make-up. She may look like a Regina, but she had the mental maturity of a Gretchen. Her blue eyes swivelled between Ivy and me, locking on me with a look of damnation.

"Who the fuck are you calling a whore?" Ivy demanded, looking ready to rip said extensions out, right there. I grabbed her arm and forced her to keep her butt in her seat, then met Kaitlyn's gaze coolly, suppressing my own urge to punch that patronising smile.

"I don't have to justify my relationships to you," I said calmly, packing my laptop and books away. "I'm a grown woman, but call me a whore again, and I'll have to rearrange that nose Daddy paid for."

Her hand flew instantly to her nose. A reflex – guess her father *did* pay for that nose. She was taken aback for the briefest moment but recovered with a haughty laugh. I stood with my laptop bag slung around my shoulder and carrying my textbooks, pointedly looking to walk past Kaitlyn. Kaitlyn ignored the hint, not wavering when Ivy got up.

"Didn't think a hotshot would go for this nerdy, whatever it is you got going on." She looked me up and down with vague disdain, but her delayed brain caught up with her mouth. "Wait, you said relationship? Are you actually *dating* Jonathan Adeola?"

"No!" I hastily said, at the exact moment Ivy proclaimed boldly, "Yeah! And what?"

Kaitlyn gazed from one to the other, uncertain of who to

believe. Her eyes widened, and her mouth gaped open, her glossy pink lips somehow still making a perfect O. I didn't give her the chance to voice her questions. Grabbing Ivy's arm and nearly dropping my books in the process, I barged past her and out and into the corridor.

"What the hell was that?" I whispered as we moved through the metal detectors. She waved off my mortification like an annoying fly.

"Oh, calm down!" She laughed dismissively. "A little fable never hurt anyone."

* * *

It seemed there was truth in that statement because I went through the rest of my classes unbothered by interrogations of my celebrity conquest. As the day drew to a close, I headed to my supervising lecturer's office and waited with my printed screenplay in hand. Film Production students were required to produce a final piece for the third-year dissertation – it varied based on your specialist subject; mine was pretty straightforward. Scriptwriting student? Write a script.

They say write what you know, so I did. My stomach still churned at the thought of just how personal this script had become for me. My heroine and I had very similar backgrounds and traits. But whereas Georgina was outspoken and confident, I preferred to sit in the background and be the quiet observer. My protagonist fell for her childhood best friend; the writer has a casual hook-up with an A-list celebrity. Okay, there are clear deviations here and there. I suppose the most similarities are visible in the mother archetype. I doubt even my mother would be able to miss the subtle similarities between her and a fictional character I had written.

It was her, actually, who unwittingly nudged me into writing. As the default introvert of the family, I was usually spotted reading alone or content sitting by myself scribbling a mini-story or character arc.

"That girl," Mum openly boasted, usually after a couple of glasses of red, "she's always got her nose in a book. Sometimes I wonder if I actually gave birth to her; she's too smart for her own good! Trust me, don't be surprised if she's a private investigator or a writer."

Being a writer was way more appealing. Stories were my escapism, and my many trips to the cinema had ignited a love for visual storytelling that only strengthened as I got older. No one in my family understood my passion for screenwriting, but how do you explain the thrill it gives you to write a script and watch it slowly become a reality? Even seeing actors bring to life characters that only existed in your head or on-page, the creative buzz it gives is indescribable.

I waited patiently, relieved when Emma Willis – one of the few screenwriting students on this course I liked – walked out. We gave a polite smile to each other, neither being much of a talker. I gave it a beat, trying not to seem too eager before I entered the office.

I was thrilled to get Amanda Egbe as my dissertation supervisor. She was instantly approachable, with some of our meetings just turning into animated talks about the latest TV show or films. She was a head shorter than me, with cropped hair, dark skin, and Harry Potter glasses that made her almost black eyes look huge. I secretly looked forward to our chats because she never bullshitted and gave upfront feedback, which I always appreciated despite her straightforward nature.

She looked up from her desk, her bright smile making me feel welcome as usual. Finally, something normal to discuss. Celebrity one-night stands? No. Fictional characters that come purely from my imagination? Hell yes.

"How are you doing today, Tessa?" Amanda asked breezily as I sat down, putting out a copy of my screenplay which was currently under the working title of *Innocence.* It had felt appropriate at the time, and now it had just stuck.

"Fine," I lied, relieved that I was speaking to one of the few people on this campus who did not know about my close and personal encounter with Jonathan Adeola.

"Terrific," Amanda said, thumbing through a copy of *Innocence*. "Now, I've had a chance to read your script, and honestly, I think it's perfect for your dissertation."

"Really?" I breathed a genuine sigh of relief, glad I was sitting down because my knees felt weak right now.

"Absolutely," Amanda reassured me, her smile looking somewhat perplexed as she surveyed me over her glasses. "Your writing here is as beautiful as ever. Your characters have a real vulnerability and authenticity, and the dialogue just flows so naturally. I wouldn't expect anything less based on your previous work."

"Thank you, but is there anything I need to improve on?" I asked seriously, the critic and editor in me kicking into gear. In my mind, continuous praise was worse than no constructive criticism at all.

"Tiny details that are easily fixable," she said casually, too casually (which instantly made me start thinking about every direction and line of dialogue I'd written, mentally editing it myself). "But there's something else I want us to discuss beforehand. Are you still considering applying to do your master's at the National Film and Television School?"

My heart skipped a beat at the mention of the NFTS. Since I had written my first ever horrendous short script, it had been common knowledge that I wanted to go to that school. Only the best went there, and every year only ten students were accepted onto the Screenwriting MA. As graduation was drawing nearer and the deadline for the submissions to the National was approaching, that dream was becoming all the more petrifying. Last year, I'd gone around that campus like I had just stepped into Hogwarts – amazed at the facilities and captivated by every word of the head-of-course tutor. What brought me crashing down to reality was meeting the other applicants, most of whom came from money or had contacts in the industry. I was just a girl from a low-income family from a small country town, the first of my siblings to go to university and the only one to have an interest in the arts. How in the name of Gallifrey was I meant to stand out against them?

Plus, there were the financial aspects. My undergraduate degree was currently being paid for by student finance and scholarships, which were based on my academic grades being high constantly. That support could vanish if those grades slipped. Even the thought of trying to pay for somewhere like NFTS with all of that in mind was like being given a hard dose of reality.

"I was thinking about that," I said truthfully, suddenly not wanting to meet Amanda's eyes, "but I'm not so sure I'm what they're looking for."

"Don't be ridiculous! Based on what I've read here, they'd be foolish not to accept you." The confidence Amanda had in me was jarring. "We just need to make sure your application stands out amongst the rest. Now, I think this should be your sample writing – the first twenty pages, in particular, are superb and showcase what you can write visually. The fact you've won a few writing competitions is also good. We just need something to show your writing on a public scale."

"Public? Like one of my scripts filmed and submitted into festivals?"

"In an ideal world, yes, but with the deadline in May and graduation not far off, you really wouldn't have the time."

Another dose of reality slapping me in the face. Lovely. But surprisingly Amanda didn't look deterred.

"What about a script reading?" she suggested, grinning as the idea was forming in her head. "Yes! We'll get together a full cast of actors, and you could stage it during the media production student showcase. You could even direct. That way, no one can take away the fact that this is your work."

"That's a great idea, but I don't fancy trying to get a bunch of students to take one of my scripts seriously," I said, already imagining the juvenile behaviour of several performing arts students. "And no offence, but the acting quality …"

I held off, biting my tongue before I could say something that would be frowned upon. Amanda nodded, seeming to understand all too well what I meant.

"Oh, of course, which is why I think you should look at some professional acting talent," she mused. "Maybe a few name casting wouldn't hurt?"

For one weird, stupid moment, I genuinely thought she knew about last night. I quickly dismissed that fear, noting how calm and nonchalant she sounded. God, I really needed to stop being paranoid. Especially if I was going to try and get a whole cast to take me seriously as a screenwriter – and now it seemed, a director.

"Yeah," I said, slowly finding my confidence the more I considered the prospect of a live reading of something I had written. "Yeah, I think that's a really good idea."

It was daunting and absolutely terrifying. But if I could pull this off, maybe – just maybe – my postgraduate application could make me shine amongst the rest. Maybe my dream school could become a reality.

4

Jonathan

I was trending. Again. Fuck's sake.

I knew it wasn't good when the entire cavalry was brought on board. The response on Twitter had been insane, with one half of the socials condemning me and the other half calling for Yana to be fired for racism. The majority saw this as headline gold, with multiple outlets rewriting and sharing the same story from various angles – the one constant was the screenshot of my face mid-shout, looking furious. It looked bad. Really bad.

Sitting in my parents' ridiculously lavish living room on their massive sofa, I felt like a kid on the verge of getting the lecture of a lifetime. Mother was pacing, unable to keep still as she angrily barked orders in French over the phone.

She was tall and willowy, a descendent of the French New Wave. She had the looks of a Hollywood starlet ageing grace-fully, always dressed properly, and the terrifying personality of a spiteful dictator. She'd been deflecting publicists and reporters' calls like this for the best part of an hour, wanting someone to blame, and she had achieved the impossible and

27

reduced Mia to tears. That sat like a rock in my stomach. I'd rather a punch to the gut than the guilt of seeing her stricken face as Mother let loose.

"*Cette interview était une imposture! La femme a décidé de détruire la carrière et le caractère de mon fils.*" Mother said rapidly, her words coming out in a hiss. She was determined to get Yana's reputation tarnished for her racist commentary. That was tough to do when half of the public saw her as a victim in an "unprovoked" shouting match.

"*Maman, calme-toi. S'il te plaît?*" I said softly, but she shot a look at me and I continued my vigil, staring at the carpet.

"English when your father is home, Jonathan!" Mother reminded me curtly, not giving me a chance to respond before snapping back at whatever her publicist said next.

Oh. The irony of Father's distaste for the French language when he'd married the only daughter of one of the most notorious French directors. He secretly hated the fact Mother had taught me her native tongue from a young age – I reckon he was paranoid we'd bitch about him, and he'd have no idea. On the other hand, Father's story was the stuff seen in movies: while Mother was born into the industry, Father had to build a name for himself. Growing up in the heart of St. Louis, Missouri, he was as poor as you could be without being homeless. Yet, he got a full-ride scholarship to Juilliard and steadily built a name for himself as one of the great African-American actors of his generation.

He caused quite a stir when he married and impregnated Ophelia LeMahieu, a French white director. Michael Adeola was suddenly betraying his entire race by marrying this person his fan base did not approve of. They stuck it out and proved the critics wrong, but I think whatever feelings were between them died long ago. Although it may have started as love, it was clearly just convenient for them now. Hollywood may see them as the longest-running power couple. I see two people who've spent so many years defending their relationship that now they don't know how to have one.

Funny, I'm the son of a Cannes Film Festival legend and a once celebrated rags-to-riches success story, but I can't seem to find my identity within my craft. I have to defend my race, who my father is, who my mother is, the fact I am the prodigy of that union. No one knows what to do with me as an actor because I can't be fitted into their ideology of what I should play. I've had casting directors have the nerve to say "he's too dark, we wanted someone more light-skinned" in front of me, but they all know what they want to do with me if I lose my temper. Just once, one time, I got rightfully upset, and the butterfly effect has been like a tornado.

"Fix it!" Mother shouted at the phone, hanging up and oblivious that I jumped a foot off my seat. She went to the liquor cabinet and poured herself a healthy glass of bourbon, knocking it back in a more masculine way than I'd ever seen any woman drink. She breathed a sigh as she poured another drink, taking her time. Her eyes met mine.

"Would you like one?" she asked, and I shook my head. I'd just survived one hangover; I was not in the mood for another one this soon.

"I'm sorry," I said quietly, unable to meet her gaze. The huff I got as a response was hardly comforting, but I would not expect anything less. She sat in the armchair opposite, nursing her bourbon more slowly.

"Of course you are," she said softly, then almost to herself, "*Tu es toujours désolé après …*"

You're always sorry afterwards. That hurt more than expected. Like she thought I enjoyed this level of chaos always coming my way. I'd deactivated every social account I had online, I let whoever write my statements and I was staying put while they attempted damage control – all without complaining. I opened my mouth angrily to tell her as much, but Dad entered with a red-eyed Mia in tow holding a folder in her hands, and I snapped my mouth shut.

Michael Adeola had the confidence and presence you couldn't learn or fake; some actors just had it. Directors had declared I'd inherited many of his good looks, making me a more "desirable" casting for roles. My face was the moneymaker; my insane workout was the bonus that casting directors creamed themselves over.

Dad's eyes cut to Mum's glass, and his almost black eyes narrowed, but she looked defiant as she took another deliberate gulp. He bit back whatever snide remark was on the tip of his tongue. I envied his self-control sometimes. He and Mia sat on the other sofa; I tried to communicate how sorry I was with my eyes. Mia's small smile gave me more comfort than anything Mother ever gave me.

"Mia has come up with a solution for this entire mess," Dad announced, ignoring the scoff coming from Mum as his eyes remained fixedly on me.

"Marvellous timing, after the event," Mum scolded, her tone indifferent. "Remind me why we hired you to represent our son?"

"Because she's good at what she does," I retorted, glaring at Mum now. "I lost my temper. I shouldn't have let that interviewer get to me."

"But *she* shouldn't have let it get that far!" Mum snapped, her accusations directed at Mia while facing me. "It's like she wants to see you be eaten alive by those media vultures. I mean, honestly, how can she expect you to recover from this?"

"Maybe if you actually listen, *dear*," – the last word sounded physically painful for Dad, but it caught Mum's attention – "you might see how."

Before Mum's next wisecrack could be uttered, Mia got to her feet. Her attention fixed on me, she slowly regained her authoritarian edge.

"The shaky responses online are mixed, that is true. But we can take back the narrative," she said, reading the perplexed look on my face and continuing. "So far, those who have seen the interview in full are rightly criticising Yana Marcus' behaviour. But we need to give the critics something else to focus on. You need a new angle."

"Like what?" I said, still not getting it.

"You need to sell them a story, Jon," Dad said, exasperated that I didn't click even with Mia's cryptic clues. "What better story to sell than a love story?"

Mum roared with laughter, nearly spilling the last of her bourbon on the perfectly white material of her chair. We all stared at her, waiting for her to stop. It only got worse.

"HIM?" Mum gasped, clutching her side as she attempted to regain her regal composure. "Chéri, that boy has been through so many women's beds he lacks the capacity to remember their names. Who will believe that?"

"That's not true!" I said, affronted. Wow. I just got called a whore by the woman who birthed me. Just when I thought I could sink no lower in her eyes.

"They'll believe it," Mia said with conviction, her confidence hiccupping my mother into silence. "We'll give them enough to fill in the blanks for themselves, and the conversation will soon be about love's young dream."

"You want me to pretend to be in love with someone?" I asked, waiting for one of these guys to shout April Fools or something to that effect. Nope, deadpan eyes met my incredulous face.

"You're an actor, aren't you? It'll be only for a few weeks. A couple of months at most," Mia rushed on, looking giddy as she flipped through that mysterious folder. "And we have just the candidate!"

She dropped the folder on the table, revealing – to my horror – a smiling picture of my conquest from last night. Seeing her face, the mysterious brunette with green eyes, made me momentarily speechless. I grabbed the folder before Mum could, shocked to read a complete and detailed background check on a Tessa Granger.

"You've got to be kidding?" I said, dropping the file before I could incriminate myself further by reading any more. "For starters, this shit is illegal! How did you even find this stuff?"

"You told me her name, and a friend of a friend did the rest," Mia said casually. "Nothing is private these days. You know that better than anyone."

I thought back; I had mentioned Tessa's name briefly, in a sleepy sex-haze. *I* wasn't even sure that was her name this morning! Fuck, this makes me look like a fucking stalker. And these morons want to try and convince this girl to pretend to be my girlfriend?! This is madness.

"She's got that girl-next-door vibe the media loves!" Mia gushed, browsing through Tessa's private and personal papers and then handing them to Mother to skim-read. "Single-parent family. Scholarship to Whitmore University. Studying screenwriting. Very down to earth, the media will adore her. Think about the headlines – it could be the next Harry and Meghan romance!"

"Hardly." Mother snapped. "More like 'poor white trash benefits from fortune of one of the industry's most respected families'. Is there no one else?" Mother glanced between Mia and me. "Why this girl specifically?"

"Jonathan and Tessa were already spotted together by the paparazzi," Mia answered. Mother noticed how carefully she'd worded that.

"When?"

"Last night …" I said sheepishly. Both of my parents knew what that meant and the annoyed look they exchanged said as much. "She didn't even know who I was …"

"That's even worse!" Mother exclaimed, spilling the last of her drink onto the carpet. "How are we supposed to trust her with your career!"

"Because if we don't," Dad said, finding his voice in all this back-and-forth bickering, "Jonathan's chances of keeping his role in that film series is next to none. I spent the last hour on Zoom with the director. She wants to keep him, but he'll have to be recast if the backlash continues."

Fuck. That hit home for everyone, including me. All that work, everything I'd achieved, could be obliterated because of public opinion. I could play a part for a few weeks, but it all hung on whether Tessa agreed to play along. After all, she had no obligations to me. She was well within her rights to tell me to piss off.

"Let me talk to her first," I said, which soured everyone's mood even further. "That's the least I can do before asking her to pretend to be my beard."

"We're doomed already then." Mother sighed, throwing me the file before getting up to pour herself another drink. I left the folder on the coffee table. I couldn't go into this with a handbook on Tessa. I was going to be doing enough acting for the press – I needed this girl to trust me if she was going to play the part.

* * *

The timing of this had to be perfect. If we came out with the story too soon, everyone would know it was a cover-up. If we left it too late, the Tessa angle would be yesterday's news. Thankfully, she had miraculously remained anonymous during our media spell, maybe because my horrendous interview was more newsworthy and interesting to readers, and a nobody like Tessa Granger wouldn't capture headlines. Yet.

Mia wanted the hype to calm down a bit first, but that did not seem to be happening anytime soon. The vloggers had got a hold of the interview and analysed my reactions from multiple angles. The hype was now being dissected by a whole new audience. So before Mia could try and talk me out of it, we headed to Whitmore a week after the scandal erupted.

I didn't have her number, and she was a social media ghost, so I was going to be looking for someone I'd met once, in the vague area of where she might be. How did I have nearly three million followers who went out of their way to meet me just for a selfie or a scribble? I never got the appeal, but here I was in a car park, embracing the stalker vibes the situation brought. My sunglasses were making it harder to distinguish a brunette from a redhead. I lifted them slowly, but Mia glared from behind the wheel.

"Keep them on," she ordered, frowning when I took them off entirely and hooked them into my shirt. She tutted when I ignored her. It was nice, seeing her back to her glass-is-always-half-empty-self.

"We're behind tinted windows. No one can see in here," I pointed out. Her silence was the closest thing to an acknowledgement I would get. "We should have doughnuts."

"Doughnuts?"

"Yeah." My lips curved into a grin, sensing Mia's frosty demeanour soften as she got the joke. "Come on, this is like a proper stakeout. You're like Judi Dench's M, and I'm like the black James Bond. Hey, why haven't we had a black Bond yet?"

"Lashana Lynch played double-oh-seven," Mia mused, thinking back on cinematic history.

"Yeah. But she was a new character who just had the codename," I countered. "We haven't had a black actor as an actual James Bond yet. Which is mad because we've had to watch the same generic white guys play the part over and over again."

"Maybe you'll be the first." She paused as something caught her eye ahead. "Is that her?"

My head turned so fast I got whiplash. Yep, that was her. Her face in my memory had been hazy at best, that night a mixture of good sex and too many shots. But in the cold light of day, I could see just how beautiful this girl was – not just sexy in a killer red dress, but actually attractive in real life. Tessa's cheeks were flushed against the cold, and she was carrying several textbooks, careful as she walked over what I assumed was an icy pavement.

"We need to approach this delicately," Mia said, not noticing I was already unbuckling my seatbelt. "We don't want to scare her off."

"Course not," I said, hopping out of the car and giving her a wry grin. "I'll take it from here!"

"Jonathan, don't—" The sound of the car door closing cut off whatever she was going to say next. Before she could get her bearings, I jogged over to where Tessa's back was retreating to what I assumed was the library building. Okay. Don't be stupid. Just play it cool.

"Tessa!" I called, not having the reaction I was expecting. She turned fast, so startled by the unexpected shout that she swivelled and then skidded to the ground. Her books cascaded everywhere, and her head missed colliding with the pavement by a sheer miracle. Whoops.

My grin evaporated as I rushed to help her up. Her eyes widened in recognition, quickly turning to slits of annoyance. She was clearly torn between indignation and pride, trying as much as possible not to lean on me. She stood back, flustered, as she hastily started picking up her books.

"What the hell are *you* doing here?" she blustered, her pink cheeks turning slightly redder as she glared at me. "Is this your pastime or something? Just go around screaming at people?"

"Sorry. I didn't mean to scare you." I picked up a textbook, which she snatched from me. Now she was deciding to put them in her rucksack, logically. She barely looked at me. This wasn't usually the response I got from women after a night with me. Usually, they're gagging for a second round. "I just wanted to say hello."

Tessa looked cautiously at me; judging from how she glanced around the deserted walkway, she was relieved we had some privacy. So was I: I couldn't do this with an audience.

"I'm Jonathan," I introduced myself stupidly, and her raised eyebrows made me want to punch myself in the face. Of course, she knew who I was; I was inside her no less than seven days ago. Plus, not to brag, but I am very memorable in that department.

"Yes. I know who you are. What are you doing here?" she questioned warily. Affronted, I had either implied she was too drunk to remember, or that she fucked actors on the regular, and I was one of many. I shoved my hands in my pockets, feeling my face burning.

"Don't worry. I'm not stalking you!" I attempted humour, her somewhat polite confusion turning to full-on alarm. Fuck, *now* she's thinking I'm stalking her. Shit, shit, shit!

"Listen, this was ..." Tessa struggled to find the right words. Clearly she was looking to escape from the celebrity that she'd be taking a restraining order out on the minute I was out of sight. How could I have fucked this up so badly? What was it about this woman that had turned me into a bumbling prat?

She went to sidestep past me, but I hastily held my hands up as a sign of peace. If she walked away now, she'd never give me the time of day again.

"Hang on!" I said, bracing myself for the rejection that would end my career. "I ... I wanted to see you because I had a great time with you the other week, and I hated that it was left on an awkward note. I felt like I must have been a dickhead for you to do a runner like that. I remembered you told me you went here, and I was just passing and wanted to ask you out for a coffee, just to chat and apologise – if I needed to."

Her expression softened. Amazingly. She gave a small smile, looking just as embarrassed as I felt.

"You weren't a dickhead. An idiot, though, based on your social skills today." She laughed, and I couldn't help but laugh too. "But I had a great time. Really. I was just embarrassed, more so when I realised you were … you."

She gave a vague shrug, that smile creeping back in. It was infectious, that smile of hers. It was a genuine reward and progress all at once. The fact she wanted me for me and not my name or fame was weirdly elating. Like I'd had an out of body experience, the freedom of being unknown was something new and alien to me.

"Don't be. It was nice just being—" I stopped myself. This conversation was running away from me. I cleared my throat. Back to business. "Listen, I wanted to talk to you upfront about something. It's pretty important. Can we go somewhere a bit more, less in the open?"

She looked sceptical. I didn't blame her. Before I could explain anything else, Mia slammed the car door and marched over. My time was up. Tessa looked even more confused, looking to me for an explanation. How were you supposed to begin a conversation like this with someone you met once? Even worse, have this conversation with this stranger when your agent, your borderline-alcoholic mother and your emotionally obtuse father were hanging their every hope on this? I swear you couldn't write this shit.

5

Tessa

If I had to name the two people I'd bet on my immortal soul I'd never see again, it would be Jonathan Adeola and his giant of a handler. Yet, there I was, sitting in a car that probably cost more than my entire university education, with these strangers.

I was already regretting my decision to go with them for "a little chat", but I'd dare anyone to try and say no to that woman. Seriously, I never got the term "piercing stare" before I met Mrs Robinson. The irony of that surname … but I highly doubted these two had a *Graduate* dynamic going on. He looked equally intimidated by this woman when she marched out of that car, all his charm and banter vanishing. No, he wasn't charming. The bruise most likely developing on my hip proved he was a bumbling idiot … a strangely cute, and— Ugh, I needed to stop that train of thought. He may have been sweet, but this whole set-up was still creeping me out.

"Am I being kidnapped?" I blurted. Both Mrs Robinson and Jonathan glanced at me in alarm. Okay, a tiny bit reassuring.

"Of course not!" Mrs Robinson barked, glaring daggers at

Jonathan. "What on earth did you say to her?"

"I didn't mention kidnapping!" Jonathan defended hastily, turning in his seat to face me – his annoyingly handsome face somehow dreamier with those sincere eyes. "I promise, this is not a kidnapping. Stop saying kidnap; I'm not into that. It's not my kink."

His half-smile evaporated when my eyes widened. If this rich boy was thinking of casting me in his remake of *Fifty Shades of Grey*, hell was definitely about to freeze over!

"No!" He hastily backtracked, seeming to read my mind and looking mortified. "I'm not into anything weird, you know? Course you know, I mean – I like normal sex, good, consensual and non-kinky—"

"Stop talking," I begged. His mouth shut as if I'd found his mute button, and the silence that followed was uncomfortably long. Movie magic must exist. Jonathan was nowhere near how I remembered him – he was like a deer in headlights today. My face burned, berating my drunk self for falling for those brown eyes and his general hotness. I felt Mrs Robinson's incredulous eyes glancing between the pair of us, probably wondering how we ever ended up in that hotel together. I took a deep breath, finding a calmness I did not feel. "Okay, no to the kidnapping. Great. But what's with the whole *Godfather* act?"

"I'll explain shortly," Mia said, pulling up outside a coffee shop not far from the university. She gave exasperated looks to both of us. It was nearly empty, judging by the windows. Actually, this street was oddly quiet for a Thursday.

A bloke who you could only describe as "the muscle" walked out – in a suit that barely concealed his muscles and with a thuggish, grim face and a bald head included. I watched with my mouth agape as he ushered out what looked like not only the stray customers with dishevelled grimaces, but also the majority of the staff.

"Umm," I said, my vowels and consonants unable to fathom what I saw into words. I watched as the entire café was evacuated quickly and silently. The Muscle tapped on Mrs Robinson's window, waiting till it slid down.

"Perimeter has been cleared," The Hulk grunted, sounding way too serious. I actually snorted a laugh, more in shock than actual humour. He either didn't hear or chose to ignore. Good thing, too. My face was burning. I bit down on my lip.

"Anyone else inside?"

"The owner, but she's staying in her office for the duration of this meeting."

"Did she sign the NDA?"

"Of course." He-Man's mouth twitched into what I guessed was a smile. "But I had to give a false name. She didn't seem trustworthy with that information; would you like me to keep an eye out? Make sure she doesn't try and listen in?"

Was I witnessing a potential hit on a nosey coffee shop owner? I looked at Jonathan. He merely shrugged. That grin on his face told me he found my reactions to this situation amusing.

"I think that will be best. Wait in the corridor outside her office," Robinson said briskly, and just like that, off he went. She turned to us. "Follow me inside and don't say a word till we've sat down. Understand?"

"Yes," Jonathan said. They both turned to me, and it took me a second to realise why before I quickly repeated, "Yes!"

We headed inside. It felt eerily quiet and bizarre to be inside an empty café, like the love child of a ghost town and a crime scene. Jonathan led me to a booth, and I slid in next to him, deciding he was the lesser of two evils. And as much as I hated to admit it, we knew each other intimately now.

"Right, everything is paid for," Mrs Robinson said, sitting opposite us and almost coming across like a weird chaperone. "So if you two want anything to eat or drink …?"

"I'm fine," I said, hearing my phone vibrate in my rucksack and pulling it out. Ivy was calling. Before my finger grazed the screen, Robinson yanked it out of my hand. "Hey!"

"This is for your own safety as much as ours," Mrs Robinson said grimly, declining the call and pocketing my phone. Was she freaking kidding me?

"My safety?" I asked incredulously. I turned to Jonathan, who went to speak. I swore to god he better not be thinking about asking for coffees. He closed his mouth, clearly changing tack. "What is this about?"

"I need to ask a favour," he said, sounding genuine, and normally I would have been a bit more sympathetic. But not today,

"A favour?" I repeated, the word sounding ludicrous from my lips. "Spoiler alert. This whole set-up is not how a normal person asks for a favour!"

"He's not normal, which is why you're here." Mrs Robinson butted in, cutting off whatever Jonathan was going to say – I was sensing a recurring theme here with these two. Robinson pressed on, finally revealing the reason for this unusual meeting. It was the furthest from any theory I could have imagined.

I listened, partly stunned and thinking this was an elaborate (and very theatrical) joke. It had to be a wind-up, surely? My eyes snapped between Robinson and Jonathan, waiting for one to scream April Fools – despite it being October – but neither even cracked a smile. They were dead serious. This woman and her privileged ward wanted me to parade around as his fake girlfriend to dig him out of a scandal HE got himself into. I mean, I'd heard that interview hadn't gone well – granted, I didn't go out of my way to watch it on YouTube or anything. I didn't even see it, yet the social media buzz had spread like wildfire. But this was his mess, not mine!

"You can't be serious?" I demanded, a tiny part of me hoping in vain this was still a joke. "This is crazy, you know that?"

"Believe me, I know." Jonathan grimaced, looking like he'd rather be anywhere but here, having this conversation. "But my career is kind of in your hands at this point. It'll just be for a few weeks, I swear. Just till the media buzz dies down."

"That is not my responsibility," I retorted, glaring as he had the nerve to look frustrated now. "No, you want a new angle – do some charity work or something worthwhile to improve your image. I'm not becoming your human prop to rewrite your little narrative."

"Whether you like it or not, Ms Granger, you are a part of his little narrative," Robinson snapped, her nostrils actually flaring. "You were spotted with him on multiple media outlets, and it's only by a small miracle your name was not leaked. We have a chance to take control of the narrative that will benefit you both. But if you refuse to work with us, an alternative narrative may not reflect kindly on yourself."

I felt like I'd been dropped in icy water as the undisclosed threat crawled all over me. Clearly, they were pretty happy for the witch-hunt to be redirected at me if need be. Robinson probably had the power to destroy my reputation in seconds, all to save his. Instead of being terrified, anger overshadowed me.

"Are you actually threatening me?" I asked coldly, the tone of my voice surprising us both. "Really? When you're the ones asking me for help?"

"That's not what we talked about." Jonathan glared at Robinson, sounding just as insulted as I felt. He took my hand in his, his eyes pleading for me to not look at him with quite so much rage. "Tess, I swear I'm not trying to force you into this. This is not what this is; I wanted you to be okay with this."

"How could anyone be okay with this? You're both insane!" I yanked my hand away, hating that my skin still felt warm from his touch. I needed to get out of there. I turned on Robinson. "Give me my phone. Now."

"We're not finished—"

"Yes, we are! The only way you're keeping me here is if this is an actual kidnapping." My voice rose, the borderline shouting masking the fact my hands were shaking. "Otherwise, I'm going."

Robinson hesitated. After meeting Jonathan's eyes, she reluctantly handed over the phone. I snatched it back and hurried out of the booth. Jonathan looked lost for words; he made to follow me.

"Tessa, please," he said, almost breaking with genuine fear. "I'm so sorry, can we just talk? Just you and me?"

"I think we've said enough. The answer's no, by the way," I said through gritted teeth. I made for the door, secretly relieved that Popeye was too occupied with the Gossip Owner to give chase and drag me back. I yanked the door open and ran out into the harsh cold.

6

Jonathan

Shit. This had gone from bad to fucking horrific. Without thinking, I bolted after Tessa, ignoring Mia completely this time. My future was hanging by a thread, with one person having the power to snap it or save it.

The cold breeze hit harder than expected, but I ran up the pavement as Tessa marched up the street. She knew this area better than I did. If she took an unexpected turn or jumped in a taxi, I was a goner. My legs were much stronger than hers, and within a minute my hand caught her arm and she whirled around to face me. Again, she nearly slipped over.

"What?" she snapped, her eyes fixed on me. There was anger and something else behind those green eyes. "And stop doing that!"

This was it – I was throwing myself at the mercy of this screenwriting undergraduate.

"Sorry!" I said in a rush again. Fuck, that was going to be the word of the fucking year.

7

Tessa

"I had no idea she was going to say that," Jonathan rushed earnestly, running a hand over his short hair. A nervous habit. "This is not how I expected this to go …"

"What *did* you expect?" I demanded, waiting as he searched for an answer. Clearly nothing was coming to mind, and the guy had left his jacket; he must be colder than he was letting on. His brown eyes were so pleading. He looked the definition of lost. I felt for him, and I actually believed he had no intention of coercing me, but his plan was crazy!

How was I supposed to pretend to be this guy's girlfriend? I didn't even know him. When we first met, I thought he was just a regular guy. He seemed genuinely interested in what I had to say, and we had fun – not just the sex, but he could hold a good conversation. Now, he was one of the most talked-about celebrities, and he wanted me to save his career … God, my Mum would go ballistic.

"Tessa—"

"Can I ask one question?" I interrupted. He nodded, and I took a breath before going on. "Why me? I mean, I get the overall plan; it's a smart one. But why not ask an actress or someone in your line of work to play this part? I'm nobody, and I'm sure there are loads of girls who would jump at this opportunity."

"Exactly," he said. "I don't want someone who will suck this situation dry. You're genuine, that's what I liked about you. And if I were going to trust anyone with my career, I'd want it to be someone like you. Someone I can have a conversation with. Someone who will take this seriously."

I laughed, but not cruelly. Our one time having a conversation was hardly enough for him to have this much faith in me – I could actually worsen the whole situation. My ambition to be a screenwriter was to avoid precisely this, to stay out of the spotlight. His face pleaded with me, and I felt myself soften slightly. Those brown eyes – it should be illegal to have those eyes. Then he ruined it.

"If it's about money …"

8

Jonathan

"Money? That's what you think this is about?" Tessa asked, her voice rising in anger again. Fuck, any progress I was making just shattered right in front of me. She stared at me like I was someone who'd never met or conversed with someone. I'd probably think the same if I was her.

"No!" I said hastily, mentally proof-checking whatever was going to come out of my stupid mouth next. I needed to wrap this up. Technically this should have been wrapped up before the money offer and definitely before the intimidation comment. "I just meant, I know there are risks with something like this, and I want you to know I'd make sure you were protected."

A thought occurred to me, and I held my hand out. Her eyes narrowed at it. "Give me your phone," I answered her silent question.

"Why?" she asked, holding it tentatively in her hands.

"Because whatever you decide, I want you to tell me first. Not Mia," I said truthfully, trying to put as much honesty in my voice as I could. "And whatever you decide, I'll respect.

No intimidation or bribery, I swear."

I could practically see her brain weighing the pros and cons. A tiny ray of hope flickered in my chest as she cautiously handed me her phone.

"I'm not saying yes, I'm just agreeing to think about it …" she said, but her voice sounded less confident as she watched my thumbs tap across her screen. "You better not be putting a tracker on me."

"I wouldn't have the first idea how to do that." I half-laughed, relieved when she cracked something that resembled a smile. I kept my face smooth and relaxed as I typed in my digits, praying this would work in my favour.

9

Tessa

For the entire walk back to campus, I kept glancing over my shoulder, half expecting The Muscle or Robinson's car to be tailing me. They weren't, but I still took the long route back to the student accommodation building, only feeling safe once I was back on familiar ground and inside my room.

As they hadn't made me sign an NDA, I immediately texted Ivy to come over. I still felt shaken when she arrived, which she seemed to notice and thankfully was serious for once. She listened quietly as I told her everything that had happened within the last couple of hours; I sat crossed-legged on my bed and she perched on my desk. When I'd finished, she seemed to be debating with herself and finally settled on: "This is some Julia Roberts and Richard Gere shit!"

Surprisingly, I was able to laugh insincerely at that. Accurate. Although somehow this feels more like Jonathan Lawton's original version of *Pretty Woman* – where Roberts' character is dragged out of the car by Gere after feeling used and hollow, even having the agreed money chucked at her dismissively as she was left in the dust. Yeah, I'm one of those weirdos who would have preferred the darker *$3,000* ending than the cheesy "rescues him right back" Hollywood cringe-fest. But I didn't want to live that scene out in real life.

"So he offered to buy your time for his image," Ivy began, stunning me when she added, "and you said no?"

"What? Of course, I said no!" I defended, unable to believe this was the response I was getting. "What did you expect?"

"That you'd use this to your advantage," Ivy pointed out, her conviction causing me to pause briefly. "Think about it. You're the one with the power here. Why not get something out of it for yourself? Not just money, but exposure or something. He's an actor, and screenwriters tend to need good connections to be taken seriously."

Huh, I hadn't thought of it like that. Actually, she'd made an excellent point. I kept thinking of myself as the vulnerable party against Jonathan's team of bodyguards and manipulators, but he at least didn't treat me as such. Plus, with the deadline for NFTS just a few months away, my application needed to stand out. Having a name casting for the script reading was recommended by my supervising lecturer … could I do that, though? Would Jonathan see it as beneath him to read an unsolicited script on stage among amateur actors? He'd care if it meant I'd pose as his girlfriend to save his butt, but this was still mad.

"Amanda suggested I use *Innocence* as my submission to the NFTS," I said, cautiously testing the idea aloud. "Maybe Jonathan could read for one of the leads. That way, I get exposure for my writing and his boy-next-door image is back on track. Just a few months, right?"

This was mad, this was mad, this was–

"There we fucking go!" Ivy praised, only making my face

burn with the proud look on hers. "What do you have to lose?"

"My privacy, my dignity, my integrity?" I offered, but I was warming to the idea more than I cared to admit despite my words. Hell, having him pretend to be my boyfriend might redeem me in Mum's eyes. She couldn't exactly ridicule me for being out with my boyfriend – pretend boyfriend – no way I'd let her or the rest of the family know it was a ruse. Ryan would go all caveman, and Vee couldn't keep a secret to save her life, and even when she tried, somehow several people already know.

This could work in both of our favours for a multitude of reasons. Before I could talk myself out of it, I grabbed my phone and found his number under JA. I hit dial.

"Are you calling him now?" she loudly whispered, I waved her to shush, and she practically dived onto the bed next to me, tapping my shoulder and mouthing, "LOUD. SPEAKER. LOUDSPEAKER!"

I reluctantly obliged, waiting with bated breath as the call rang … and rang. I was just on the verge of hanging up and thinking maybe fate had declared my idea was insane when he answered, "Hello?"

"Hi!" I said, forcing the breeziness in my voice so much I wanted to curl up and melt, Wicked-Witch-of-the-West style. I rushed on before I bottled it. "It's me, I mean, it's Tessa. From earlier. Are you okay to talk? If you aren't, I can call you back?"

"Oh, hi. Course. Just give me a minute, okay?" I heard some rustling and footsteps. I imagined he was going upstairs. "Figure it's best to have this chat in private."

I suddenly felt terrible I wasn't giving him the same courtesy. I missed whatever he said next and opted to answer stupidly,

"Huh?"

"I said, I'm really sorry about earlier. Again." He spoke softly, and my mind's eye flashed that crooked smile. Focus. I floundered for a response. Ivy stared incredulously at me, somehow keeping her mouth shut. This was a struggle.

"Yeah. I know, but that's the thing I wanted to talk to you about," I said. "If I were to do this, you'd have to agree to a couple of things too. This can't be all one way."

"Absolutely," Jonathan agreed a bit too quickly, but continued more casually, "what do you have in mind?"

"My family can't know about this, so you'll have to play my boyfriend around them."

"I can do that. That's no problem—"

"That's not all," I interrupted. "I'm applying to the National Film and Television School for my master's, and I'm putting on a cast reading of my dissertation screenplay. So as you're an actor who acts, I thought you could read one of the leads. It'll bulk up my application too."

He didn't answer as quickly, and I stopped myself from rushing on or elaborating. Nope, I wasn't going to beg; I'd never do that. I may be selling my dignity down the river, but my pride was staying put.

"Okay," he said brightly, and I breathed a sigh of relief, but that was short-lived. "I'll have to read it first, though."

"Read it?" I asked warily, ignoring Ivy's eye-roll. I didn't like other people reading my work, which was ridiculous for a screenwriter. It was part of the game. But whenever I had to hand over one of my scripts, I immediately started thinking of how it could be better.

"Yeah, of course," Jonathan said, his voice sounding like he was smirking at my silent freak-out.

"Great, I'll send it over tonight." I forced my voice to sound cheerful. Ivy silently whooped, looking ecstatic. That made me feel a bit better. On the plus side, I wouldn't be able to torture myself with rewrites. I'd just send it before I could chicken out. The torture would be reserved for the fact I'd sold my soul for my educational prospects. This felt a bit too *Dorian Grey* …

10

Jonathan

Rarely do I sit up till late re-reading a script, but it was just that fucking good. Even now, I was sat re-reading Tessa's screenplay on a bench in Leicester Square, with Paddington Bear's statue eating an eternal marmalade sandwich for company. It felt appropriate to meet here, surrounded by the physical embodiment of cinematic history.

I didn't know what I'd been expecting – okay, that was a lie. I thought Tessa would be a shit writer and for this to read as a horrific student film – but she had some actual skills. Everything from her descriptive language to the dialogue was insanely good. I was amazed she wanted to pursue her master's, she already wrote like a professional.

Despite the cloudy sky above, tourists were still bustling up and down the square, snapping photos on their phones, and one or two were talking animatedly on FaceTime as they passed me. It was weird how invisible I felt and yet more bizarre that these people didn't appreciate the beauty of London; everything was lived through a lens these days. Funny, that's how I'd spent my whole life – seen through other people's lenses to spectate and analyse.

I told Mia this morning that I was on good terms with Tessa, and she had agreed to the arrangement reluctantly. I was totally fine with Tessa's terms, but I could tell from Mia's cynicism that she thought a cast reading directed by an undergraduate screenwriter was beneath me. Maybe she was right, but I'd never had the university experience – my career had suddenly soared at eighteen. As I'd no longer needed a tutor on set, acting became my full-time occupation. I sometimes wondered what I'd missed out on and what I could have gained if I'd stopped and taken a breath, but that was impossible in my family. A degree was irrelevant when you had directors and casting directors gagging to get you in their production, but hardly any of their scripts moved me as Tessa's did. Truthfully, *Awakened* was the first script I'd read in months that I'd enjoyed … which is why I was eager to do that project instead of others.

Maybe when this media mess was cleaned up, I should start auditioning for more independent projects – less mainstream and more risqué; I needed more of those characters on my reel. I barely glanced up when a woman sat on the opposite side of Paddy, her enormous green hat obscuring most of her face. She seemed to be wearing massive sunglasses. Which was weird, given the dark clouds overhead.

"Hi," a familiar voice whispered, and I did a double take when I clocked that the hat wearer was Tessa herself. She stuck out like a sore thumb, which was saying something for central London.

"What are you *wearing*?" I answered as a form of greeting, unable to suppress the laugh that escaped my lips. She lowered her glasses to glare at me, making me notice the hat atop her head paled against the emerald of those eyes. Her frown was meant to be intimidating but actually had an opposite effect. An unintentionally sexy effect.

"Oh shut up!" Tessa snapped over Paddington's sandwich, her face flushed under the glasses, and that only made me laugh harder. "Seriously? I'm trying to be inconspicuous!"

"Excellent job there." I chuckled, then I said more softly, "The hat's a bit much, no? I'm sure they can spot us from a space station up there or something."

"Oh, be quiet!" she muttered, her annoyance making her even more rattled, and I loved it. It was funny to see this girl who was so sharp-tongued could be so flustered; she had no idea she made me feel the same whenever she caught my eye.

"I'm only messing," I said softly. She seemed to sense my sincerity and met my eyes. "We're safe. Promise. You don't have to do all that, I swear."

She considered this, then reluctantly took both the hat and sunglasses off. Her hair fell in loose waves to her shoulders. I suddenly recalled how soft it was that night, my fingers remembering the sensation. I pushed those thoughts away. I needed to keep it professional. Feeling bad for her, I got off the bench and casually sat next to her, very aware of our closeness without stony chaperones sitting between us. I nudged her with my shoulder and was rewarded with a small smile.

"I just didn't want to draw attention," she begrudgingly admitted, shoving her marvellous disguise into her rucksack. Thank Christ.

"A for effort," I said, smirking as her face flushed and she visibly relaxed more. She wasn't MI5 material, but if I admitted I thought this act was cute I'd probably get a punch in the mouth.

"Okay, okay." She sighed, smiling despite herself. "You've made your point, Jon."

Somehow that nickname sounded nicer from her mouth. We sat in surprisingly comfortable silence. She glanced at the screenplay in my hands, clearly itching to ask what I thought of it.

"You read it?" Tessa asked coolly, her breezy tone masking a slight pitch of nerves in her voice. Was she mad? Did she not know what she had written?

"Yeah, four times," I said incredulously, barely concealing my enthusiasm. "It's brilliant."

"You think?" Tessa winced. "I mean, you like it?"

"Would I say that if I didn't?" I half-laughed, which she seemed to believe. "This is really good, and I've read enough scripts to say that. The characters are so vivid, it feels like a Barry Jenkins piece, but British."

"Wow. Um. Okay," Tessa said, flushing for an entirely new reason. That smile was back. It wasn't arrogance; she was genuinely touched by what I'd said. "Thank you."

Was she not used to accepting a compliment? Or was she one of those writers who constantly self-analysed? I could relate to that. I could hardly watch myself back on screen without seeing how I could have played it differently. It must be a nightmare for a screenwriter. They'd do that throughout the entire film.

"So why are you applying to a film school when you write like this?" I asked, turning on the bench to face her. "Do you even need a master's?"

"In my case, yeah," Tessa responded. But she hesitated before admitting, "No one in my family are writers or involved in the industry. Actually, I'm the first to even go to university, and that's a big deal in itself. So I don't have any connections to get my work seen by the right people. I'm an unknown, and anything I write would go straight into the unsolicited pile. Getting into the NFTS will not only help me develop my writing and have some of my scripts made, but people outside will take me seriously."

I already took her seriously. She was so honest; it was infuriating to imagine someone with talent must rely on luck or chance. Countless shit screenwriters had agents and had their scripts produced. Honestly, there were a lot of writers that I'd immediately rejected on the basis they lacked the ability to write good characters and a consistent plot. Those screenwriters also tended to write uncomfortably detailed sexual scenes that some had me in mind to play, not even using the Female Gaze and instead going for sensationalised shock value. Those writers should be contemplating the unsolicited pile, not Tessa.

"Well, anything I can do to help, I'm in," I said. "And not just because you're saving my butt agreeing to this insane plan. Your writing deserves to be seen."

"Thanks." Tessa smiled, tucking a loose strand of hair behind her ear. "You're also saving me from the wrath of my mum. She'd approve of my choice of fake boyfriend now."

"Don't mothers usually want their daughters to get with doctors or lawyers?"

"Not mine," Tessa laughed. "She'd think it's very progressive that I'm getting a university education and dating an actor who will be reading my words. Much better than a one-night stand becoming a fake romance."

"I don't think this is fake," I said without thinking. Her eyes widened and I berated myself mentally. "I mean, we like each other. As mates at least, no?"

"Oh, yeah," Tessa said. She breathed out and then added gently, "You're not like what I expected."

"What did you expect?" I asked, suddenly craving the answer more than I should.

"Not this. Real. Actually, sweet. As crazy as this ruse is, at least it's with you. And it benefits us both, so that's a bonus!" She playfully bumped my shoulder with hers and gave me a little grin. I casually draped my arm over the bench, my fingers inches away from her shoulder, and looked around for something to say. She beat me to it.

"Have you seen this *Scenes in the Square* exhibit before?" she asked, indicating the cinematic statues around us. I shook my head and she grabbed my hand and pulled me up with her. "Me either. Let's have a look. Come on."

As if it was the most natural thing in the world – because that's how it felt – I entwined my fingers through Tessa's and allowed her to pull me through cinema history. We left Paddington and headed over to Laurel and Hardy, who were playfully teetering on a rooftop and depicting that insane stunt from 1929's *Liberty*.

From Bugs Bunny, and Harry Potter sat on his Nimbus 2000, we also spotted the modern classics with Batman standing on a rooftop – apparently, the Bat-Signal was visible at night – and even Wonder Woman dramatically bursting out of ODEON's wall. We paused at Julie Andrews, immobilised as her Mary Poppins incarnation, umbrella in mid-flight included. I frowned at her smiling face, childhood memories making an annoying appearance.

"Her film scared me as a kid," I admitted, and my eyebrows rose incredulously as Tessa tried unsuccessfully to hide a snort.

"What? I'm serious!"

"I'm sorry, but how?" She giggled again, trying to control herself. "How is *Mary Poppins* a scary film?"

"A strict white lady descends from clouds on a talking umbrella and gaslights the kids she's looking after that the crazy magic happening is in their heads?" I explained with a reluctant grin, only making Tessa laugh harder. "That is some scary shit!"

I couldn't hide my smile as Tessa took my arm and led me away from the woman who'd haunted my childhood. She was the first person I'd told that silly childhood anecdote. I don't even know why; it just came out.

"Don't worry; I'll protect you from any flying nannies coming our way," Tessa said teasingly, but not in a mean way. I noticed she kept her arm hooked through mine as we made our way back through the square. We passed the joyful and iconic figure of Gene Kelly on a lamp post from the dance sequence he'd directed and choreographed for *Singin' in the Rain*.

"Who's that?" Tessa asked, frowning at Rowan Atkinson's incarnation of Mr Bean smiling a hapless grin at thin air. I looked at her in disbelief. No, she must be joking. Surely, she'd know the Bean?

"Mr Bean," I answered, her blank face not showing a hint of recognition. "Tessa, what the fuck was your childhood? Everyone knows Rowan Atkinson!"

"Oh!" she said, dawning comprehension. "He played that weird hotel manager in *The Witches*, right? And Zazu in *The Lion King*, I remember."

"You know that, but not the Bean?" I said in mock horror. "And you're meant to be a film student!"

"Okay, okay. It's not like he was in *Citizen Kane*," Tessa defended, her pout making me take note of how full her lips were.

"That film was horrendous, a complete bore and pretentious as fuck," I said, leading her to Mr Bean's bench. "And you can't convince me otherwise. The Rosebud reveal? That was ridiculous!"

"Yeah," she admitted, a grin spreading across her face as she sat down beside Bean and, with a gentle pull of her hand, I joined her. "So what's the big deal about Bean?"

Her look of undivided attention instantly told me she was more than the academic type. She was a Hermione Granger type: any chance to be educated or expand her knowledge, she was interested. Something caught my attention as I began to explain the absolute masterpiece of cinema that was the *Mr Bean* film.

So small, but the sound was instantly familiar.

Click!

In my peripheral vision, I saw him. Paparazzi. He was standing in the doorway of an Italian restaurant across the greenery, rudely blocking the entrance and attempting to look casual as he snapped another picture. He was some middle-aged prick who probably had us from multiple angles on that camera. How could I not have spotted that? I clenched my jaw, not wanting to ruin this moment or cause a scene.

"What's the matter?" Tessa asked, turning to follow my gaze. Her small, "Oh …" told me she knew what was happening. She turned to face me, giving the cameraman her back, and determinedly took my hand in hers, most likely for show – it felt nice, though.

"Do you want to go?" I offered, secretly relieved when she

shook her head.

"I'm good here," she said. So was I, and that did not have to be put on for the cameras.

11

Tessa

Time seemed to fly when I was with him; it was easy to get lost in conversation with Jonathan. And I did; I even let him drive me back to campus – not only because it was practical, but it allowed us to keep talking. I learned he was an only child and the son of the actual filmmaking legend Ophelia LeMahieu, so he was literally born to be in the industry in some way or another. I stupidly told him that although I had seen a few of his mum's films due to Cinema Culture seminars, I wasn't really a fan of her style.

"Really?" he asked, his interest in no way soothing my desire to rewind time and praise his mum's work like a fangirl instead. "Why is that?"

"Well," I muttered, thinking I might as well throw myself entirely on the sword of mortification. "Her films are dark, like doomsday dark. I mean, she's got an excellent eye, and every frame is gorgeous. Just, I don't think she strikes the right balance with intimate or even funny moments …"

He tilted his head to one side, a wry smile on his lips as he watched the road. That was an odd reaction to criticism from a nobody writer against a French Noir icon and the woman who had given him life. Instead, he laughed.

"Thank god someone finally said that!" He chuckled, confusing me even further. "I can't sit through her films any more. They're all so fucking depressing!"

"You can't say that about your mum," I said, fighting my urge to laugh. "She's won awards and—"

"That doesn't matter," Jonathan retorted, smirking at my evident discomfort. "If you didn't enjoy the film or feel invested in the story, she's failed as a filmmaker. No amount of awards can make you a good storyteller."

I wasn't sure whether that was supposed to make me feel better or worse … how could he say that about his mum? That continued to play on my mind as we drove in silence. I could feel him glancing at me whenever it was safe to do so. Like he wanted to ask something but was scared of the answer.

"Did you google me?" he asked apprehensively. I frowned in confusion at his random question. He hastily added, "I wouldn't blame you if you did. Just, not everything you read about my parents or me is true. Really."

He was worried I'd spent hours trolling gossip columns looking for all the sordid details of his past. I felt a twinge of pity, realising that this must be new for him too – except where I was getting mentally psyched to debut as his fake girlfriend, he was wrapping his head around putting his faith in a complete stranger. We both were. After the incident with that random photographer, I wasn't surprised he had trust issues. I was determined for that not to spoil our day, but I'd be lying if the sight of that photographer taking our photo hadn't made me feel uneasy. We both knew exactly how the other was feeling, which was oddly comforting despite everything else.

"Of course not," I reassured him, noticing his shoulders relaxing a fraction. "Okay, I checked out IMDb to see what kind of stuff you've been in – I was curious – but I'm hardly going to look for dirt on you, Jon. If this is going to work, we'll have to trust each other. At least, I hope we can."

The smile he gave me was so genuine, I actually couldn't help my goofy grin back.

"I do trust you," he said so softly and intimately I momentarily became speechless. Did he mean it to sound so sexy? Did he even know when he was being sexy, or was it like some mythical energy this guy gave off? I floundered for something to say, trying not to drown in those brown eyes. Thankfully, they were back on the road and, sooner than expected, we were pulling up outside the student accommodation.

"Thank you for driving me home," I said, and without thinking I leaned over and kissed him on the cheek. What had I just done? I was mentally screaming but keeping a somewhat casual demeanour, and his voice stopped me when I moved to get out.

"Are you free tomorrow?"

"Why?" I replied without thinking. He sighed, probably because I'd answered a question with a question, and I cautiously said, "Yeah …"

"You wanna go somewhere with me?"

I raised one eyebrow. "Somewhere?" I asked.

"It's a surprise."

"I don't really like surprises," I admitted, omitting that this was a massive understatement – I hated surprises, even as a kid. But this only broadened his smile, and a mischievous glint appeared in his eyes. It was annoying how cute that was.

I felt my resolve against this spontaneous day trip wavering ever so slightly. Bloody hell.

"I'll call you tomorrow." He winked, clearly giddy with the air of mystery. There was no way of talking my way out of this.

"Fine," I said coolly, fooling myself into thinking I had some say in the matter, and with a reluctant smile I hopped out of the car.

* * *

Night had always been my favourite time to write. There was something about the quiet and stillness that was strangely comforting. Like when you sat under your duvet reading late into the night, it was like being in your own little world. No interruptions, no questions or prying eyes, just me and my laptop. Me and my story.

I sat crossed-legged and still fully dressed on my bed, my laptop screen illuminating my face as I decided to bite the bullet and start my NFTS application. To save my brain from going into overdrive as I tried to pitch myself as a writer and human in two hundred and fifty words or less, I switched between my application and the less stressful task of looking for actors for my reading. Funnily enough, I wasn't as stressed about this as I had been yesterday. Maybe Jon's easy-going nature was influencing me. I smiled at that thought.

Coming back from Leicester Square and back on campus was the equivalent of when the Pevensies stumbled out of the wardrobe after living a whole different life in Narnia, back to a former version of themselves. Here, I was Invisible Tessa, the one who tidied up after her messy flatmates, listened to the latest boy drama from whoever got dumped or even helped with their last-minute studying as they asked to *borrow* my notes. Aside from Ivy, I doubted my three other flatmates would notice if I walked out that door and never returned.

With Jonathan, I was Tessa, the Screenwriter. He'd read my work and loved it, and he genuinely thought I was good. He wanted to know everything and was completely interested in hearing about it. He saw me as an actual writer, not someone wasting time on a hobby or as the scholarship charity case. I felt visible when he looked at me, especially how his eyes met mine.

Ugh. I mentally shook myself, chasing those thoughts away as I continued to type up a casting call for my script reading online. Nope, nada, absolutely not – I refused to start crushing on Jonathan. This was a mutually beneficial arrangement between two adults and nothing more. This whole act was going to be hard enough without my overactive (and sleep-deprived) brain fantasying about him. It was bad enough lying to Mum without adding more complications, but it turned out I was a better actress than I thought. Mum believed the story I had scripted to memory – so well that my stomach knotted as she apologised over and over again during our last phone call.

"I never would have said what I said if I'd known you were in a relationship with him." Mum sounded on the verge of tears and that only intensified the guilt I was already feeling. "Why didn't you just tell me, love?"

Because he was really a drunken one-night stand, and I'm actually using his need to salvage his reputation to get into film school?

There must be a special place in hell reserved for yours truly by Satan himself. Instead of spouting the truth, I squashed the guilt I was feeling and lied through my teeth.

"We just wanted to keep things normal while we could," I said. And then added way more truthfully, "I like him, Mum. He really listens, and he's sweeter than everyone thinks."

"I'm glad, but you know this isn't normal," Mum said cautiously, her voice unintentionally sending a chill down my spine. "Once you're in the public eye, nothing you do is private. Look at the royal family."

After concluding that Mum needed to ease up on *The Crown*, what she said about privacy bothered me more than I thought it would. Screenwriters are rarely the focus, something I always found appealing. But knowing there was someone out there with my picture on their camera, someone who could be doing anything with it, was terrifying. And it was that lack of power that made this seem not as worth it as I'd thought. But if the ends justified the means, I could make a name for myself outside of Jon's spotlight.

Chatting to Ryan and Vee was less emotionally challenging. It was kept to a few short messages in a group chat. Ryan merely sent a thumbs up after I gave the same explanation, and Vee's excited onslaught of emoji messages was unreadable. It was surprisingly easier to lie to my family than I'd thought … I didn't even bother telling Dad; we hadn't spoken properly since I was fourteen, and yet I had no doubt Ryan or Vee had given him all the details regardless of whether I wanted him to know or not. Whereas I'd chosen to cut our absent father out of my life because of his toxic and flaky behaviour, my brother and sister were still clinging to the hope he'd suddenly be the dad they'd always wished he was. I was more practical when it came to Dad. I had no childish illusions. And I'd rather have one great parent than two, when one quite clearly couldn't care less.

I uploaded the casting call for four female speaking roles and three male speaking roles and saved what little progress I'd made on my application, reluctantly giving in to my body's need for sleep. As I curled onto my duvet, I was on the verge of sleep when my phone chimed on my bedside table. I grabbed it, my thumb about to silence any applying actors' emails, and stopped.

It wasn't an audition email. What I saw instead made sleep vanish from my mind. A news alert had appeared on my screen: *Actor Jonathan Adeola spotted with new flame T …*

The headline was cut off, but the glaring T may as well have been a neon sign. I quickly swiped my thumb, only to confirm my fear being realised in pixels. My name had been leaked, there in bold letters was Tessa Granger for the world to see, accompanied by a picture of Jonathan and me, smiling and looking at each other like lovesick teenagers. Had we really looked at each other like that? The camera never lied, but a picture can be interpreted in whatever way suits. As I looked at the photo taken just a few hours ago, the social media share numbers were going up and up.

I was no longer Invisible Tessa or even Screenwriter Tessa – I was Tessa, girlfriend of Jonathan Adeola, actor and offspring of filmmaking legends. Mum's warning rang in my ears … *nothing stays private.* The whole world was looking at me now, and that thought kept me awake long after I switched off my phone.

12

Jonathan

Mia barely raised an eyebrow as I barged into her office, the heavy door gently swishing open despite my hard shove. Robinson & Clarke Agency was the definition of chic, and the brightly lit interior that screamed money and stupid doors that didn't crash open properly were mocking me today.

Tessa's name being leaked on the day she agreed to this plan was no coincidence, and now she wouldn't even answer my calls. Any progress in the trust we had started to build yesterday had blown up in my face.

And only three people knew.

"Who the fuck leaked her name!" I demanded, not caring at that moment how loud I was being. I was used to personal information being leaked, but not from the people who were meant to have my back. "I actually got her to agree to this crazy idea – something you came up with too! Now any trust she might have had in me is gone—"

"Please don't shout in my office." Mia's calm voice shut me up; her stern glare made it abundantly clear she wasn't here for my bitch fit. "For starters, you should know better than to even consider I would leak that girl's name to the press. As well as this putting your career at further risk, it puts her at risk, and we now have limited time to prep her for the media attention. Why would I restrict our limited window of preparation? It wasn't me."

I knew that, which slimed the suspects down to two. I deflated. Dad had next to no input into my career, but even he wouldn't throw me to the wolves. That only left …

Fuck's sake. I felt myself sagging into the plush chair opposite Mia, frustrated and honestly feeling quite sick.

"Mother?"

"Looks that way."

"Get her on the phone, we need—"

"Hang on," Mia said, her tone serious now. "Before we confront her, we need to have a conversation. Despite what your parents may think, they do not influence how I represent you. You are my client, meaning you are my priority. Understand? From this moment onwards, anything concerning you or even Tessa goes through me."

"Yeah," I felt reassured and yet unnerved at the same time. This dynamic between us felt different; Mia was one of the few people to treat me like a human and encouraged me in my acting in more ways than even she knew. She pushed me for roles that casting directors didn't see me for, ensuring they saw my acting range before saying yes or no. Those auditions mainly turned into yeses.

How could I have doubted her?

"Sorry," I mumbled and I could have sworn that icy exterior softened. She glanced at me as she scrolled through her phone.

"You aren't the one who needs to apologise." Mia sighed, placing the phone on the desk between us with the outgoing call on loudspeaker. Mother answered almost immediately. I half expected her to deny it; on the contrary, she did the opposite.

"Of course I told the reporters her name!" Mother barked, the static in no way hiding the sneer in her voice. "I don't think either of you realises how this has impacted me."

"You?" I demanded incredulously, in disbelief that somehow she had twisted this to make it about her. "How did you come to that conclusion?"

"Because, Jonathan, critics would rather talk about my child's sex life than a film I poured my blood, sweat and tears into!" She ranted, switching to some creative French that I'm sure even Mia got the gist of, before continuing in English. "I gave those parasites something else to feed on. What's the difference? We were going to tell them this story anyway."

"Yes," Mia said through gritted teeth, mastering her composure, "but when we had the story finalised, and both Jonathan and Tessa were media prepped!"

That sunk in for a moment. I fleetingly wondered if she regretted revealing Tessa's name early. I could almost imagine her shrugging this off, her indifference overshadowing any parental concern.

"How are we prepping them?" Mother asked, and I scoffed. She had a nerve. "What was that, Jonathan?"

Fuck. She heard that. Fucking loudspeaker.

"*Jonathan* and *I* will be working with Tessa to get their story watertight," Mia said, picking up the phone, "and until they are fully prepared under my supervision, this will be an NDA arrangement between the three of us. Can't have any leaks, can we?"

And with that, she hung up on my mother. Fucking hell.

73

This woman was an actual legend. I was momentarily stunned silent. Mia sat back in her chair and, unless I was mistaken, she actually looked pleased with herself.

"That's the coolest thing you've ever done, you know that?" I said, unable to stop grinning. Mia merely rejected the incoming call – Mother probably ready to lose her shit – and turned to me, businesslike.

"We need Tessa to come in," she said sharply, her eyes narrowing at my ringing phone. "Ignore your mother. This can't wait. The sooner we get this story straight, the better. Go ring Tessa, now."

Obeying orders, I headed into the hallway and tried calling Tessa again. My heart felt like it was in my throat, and I was already on edge, but I jolted when I heard the soft "Hello?"

Shit. She'd answered. Weirdly, I wasn't expecting to hear her voice. Nor was I expecting the feeling of relief that washed over me.

"Hey, it's me," I said softly, trying to reassure her with my voice alone. "How are you?"

"Been better," Tessa half-laughed, the sound making me smile. "Sorry I missed your calls, I've been in lectures all day and had to keep my phone off."

"Don't apologise," I said and then added earnestly, "I didn't leak your name, I swear."

"I believe you." She hesitated. "Do you know who did?"

My stomach lurched at that question. Naturally, she'd want to know. I wouldn't expect anything less. I should have been prepared or had an answer ready, but like an idiot I had nothing. I couldn't tell her my mother had leaked her name; she'd back out immediately and deem me completely untrustworthy. I wouldn't blame her. That betrayal would run too deep, and I wasn't the one who'd caused it. Anger and resentment surged in my chest, but I forced myself to sound genuinely calm as I said, "No, I have no idea."

That lie made me feel worse than I expected. Somehow lying to Tessa was harder than lying to my agent, mates or even my parents.

"Oh. Okay." Tessa sounded disappointed, which added to the guilt that she'd believed me so easily. "So what do we do now?"

"Mia wants us to meet and plan just that," I told her, secretly impressed she was already thinking along those lines. "You still on campus?"

"Yeah, I can get a bus or taxi and come meet you?" Tessa offered, but I already had a plan in mind. We needed to get her here fast and unnoticed.

"I'll come and get you." Thankfully, I kept my Yamaha motorcycle in Robinson & Clarke' private parking, and it just so happened I had an extra helmet.

13

Tessa

"I'm not getting on that."

"Why not?"

"Because I don't feel like dying today."

My jaw had dropped when Jonathan rolled up outside my accommodation building on death on wheels. As much I hated to admit it, he looked good on that bike. The leather jacket and his confidence as he pulled up added a whole layer of sexy. But I was not going to put my life in the hands – or wheels – of that.

He leaned casually on the handlebars, his lips curved in a smile as he held the spare helmet. I was cautious in my stance on the pavement, feeling like my shoes were made of concrete. Nope, I was not moving. No way.

"Come on," he said, clearly fighting the urge to laugh at my absolute terror. "I'm fully licensed, and I've been driving bikes since I was seventeen. It's totally safe. I promise."

"You can't really promise that," I said. Then added in a rush, "According to the National Highway Traffic Safety Administration, thirteen cars out of every one hundred thousand are involved in a fatal accident, but motorcycles have a fatality rate of seventy-two per one hundred thousand."

"That's a small number, technically." He smirked. His confidence had no effect on my nerves. "I mean, we're barely a blip in those statistics. Come on. It's fast and a safe way for us to get through London without the paparazzi hounding us. The helmets aren't just a safety precaution. You know, if I didn't know better … I'd say you were scared, Tessa."

My spine straightened at that. "I'd say more cautiously apprehensive …"

"Scared," Jonathan said again, his smile becoming softer. "Hey, it's okay to be scared. But you can trust me to get you there in one piece. I meant it when I said I'd keep you safe."

"I'm not scared," I said stubbornly, choosing to ignore how swoon-worthy his voice sounded after the first part. Growing up with two siblings, you unintentionally developed a natural competitive streak. Despite my nerves, a part of me wanted to prove I could do this. I was finding it harder to ignore that temptation. Bloody hell. A month ago, I'd say I would never do anything this spontaneous. Yet here I am, contemplating riding a deadly machine with my fake actor boyfriend.

Jonathan raised his eyebrow, a challenge in his eyes as he swung off the bike with ease and stood in front of me.

"Yeah?" he said, flashing me a playful grin. He held up the helmet. "Prove it."

Going against every instinct inside of me, I shoved the helmet ungraciously on my head. Stupid, stupid, stupid. Clearly, I'd learned nothing from my religious re-watches of the *Back to the Future* trilogy. Sometimes it's okay to be a chicken. But not today. Jonathan chuckled and, with much gentler hands than I'd expected, he fastened the helmet more securely. Goosebumps trailed across my skin whenever his fingertips brushed my cheek. We both smiled at each other. Why did I feel so seen?

Getting on the bike was easier than I expected. I didn't fall off the other side, which was already an achievement. My hands floundered behind Jon's back, hesitating at his shoulders and then his waist. Did I hold on to him like in the films? We were already wedged together on one seat, but still. I was kind of thankful he was busy putting on his helmet and didn't see my awkwardness up close. I coughed, catching his attention.

"Umm, where do I hold on?" I asked, pulling down the tinted visor to give my hands something to do.

"Oh. That's totally up to you," he said with what sounded like a smile. Though I couldn't see. He cleared his throat. "There's a handle you can hold on to, or you can wrap your arms around my waist."

My hands tentatively reached for the handle at the side of the bike, but the engine revving made me jump a foot off the seat. I instinctively wrapped my arms around his waist, holding on tight. Over the engine, I definitely heard him laugh. He was enjoying this.

"Shut up," I said through gritted teeth, but secretly admitted that holding on to him was having a more calming effect than expected.

"I didn't say anything," he said, being less discreet with his laughter. He sobered up quickly and said more seriously, "Ready?"

Despite every nerve and impulse screaming the contrary, I said with way more confidence than I felt, "Yeah. Ready."

Jonathan kicked the bike into life and drove off-campus. It was faster than I'd expected, but he wasn't kidding when he said he was experienced. He weaved in and out of cars with ease. The feeling of the wind rushing past us and the pedestrians being nothing more than blurs was exhilarating; it was almost like flying. I kept my arms securely around him as we sped through London, the day slowly turning into twilight. And yet having Jonathan as the constant that was with me and grounding me ... it felt like the most natural thing in the world.

14

Jonathan

My entire life had been made for structure – auditions, line learning, taking notes from directors, reshoots – but this, riding the streets on this bike, was my little rebellion. My way of saying "fuck you" to that tired old structure. The speed, the rush and the control were still thrilling, even after four years of riding.

Until today, this was my time to be on my own. I'd never let anyone on my bike. Tessa was the exception. Although no women I'd hung out with in the past would have had the bottle to trust me to drive at this speed – many of them would've been panicking over keeping their hair pristine. But Tessa was braver than even she thought. Despite her nerves, she'd jumped on with a pretty cute stubbornness. I also wasn't complaining about her arms locked around me; it felt nice.

Someone must have been looking down on us; the streets were surprisingly less jam-packed than usual. I was tempted to push the speed a bit faster but decided against it because Tessa's grip was still vice-like tight.

"We almost there?" she asked, her voice muffled as we

slowed for a red light. She didn't even relax her grip when we were stationary. I used the moment to take one hand off the handle and squeeze her hands clasped on my chest. Without words, I was trying to reassure her that we weren't about to crash in a ball of fire, not with me driving, and I felt her chest heave a sigh. Her hands relaxed slightly; it took a lot to put my hand back on the bike.

"Yeah, you okay?" I said, raising my voice a bit louder as a commotion kicked off two cars behind. Cars honking like twats, even though the light ahead was only just turning amber.

"Yep. I'm fine, just—" Whatever she was going to say turned into a squeal as I drove through the green light. I couldn't help the grin as the vice-like grip returned.

Sooner than I'd expected or hoped, we were pulling up inside the underground car park. I parked in my usual spot, feeling Tessa relax her grip, and I got off the bike.

"Need some help?" I asked, pulling the helmet off as Tessa swayed in her seat. Fuck, was she going to be sick? Instead, she hopped off the bike and looked ready to run a marathon. That infectious smile was back; I'd got that same adrenaline rush my first time.

"That was so cool!" she gushed, looking like a bunny on crack. "I can't believe I did that. Wow. Wow!"

"Fun, right?" I laughed, moving close to her as she pulled off her helmet. Her hair was frizzed up, but she didn't seem to notice. Without thinking, I reached out and tucked a strand behind her ear. Man, those green eyes were gorgeous up close. Why did people hype up blue eyes so much? They hadn't met this woman.

We stared at each other a bit too long; my fingertips grazing her neck accidentally jarred us both back to reality. She laughed awkwardly, using her fingers to comb through her brown hair. I let my hand fall to my side, feeling stupid for some unknown reason.

"Do I look that bad?" she asked. She looked anything but bad.

"You look beautiful," I said softly, meaning it completely. She laughed that off. Did she think I was joking? I forced a smile, confused still by this girl. Whenever I said one thing, she automatically took it differently or dismissed it.

"Right. Okay." Tessa shrugged, looking around the deserted car park. "So, where do we go? Don't want to keep Brienne of Tarth waiting, do we?"

* * *

Mia did indeed give Brienne-of-Tarth vibes when the elevator doors opened, and her glaring stare was there to greet us. Of course, she was furious I had left without telling her, but even she couldn't deny I'd had a brilliant idea. I'd got Tessa here quickly, safely, and neither of us was seen. But she just ushered the pair of us into her office.

Tessa and I sat across the desk from Mia; Tessa's eyes roamed the office in apparent awe. This must look extravagant to her. Was it bad the sight of money had such little effect on me?

"Right," Mia barked from her desk chair, scrolling through social feeds on her phone. "We need to get your story straight. There are already networks eager to get an exclusive interview, so we need to act fast."

Tessa pulled out a notebook and pen, ready to take notes. (The blue notebook had a tiny TARDIS inscribed on the cover

– a *Doctor Who* fan. Not surprised.). I couldn't hide my grin when she looked at Mia expectantly – momentarily throwing Mia off her train of thought.

"Right," she said again, getting back into the swing of things. "How long have you two been an item? It can't be any time before March because you were linked to Nina Mikhailova around that time while you were starring in *Vampire Huntress*."

"Linked?" I said, forcing myself not to scoff. "We had one sex scene in the season finale, and that makes us linked? Our characters were linked, not us!"

Nina was someone I could have slept with if I'd wanted to – she'd made no secret of her attraction towards me, but I couldn't see her as anything more than my co-star. My first leading role on a big-budget network show, I wasn't going to jeopardise that for a fuck. No matter how fit the woman was, blurring the lines between us and our characters was a hard pass. When she clocked I had no interest in her romantically or sexually, her behaviour towards me soured. We did our scenes, but she barely spoke to me, which soon became evident to the whole cast and crew. I was secretly relieved when we didn't get renewed for a second season and *Awaken* came along. Nina and I hadn't spoken since.

"That show had such wasted potential," Tessa mused to herself, looking up when she caught me looking at her. "Oh. I'm halfway through series one. Thought I'd do a little research, but I can see why it didn't get renewed. I mean, you were good – it was just difficult to take you seriously when you had your shirt off for practically every scene, even scenes that were quite tragic. Plus, in the original books which the show was based on, your characters don't get together till much later. The writers were just feeding fan service rather than being authentic to the characters or plot."

"That's exactly what I thought," I said, amazed to hear the criticism I'd had for twelve episodes spoken from someone else's mouth. And, more importantly, "You thought I was good?"

"When the show didn't rely on the Female Gaze, yeah," Tessa admitted, almost shyly, as she went back to scribbling in that notebook. I was on the verge of craning my neck to see what she was writing, but Mia coughed irritably.

"May?" I offered. Both women nodded. "Four months is a reasonable time frame for keeping a relationship private."

"Good, but where did you meet?" Mia asked, and then she hastily added before I could say it, "And it can't be at a convention or a signing. Tessa is an unknown to the industry; we can't push a narrative that she's an obsessive fangirl. It needs to be authentic, a mutual connection."

Yeah, that would make it look staged as fuck. Well, we met in a nightclub. We did plenty of talking. It wasn't just about the sex. Her banter hooked me; the fact she was so passionate about writing – everything about her enticed me on sight. The truth was, if we'd met in different circumstances … I'd have still wanted to talk to her.

Tessa tapped her pen against her notepad rhythmically, chewing on her bottom lip. Thinking. She looked uncertain over how to say what she had in mind. I caught the glance in my direction, then she looked at Mia instead, her jaw set.

"We met in the Oxford Botanic Garden," Tessa said, hesitating for the briefest moment before continuing. "There's a bench where I used to go and read during the summer when I was younger."

"Why would you travel from Hertfordshire to Oxford to

read on a bench by yourself?" Mia asked, and Tessa's pause sent a chill down my spine. Fuck, Mia wasn't meant to know that, and she knew it. What else did she read in that fucking file?

"How did you know that's where I lived?" Tessa asked, evidently confused, and before Mia could dig herself into a deeper grave, I jumped in.

"I told her," I said casually, meeting Tessa's eyes with a relaxed smile. "You told me that night, remember? Sorry. Didn't think that was an issue."

"Oh, it's not. I was just surprised," she said, seemingly reassured. When she glanced back at her notebook, I shot Mia a glare and she had the decency to look ashamed. There better be no more slip-ups. I wished she'd never dug up that file on her; it could be the derailing of all of this.

"So why the Botanic Garden?" I asked Tessa, partly to distract her from Mia's comment and partly out of genuine curiosity. She turned to face me, and that smile of hers had my complete attention.

"Well, it's kind of sad," Tessa admitted awkwardly, grinning despite herself, "but in the last *His Dark Materials* book, there's a bench where the two main characters agree to meet in their parallel universes. Even though they can't be in the same world together, sitting on that bench every year keeps their love for each other alive. It's a sad but kind of beautiful ending. A couple of years ago, they unveiled a dæmon stainless steel sculpture of Pantalaimon and Kirjava behind this bench – those are Lyra and Will's souls manifested as talking animals. My mum used to take me to that bench, but then I started going by myself. I guess it was my little tradition. Stupid, really."

"No, it's not," I said earnestly, meaning it. Why would that even be stupid? It was actually kind of cool but also made me have a ton more questions. Why would Tessa go so far for alone time? What was she trying to escape from? There was no way I could ask such personal questions, especially in front of Mia – who was glancing between the pair of us, utterly perplexed.

"So, we met in Oxford and started chatting, and it went from there," I said, already visualising how good this would sound to the media and enjoying the fantasy myself. "Two strangers on a bench, getting to know each other."

"Simple, but romantic," Mia pondered, looking more than satisfied. "We'll run with that story and go through potential outlets to have your first interview."

"Interview?" Tessa's eyes widened and she was suddenly completely motionless. "You'll be prepped and ready in no time." Mia's dismissive reassurance was not working on Tessa, even I could see that.

"You'll be fine," I told her gently, but instead of giving the smile I was getting used to seeing, she merely nodded. Her thoughts were elsewhere.

My mind drifted to Tessa's Botanic Garden, thinking how great that would have been. If parallel universes were a thing, I hoped there was a universe where another Jonathan and Tessa could have met like that. No media staging or being forced to pretend for their respective futures. Instead, just a bloke who saw a beautiful girl reading and had the nerve to have a conversation with her. As normal people.

That universe sounded way more appealing.

15

Tessa

Mrs Robinson was efficient; I'd give her that. She made sure Jon and I had crucial elements of our lives scripted to memory: he'd spent the first seven years of his life in France, trailing after his mother's production schedule; I'd spent mine in the heart of the countryside … my only real company was the pages of the books I read or the indie films I watched. I stayed with the loner vibe, only really elaborating on parts I had to. I was surprised by Jonathan's origins – drifting between Paris, London and the United States; amazingly, the British accent had stuck.

Robinson didn't ask as many questions as I'd expected; it seemed I just needed to memorise Jonathan's life. But then he started asking me questions. He wanted to know everything. I skimmed over most of it, cautiously explaining the aftermath of my parents' divorce. He could tell I was omitting but didn't push it. Would he know everything if he was my real boyfriend? No, not this early. The office seemed to fade into the night around us; I didn't realise how late it was till Mrs Robinson snapped on a lamp.

"I should probably get back," I said, jarring both Jonathan and Robinson out of their background checks of potential interviewers. Yes, the prospect of performing our staged romance on national TV was still gnawing at me. Would I be able to fool thousands of viewers? I wrote the parts; playing them was another story.

"Oh. Christ, is that the time?" Robinson asked, looking genuinely surprised at the time on her phone: 22:47 to be exact. "Right. We should wrap this up. Just one more thing, Yana from *Cine-Chat* has been spamming my inbox. She wants the first scoop."

"Fuck no," Jonathan said firmly. I couldn't blame him. I turned to Robinson.

"She's got some nerve," I added, surprised to see Robinson give a slight nod of agreement. "What is she thinking?"

"About her reputation, Teresa," Robinson answered coolly. "It's a career-saving move for both of them, but I agree with Jonathan. She'll try and twist the narrative or catch one of you out, which is why we need a sympathetic ear. Someone like …"

Whether it was for dramatic effect or she genuinely couldn't find the page, a long minute went by before she pulled up a profile. Ochuole Kikelomo from *The O Show*. Her face was instantly recognisable; I had an internal fangirl moment. She was one of the few people to progress from the cyber web of YouTube and onto her own talk show. I streamed her show whenever I had the chance, mainly because her topics mostly revolved around literature and cinema. Her show wasn't as popular in the States as it was here in the UK, but she'd been known to tackle tough subjects on representation through page and screen.

"She meets the demographic you appeal to." Robinson ticked off an invisible checklist. "Her viewers are all film and book fanatics, so that already lands with the right audience, and it helps you're both—"

"Black? You mean it'll help that the host and I are both black?" Jonathan finished for her, a hint of exasperation in his voice. "I fail to see why that matters?"

"It doesn't, but it does to the media – it's about meeting all demographics that you apply to," Robinson said heavily, hastily moving on because even I noticed how uncomfortable the air had suddenly become. "What matters is that we have a sympathetic ear who will help push this narrative. We need the world to believe you're in love!"

* * *

The ride back felt slower – whether it was because the engine was lulling me to sleep or Jon was driving more cautiously, I had no clue. Either way, I found myself leaning my head against his back as my eyelids felt heavy.

A sadness had swept over me that I couldn't really name, but it was there. It started when I told that bench story; it felt like I'd given away something precious. That bench was my special place. It had been twisted into a lie for a fictional Tessa; it was no longer private. *Nothing stays private* – I was starting to see just how true that statement was.

"Fuck," Jonathan breathed, and I looked around, spotting in horror what had caused the bike to slow to a stop at the end of the road. Outside my building were at least forty photographers. They were huddled against the cold, but all eyes seemed to be on alert. They were ready at a moment's notice. No one noticed us, whether it was the darkness or that we were too far down the road.

My heart felt like it'd been dipped in ice. Seeing those paparazzi and knowing they were specifically looking for me made this charade seem all too real. I tried to clear my head; I needed to be rational. If it was just me, then there wasn't much of a story. Once I'd made my way through the mob and scanned my student card, I'd be safe.

I unwrapped my arms from Jonathan's waist and started to get off the bike, trying to calm the utter terror swirling in my stomach. If I was quick, this could be over quickly.

"You're not walking into that!" Jonathan snapped, his voice causing me to hesitate. I shook my head. What was the alternative?

"You have a better idea?" I retorted. "I'll be fine; it'll be worse if they see you here. I'll just pull the 'no comment' card and get inside quickly. Easy-peasy."

"Did you just—? That's not a plan. You won't be able to get near that door before they pounce on you. This isn't a private property; they actually think they have a right to be there." Jonathan sounded genuinely worried. "I'm not letting you risk getting crushed to death."

"Since when did you *let me* do anything?"

"Seriously?" Jonathan shot a look over his shoulder, pulling up his visor to show his eyebrows creased in a frown. "Everything I just said, and *that's* what you focused on? Fucking feminism."

"There's nothing wrong with being a feminist—"

"THERE THEY ARE!"

We both turned to see a stout and balding journalist pointing at us. Within seconds, the journalist and photographers surged towards us. They were running fast, despite their age and weight – the sounds of snapping and unintelligible questions were deafening on the quiet street. Terror gripped me. Now I understood why the media were called vultures. They looked like animals, and we were the meat.

"You should go!" I said, but Jonathan glared at me. I realised that what I was saying sounded stupid, even to me. Like he'd leave me to these lot. Secretly, I was glad he was as stubborn as me.

"Again. Not a good plan, Teresa." He revved the engine, and I automatically wrapped my arms around him – momentarily forgetting my irritation at his use of my full name. "You trust me?"

"What?" I asked, bewildered, noticing how much closer the paparazzi were. "What does that matter?"

"Do you trust me?" Jonathan shouted over the mob and the engine, both getting dangerously louder.

This was insane, all of this! I was almost too scared to speak, but forced myself to swallow my pride and shouted, "Yeah, I do!"

Like I'd just said the magic words, an entire sequence of events followed in a blur. Jonathan kicked the bike into life and drove at the oncoming mob at a dangerous speed. My arms locked around him; I caught a glimpse of their eager eyes turning to terror as the sweaty middle-aged journalists realised we were driving right at them. My mouth opened to shout a warning or scream, but my throat tightened around any noise I might have made.

It was a game of chicken, and Jonathan was not going to let up. The shouter who'd alerted his cronies widened his eyes in panic and he dived out of the way. Jonathan swerved when the others followed his actions, deliberately avoiding the fallen mob. Somehow, flashes were still blinding us, and the snapping of the cameras followed us into the night.

16

Jonathan

So much for reviving my good boy image. Shit. A cocktail of anger and adrenaline was coursing through my veins. The thought of what could have happened if Tessa walked into that … they were animals, fucking animals. I'd grown up used to the chase, familiar with avoiding those flashing lights and invasive questions. But seeing Tessa's fear had triggered something in me. I just wanted to get her away. I just wanted to keep her safe, but of course … that's not how the papers would report it tomorrow. They'd make those fuckers out to be the ones in danger.

The further we drove, the calmer I seemed to feel. Tessa's fingers trembled against my stomach, whether from the cold or the aftermath of that getaway; I slowed and pulled the bike up in a deserted car park. The orange glow broke the darkness around us; the distant cars broke the eerie silence between us.

Tessa unwrapped her arms from me and slid off the bike without a word. She handed me her helmet wordlessly. She didn't look at me. I watched her pace away from me. She stopped, staring up at the sky. It was so quiet I could hear the precarious breath she released.

Guilt flooded through me. I didn't mean to scare her. Fuck, I was scared just as much as she was. Despite my façade, I was terrified at what could have happened if they caught up with us or I accidentally hit one of those bastards. I took off my helmet, realising how sweaty I was when the cool wind hit my face.

I got off my bike, hesitantly walking over to her. Now I was closer, I could see her face had paled and I momentarily panicked that she might faint. Instead, she turned to face me and had the nerve to smile. Like she was reassuring me or something.

"Sorry," I said, the first thing that popped into my head, then rushed on when she looked confused. "About earlier. I just wanted to get us out of that before it got ugly."

"Why are you apologising?" Tessa said, a disbelieving laugh escaping her lips. "I'm actually glad you didn't let me walk off into that. That was a stupid idea."

"No, it wasn't," I assured her, stepping closer and taking her hands in mine. Her skin was cold beneath my fingers, but she didn't pull away. I was just trying to warm her hands up. That's what I told myself. "No one can be prepared for that. The media have no shame sometimes. Anything to get a story."

"Has it always been like that for you?" She looked at me with eyes wise beyond her years and threaded her fingers through mine. "Even when you were little?"

"Yeah." I shrugged, surprised by the way she was looking at me. Like she was seeing something I had hidden and wasn't judging. I tried to laugh it off, but it sounded hollow to my ears. It had become normal. Some of my earliest memories were of paparazzi chasing after us. No personal space or boundaries.

94

I even remembered Mother causing an uproar when grown men were crouched in bushes outside my primary school, selling pictures of me as a kid for a story.

An unease crept over my skin. Why was I seeing this through Tessa's eyes? Why hadn't I really thought how disgusting and invasive my upbringing had been? Instead, I'd just brushed and laughed it off, thinking it was normal. I mean, what did you expect with the parents I had?

Tessa's fingers tightened on mine. I was shaking. I didn't know what I was feeling, but this girl was tethering me to reality. Her gaze was understanding, like she could see the storm of emotions fighting to surface. I felt too exposed. I wanted to pull away from this anchor and started to do so.

"Hey," she said softly, taking my face in both her hands and keeping my eyes on hers. I couldn't pull myself away from her now. "It's okay. We're okay."

"How are you so sensible?" I asked, unable to stop myself from grinning at her. Her smile was more hesitant, and she briefly glanced away – something dark and troubled brewing behind those eyes.

"Someone had to be, in my family," she said, sadness creeping into her voice. It was her turn to try and pull away, but my hands found hers and held them tight. We stared at each other, something different holding us both in place.

"Don't …" I said so softly. It almost sounded like a plea. I leaned closer, my hands tentatively moving to her waist. She gasped as I pulled her close, my lips moving slowly to meet hers. I didn't want to break the spell between us, and I was hesitant to cross the line. I sensed that Tessa felt the same way. This wasn't a drunk night of passion. This was in a darkened car park. And yet it felt way more intimate.

She tentatively closed the distance between us, her lips grazing mine, and any restraint we were both clinging to crumbled. I crushed my lips to hers, her body moulding perfectly to mine. I felt like I was on fire. Every detail of this kiss was in fucking HD. The way her lips parted for my tongue, every moan or gasp that escaped her lips, how her body felt against my hands.

"Jonathan …" she breathed as she arched her neck back to allow me more access. "Maybe … we should … stop."

"Do you want to?" I asked genuinely, despite how much I wanted her – if she wanted to, we'd stop.

She stared at me, and answered by kissing me back just as enthusiastically. My body sang with pleasure. This quiet car park felt like our own safe haven. This right now was the only thing that mattered. It was fucking heaven.

17

Tessa

Oh … My … God.

Two sides of me were at war. The sensible part of my brain reminded me that kissing Jonathan Adeola was a terrible idea, but the part of me enjoying the way his lips tasted and how strong his arms felt around my waist was winning. I moaned as the kiss deepened, the heat of his body against mine warming me from the cold.

My arms wrapped around his neck, feeling like I was about to melt in his arms. I was breathless, my head was spinning, and it felt like time had come to a halt. That now-tiny, sensible voice was trying to point out this would get complicated or messy, but the sensations Jonathan's lips and body were igniting in me drowned those fears completely.

What was I even thinking? Why had I even wanted to kiss him? I'd wanted to kiss this annoying and cocky guy since that night. Because I was seeing sides to him that the tabloids didn't, and that was the Jon I've secretly wanted for weeks. When he asked if I wanted to stop, the answer was absolutely and definitely no.

"Oi, oi!"

The sound of a car honking caused us to break apart, the headlights of a car momentarily lighting the car park before disappearing into the night. Reality had come crashing back to me, and I hastily stepped out of his arms, avoiding his flirty little eye thing. That was stupid – really, really stupid.

"Where were we?" Jonathan asked, his smirk turning to confusion when I put a hand on his chest, stopping him from coming any closer. I took a deep breath, the breeze cooling my flushed face. "What's the matter, Tess?"

"We can't do that again," I said, sounding harsher than I wanted to and Jonathan looked hurt. "I mean, it was nice. Really nice. But we shouldn't let that happen again, seriously."

"Hey, you were the kisser here," Jonathan annoyingly pointed out, that cockiness creeping back in. "I was an innocent party."

I scoffed, trying to appear more aloof than I felt. My lips were still stinging from the intensity of that kiss. It was meaningless, a spur-of-the-moment thing. Okay, that was a massive lie. A titanic-sized fib, and I think he felt the same. No one was that good an actor.

"It was …" I struggled to find the right words. Irritatingly his smile broadened at that. "Shut up. It was a momentarily lapse of judgement. That's all."

"That's all?"

"Yes. It's been a crazy night."

"You're a terrible liar, Tess," Jonathan said softly, his voice magnetic in the darkness. He moved closer, but I shook my head. No one had called me Tess, ever. Why had he started?

"I was caught up in the moment, that's all," I said firmly, his eyes widening when I added angrily, "I wouldn't be in this mess if it weren't for you."

The words hit harder than I'd expected. I didn't mean it the way it sounded. I wanted to take it back as soon as I said it, mainly because he looked so hurt. An invisible force field had shot up between us and the last twelve hours felt like another lifetime. His face shifted into an emotionless mask. The glint in his eyes was gone.

"Fine," he said curtly, his voice turning scornful. "But do me a favour, don't rewrite what just happened here. Don't try and paint me as the bad guy to make yourself feel better."

"That's not what I'm doing—"

"Isn't it?"

"No!" I said defensively, even though that was exactly what I was doing. "I just don't want this to get complicated. More complicated than it is!"

"Know what I think your problem is?" Jonathan said coolly. "You'd rather hold people at arm's length than let someone see you. The real you, Tess."

"Coming from you, the actor?" I asked cynically, hating how mean I sounded and furious that everything he'd said hit a painful nerve. "You don't need to know me. You just need me to revive your squeaky-clean image, and I need to strengthen my application for film school. Let's just remember what this is."

"Do you think that little of me?" he asked quietly, sounding like I'd punched him in the gut.

"No …"

Tears burned my eyes, but I angrily brushed them away. A chill had descended between us that had nothing to do with the weather. I couldn't believe I'd just thrown that in his face. Why was I being such an idiot? Maybe because he was right, the idea of letting my guard down was terrifying. I would rather keep this dynamic playing pretend; treading into anything real was out of the question.

But I couldn't hurt him just because I was scared. I wasn't my dad. I couldn't stop the tears as I realised that I'd resorted to his behaviour. If the truth hurt, hurt them back. Even Jonathan's eyes widened in shock when I started blubbering in front of him.

"Tessa—"

"I'm sorry!" I cried, backing away when he moved to hug me. That only made me feel worse. "I didn't mean any of that. I'm sorry. Sorry."

"Let's just get back on the bike," Jonathan offered, but I shook my head, and he actually gave a half-grin. "We can't stay here all night, let me take you home."

"I think I'll walk," I said, adding quickly, "I can get a bus. They'll be looking for a bike, that's if they're still out there. I'll be fine."

"Don't be like that," Jonathan sighed, a hint of frustration in his concerned voice.

"Seriously, I just need some time to be alone," I said, taking a moment to put some distance between us. Was I being stupid and stubborn? Yes. But I'd spent my entire life riding night buses by myself. And right now, I'd rather that than let myself get back in a situation with my body pressed against him. Not when I was a crying mess and had made a twat out of myself.

So, with nothing but my weak pride – and ignoring Jonathan's pleas – I turned and walked off towards the bus stop down the street. The word sorry was used a lot, but I'd heard it so much … it was just a meaningless saying, but I never thought I'd be the one saying it.

Pride could only get you so far, especially sitting alone and snot-ridden on an almost empty bus. I cautiously pulled my hood up and sank in my seat, even though my only companions on this night-time travel were a couple snogging each other's faces off, and an older lady in a seat opposite me.

Weirdly, the wizened woman reminded me of my dead grandmother – tight-lipped and grim-faced, only nice to a handful of people. I was one of those people. She'd introduced me to the likes of *Wuthering Heights*, *Jane Eyre* and even slyly gave me her battered copy of *Flowers in the Attic*. That was probably why I was fascinated with Gothic horror. That and living through a twisted family horror show of my own … would Jonathan still want me as his ruse if he knew just how dark things had got?

"Sherbet lemon?"

I jumped, my head whipping round in alarm to see I'd startled the little old lady just as much, making her nearly throw the bag of yellow sweets in the air.

"Oh!" I gasped apologetically, trying to calm my erratic heartbeat. When had I become so jumpy? "Sorry. No, no. Thank you, no."

"Sorry, dear," the woman said, surprising me by clumsily standing and sitting next to me. She took her time picking another sweet, even though they looked identical. "Sure I can't tempt you?"

"Positive," I said, managing a weak smile. "I don't like sweets. Anything sweet actually, especially chocolate."

"Never!" The woman gasped, her eyes widening when I nodded. "Your mother must have had a field day with you."

"My brother and sister made up for my lack of sweet tooth," I said, smiling more genuinely this time when she grinned. I let her eat her sweets in silence; my attention drifted to the window.

"Rough night?" she asked randomly, and I instinctively wiped my nose with my sleeve, as if my puffy eyes and red nose were to do with the weather. "Boyfriend trouble?"

"Yeah, you could say that." I laughed dryly and shrugged. "It's complicated …"

"If I had a tenner for every time I'd heard that, I'd …" She never said what she'd be. Instead, she spotted a sweet that caught her fancy and munched on that before continuing. "What did he do?"

What did Jonathan do? Kiss me in the heat of an intense moment, after first making sure I wanted to kiss him. It was totally consensual. He didn't do anything I didn't want to happen, and then I went on the defensive. It was getting too real. The line between pretending for the media and us had blurred. No, it had vanished completely.

I had a feeling this wise older woman wanted an answer. Those steely grey eyes said as much.

"Things between us have been good." I opted for instead, a half-truth. "But it's getting a bit too real. There are things I don't want him to know. We both knew what this was and now …"

"Now, you're terrified of being vulnerable with him?" this creepily wise lady finished for me, and I nodded feebly. "Young people these days. You can't script or plan these things. Love happens when we least expect it. If you're thinking this way and he's willing to listen, maybe he's not so easily scared off."

Love? Who mentioned love? I definitely hadn't! If anyone should be scared off, it's me linking myself to a celebrity. A celebrity had shown more genuine interest in me than my family had, and opened up to me whenever I asked an inappropriately personal question. Yet I ran a mile when he just wanted to comfort me – a total blubbering and rude mess. He was more than a tabloid or someone playing a part, and that's what scared me.

Not quite love – no way. But knowing it was treading water into something tangible had hit me earlier. Whatever this was, I didn't want to hold Jonathan at a distance. I pulled out my phone and with a deep breath, I typed him a text:

ME: Sorry. Again. Will message you when I get home. Promise I'm okay.

As if she knew, the woman smiled at me and instead of giving me some more words of wisdom she went back to her sweets. I found myself smiling too. She gave strong Dumbledore vibes. Her silence gave me the impression the conversation was over. I was fine with that, really. It was always nice to know you didn't have to force a conversation.

My heart soared when a ping alerted me but dropped to the Earth's core when I saw it was an email. Not just any email, but from my head-of-course lecturer, Lawrence Oliver. The subject: Important Meeting. With three university emails copied in to the thread. After a brief hesitation, I tapped on it, and each word made my chest tighten.

Dear Teresa,

Due to recent events and media attention on campus, we request that you meet with myself, your supervising lecturer Amanda Egbe and Dean of the University Gia Patel as a matter of urgency. Please be on campus at 4 p.m., where I will meet you in the reception to discuss how we proceed with safeguarding during your final

year with us.
  Kindest regards,
  Lawrence Oliver, Course Leader of Media Studies

Oh. This was about to become even more real.

18

Jonathan

My legs ached. I'd been jogging longer than usual – but the muscle burn was a great distraction from the two complications now a constant in my life: Tessa Granger and my career. The former was a bit more cut and dry, especially with a girl like her. The bizarre switch from that amazing kiss and then the aftermath had been jarring. I hated to see her so upset. And yes, things had got heated, but there seemed to be something deeper going on. I'd caught a glimpse of something other than her nerdy exterior, and that scared the shit out of her.

If anyone was going to be scared of being their authentic self, surely I'd own that title. I'd had enough stories fabricated about me. No woman wanted to see that side of me. Except her. That file – the one Mia had compiled about Tessa – kept niggling at my brain. I knew the answer would probably be in there. I also knew that it would be a massive violation to read something Tessa wasn't willing to share – Mother and Mia saw it as a vetting process, I was genuinely concerned. Still, it wasn't worth the guilt I'd feel over betraying her trust. So I told Mia to keep whatever was written inside that folder away from Mother and even Father.

Tessa and I spoke today, which was short and sweet. Light on the sweet. Despite the apology texts, something formal had sprung up between us, and I didn't like it. I'd just got out of the shower, nearly tripping and falling flat on my face when I hastily answered her call.

"Hi," I said quickly, trying to sound casual despite being dripping wet and clinging to the towel around my waist. I sat down on the bed, almost missing what she said. "Huh?"

"I just said 'hi' back," Tessa said, her voice sounding uncomfortable. A beat of silence hung between us. We were both waiting for something, and before I could say a word, she rushed on. "Are you dropping out?"

"Sorry?" I asked in disbelief and had to suppress a laugh when I clocked she was being dead serious. "No, of course not. Are you?"

"No," Tessa admitted, and I breathed a sigh of relief, but then her tone switched back to a forced nonchalance. "Good, great. So, I thought you could read for Josh."

"That's the main love interest guy, yeah?" I asked casually like I hadn't already memorised every word of her script. "Course. I liked his arc."

"Brilliant." Her voice softened, and again, before I could say what I wanted to, she continued. "Oh, and I met with a potential lead this morning. Sarah Dew. She's done mainly indie stuff, but she did a great audition."

The name didn't ring a bell, but my stomach dropped at the thought of playing a romantic role opposite an amateur. Worse, what if she was an obsessive fan? I didn't want Tessa to see how weird women get around me, especially when she treated me normal.

"Yeah, her boyfriend dropped her off," Tessa went on. "We had coffee, and she liked the script too. She seems nice."

Phew. It was highly unlikely this actress had written explicit self-insertion fanfiction about me then. Yes, that had happened … the internet was a scary place.

"Great, do you want to meet up later? To discuss the reading, of course."

"I have a meeting. School thing," Tessa explained, a bit too vague. Something was up.

"Everything okay?"

"Should be," she said, still being evasive, and we left it at that. I think I preferred her crying and ranting. At least that gave me a clue as to what she was thinking or feeling.

The other issue. Acting. The media storm had turned to a drizzle, with a surprising twist on the motorbike incident. It turned out Mia had planted some reporters of her own, and the narrative soon took a very sympathetic turn: ***Need for Speed: Actor Jonathan Adeola and girlfriend flee dangerous Media Mob!***

The journalists had come under criticism not just from the general public and industry professionals. Whitmore had come out with a statement of their own. Mia could barely contain her glee when I entered her office, and she immediately handed me an iPad. I read the statement on their Twitter feed, unable to stop my mouth from falling open:

> *While our students' personal lives do not influence their educational experience, the safety of each student will always remain our top priority. Therefore, we condemn the actions of those who harassed one of our students while on campus.*

We will not indulge in media speculation nor answer any questions regarding the student involved. Still, security will be added near the accommodation buildings after-hours. We are insisting any guest sign in with confirmation from the student they are visiting – to ensure the well-being of our students, staff, and guests takes precedence.

Professor Gia Patel, Dean of Whitmore University of the Arts

"How good is this?" Mia beamed, snatching the iPad back as we both sat at her desk. "Hashtag Jessa is trending, and we've got confirmation for your interview. It'll be next Friday; we need to jump on this positive response ASAP."

"Great," I said half-heartedly, still troubled. "Any news about *Awaken?*"

Mia's fleeting pause was a worrying sign, but I kept my face as composed as possible.

"*Dawn* has been greenlit, and it looks like the last book is close behind," Mia said cautiously, her tone evaporating any excitement I might have felt. "I got an email. The director is still fighting to keep you on. They want a video conference this weekend. I just think they're waiting to see how the public reacts to you and Tessa."

Which is why we had to give a fucking good show. My stomach still lurched at the thought, but what choice did I have?

"The author wants you at a book promotion tomorrow," Mia said, as if sensing what I was thinking, but I'd completely forgotten that I was initially planning on taking Tessa to that as our surprise. Yesterday had blown that plan out the window. "So as promising as that is, I think we should start looking at other projects in development. There are some great American shows in the works. One has a Roberto Aguirre-Sacasa vibe. It's a very small-town mystery. The casting director wants you to read for the star football player at his high school, who falls for the girl next door while a serial killer—"

"No more teen dramas," I said quickly. Her eyes widened in response. "Yes, I know I'm the playing age for a senior in high school or a college freshman – but there's a massive difference between playing a character who is a teenager and playing a walking stereotype. I want something more challenging, something that can show my range."

I'd wanted to say this for ages, since before *Awaken* came along. All of the auditions I'd had in the past had been jock or fuck boy – nothing new or fresh, just eye candy for thirsty viewers. Having a script like Tessa's and knowing she saw me for a character like Josh made me reflect on my potential future auditions.

Yes, Josh was written to be a romantic interest, but Tessa gave his character much more than that. While Josh was trying to be there for the protagonist, you learned he was in a toxic home situation, and his alcoholic mother was abusive. You rarely saw a female character being the abuser, and the characters and plot acknowledged Josh was the victim, and the script saw him starting to seek help. That was what made the love story so great, it wasn't all one-sided, and both characters had moments of vulnerability and growth.

Those were the characters I wanted to play. I needed that nuance to find a footing outside my typecasting. I didn't want to rely on the pretty boy role until I was too old to play it, only to be stuck because no one saw me capable of acting like anything else. I was at the perfect age to explore different stories and parts.

"What were you thinking?" Mia asked, already scanning through her emails on the computer.

"Something indie, more risky and honestly, something to keep me on my toes."

Her brow furrowed as she read something on her screen. I itched to lean over and take a look, but I knew better than to try that. Instead, I waited, my curiosity peaking when she said, "Huh …" to herself, more like a muse.

"Yes?" I asked pointedly, but she instead printed off whatever she was reading and, completely ignoring me, crossed the room to the printer. I watched incredulously as she picked up the freshly printed paper, reading it to herself again. "Mia?"

"Samuel Harrison is making his directorial debut," she said, her eyes on the page still, and she did not indicate whether she was reading aloud or speaking to me. "*Prodigal Son* will be directed from his script, chronicling a semi-autobiographical coming of age story of an African-American teenager coming to terms with the fact he's gay while his religious father condemns the love he's found with a white classmate. This is a period piece, set during the nineties in Forks, Washington—"

"Isn't that where those campy vampire books were set?"

"Where Harrison himself grew up," Mia continued, frowning at my interruption. "He is currently looking for an actor to play the leading role."

"Email him, please?" I asked, having never felt this fucking excited about getting my hands on a script before. "I need to audition for this, Mia!"

Emails were sent, and calls were made, but Samuel Harrison

didn't share my enthusiasm. Correction: he wasn't enthusiastic about me. With the briefest email, Harrison responded to Mia:

Unfortunately, your client is not what we're looking for.

What the fuck did that mean? How could he make that fucking decision without even letting me read the script? I'd been rejected for roles before, but this curt response stung more than others.

While Mia was still in email correspondence with one director who was scared of keeping me on and the other who flat-out didn't want me, I needed some air. Pushing myself physically kept me from lingering on what I was feeling or thinking.

19

Tessa

News of the series of unfortunate events from last night spread like wildfire, except for the car park kiss. That was something only Jon and myself had, without media speculation. Questions and stares followed me wherever I went, but I found allies in unlikely places. Ivy was, of course, her usual protective self, but I wasn't expecting that response from my flatmates.

People who barely spoke two words to me were suddenly checking in with me. Sid offered to make me a cup of tea, and Emmanuel didn't bombard me for notes. Small acts of kindness, but the most jarring was Fiona, our flat's resident drama undergraduate, pulling me to the side between lectures, her face a picture of empathy.

"I just want you to know I'm here for you," she said, her red hair falling in curls today – she went for a different hairstyle and colour depending on whatever fit her mood or character she was preparing to play. I thought this was her natural colouring, though. I thought.

"Thank you," I said, moving to sidestep her and a bit creeped out despite her frozen smile when she moved to block my escape. Even though we lived together, this was the longest conversation we'd had outside our flat. "I have to get to class …"

"Oh, I know!" Fiona gushed, grasping she had to get to the point. "Obviously. Okay, so I thought that I could be your decoy!"

"Pardon?" I asked, bewildered, realising there was a strong possibility that she'd had part of this conversation in her head. She often thought before she spoke.

"I can be your d-e-c-o-y." She pronounced it slowly, like she was speaking to a small child, which only pissed me off. I think it was clear on my face because she hastily backtracked. "Like I have a brunette wig from when I played Cathy in *Wuthering Heights* last year on stage. Well, it was an amateur production, and the colouring isn't as pretty as yours, but it can work for a quick getaway from the paprazzle to see your beau!"

Yeah, because I was really looking for a repeat of last night. Because I was too nice, I gave a vague mumble of agreement and made a quick getaway. I tried my hardest to focus on whatever lecture or seminar I was sitting in, but the day passed in a blur. When I wasn't burying my head in textbooks, I was pointedly ignoring sly comments from the likes of Kaitlyn and her cronies of bitches sat mere feet away. All day I managed to do just that – mainly because I had Ivy and my misfit flatmates shadowing me – but Cinema Cultures was the one seminar I found myself sitting on my own. With our lecturer running late, Kaitlyn jumped at the opportunity.

"She's not even that pretty. What does he see in her?"

"Maybe she lets him do some kinky shit in the bedroom."

"No! She's too vanilla for that."

"It's always the quiet ones that are freaks!"

My hand was hurting. I realised too late it was clenched into a fist and my nails were dug hard into my flesh. I looked at my palm, seeing the four dents from my nails. I relaxed my hand and tried to ignore the sick feeling in my stomach, remembering I had only been this stressed once before. I didn't want to go down that path again.

I glared up at the Bitch Clan. A trio of unnatural blondes that were as unoriginal as you'd expect. Kaitlyn and her minions were sitting at the very back of the lecture hall. They weren't even attempting to be quiet, which meant other people heard them as well. I met Kaitlyn's cold stare, fighting the urge to lunge at her.

"You got something to say?" I asked. A hush fell over the hall. Even Kaitlyn appeared to lose some of her nerve for a second.

"Nope!" Kaitlyn chirped in a sickly-sweet voice. Her two so-called friends laughed like they'd been given a cue from a director. "It's always nice to be proven right."

"About me being an Insta Whore?" I demanded, my anger rising, and even her hangers-on knew better than to feed Kaitlyn's ego right now. "No, I'd say you were way off the mark. So could you stop talking about me like I'm not here? You got something to say, say it to my fucking face!"

"Look at that," Kaitlyn roared, ignoring the fact that no one was enjoying her little spectacle. Most were actually trying to ignore her. "Not so innocent after all, are we?"

"I never said I was innocent," I said evenly, trying to keep calm and not rise to her bait. "But I am an adult, so I'm asking you again to mind your own business."

I turned back to my textbook, but the words blurred in

my vision – whether through tears or blind anger. I blinked rapidly and was thankful when the oblivious tutor strolled in. I tried to focus on my breathing and clear my head, but Kaitlyn's sneering words kept ringing in my head.

"She's so defensive," Kaitlyn whispered obnoxiously loudly and the sound carried over to where I sat. "But what can you expect from council scum. The girl is the definition of white trash."

My body went on autopilot, and before I knew it, I was on my feet, shoving my books back into my rucksack. Everyone was watching me now, but I didn't give a fuck. Let them stare. Why not take a picture. Apparently, mine cost a lot these days. Tears blinded my eyes as I slung my rucksack over my shoulder and hurried past students, and dashed for the stairs. The lecturer said something, but I didn't make out the concerned questions – my brain was fixed on getting through the double doors and out of here. If I stayed there a minute longer, I'd say or do something I'd regret.

Nearly there – my hand was just about to shove the door open, but that harsh voice broke through my foggy mind and caused me to stop dead in my tracks.

"I wouldn't worry," Kaitlyn told Carla, the Cinema Cultures lecturer. "I think Tessa is just having a psychotic episode. She's getting too much attention. Mental health issues usually come from the mother, I'm told. Especially with her background."

Any self-restraint I was clinging to shattered like glass. Before I could think rationally about it, I had turned and was storming back the way I'd come. This wasn't anger; this was pure and unfiltered hatred I felt right now. I was heading straight for that little bitch, not caring what anyone thought any more.

Her eyes widened briefly in panic. She had caught a glimpse of my face and was not prepared for the look she saw there. Her mouth moved to say something, or maybe she had been speaking this whole time, but no one's voice registered with my brain. All I heard was white noise. All I felt was loathing.

My clenched fist swung out, finding its target. Another punch and another cut off her scream, each one easing the ache I felt in my chest, just a bit. The iron fist around my heart lessened as I hit her over and over. Seeing someone feel a fraction of the pain I was feeling felt good. Too good. I didn't want to stop. I wanted to hit and hit until this anger had gone from me into someone else. Why shouldn't she have this pain instead? This spiteful, vapid, callous person. What had I done to deserve this?

Someone grabbed me around the waist and pulled me back off her, but I didn't fight against the arms that now had me. Instead, I pulled free of the lecturer or student retraining me and backed away from the bloody scene. The bloody scene I'd created …

Kaitlyn sat slumped in a crying heap in the chair, clutching her nose as blood pooled through her fingers. The same crimson that was now coated over my knuckles, but I felt numb. Worse than that, I was not scared or regretting my actions. Chaos was all around me, as students and staff rushed about, but I felt calm. Calmer than I'd felt in years.

Medics were called, lecturers bustled in and out, stories were exchanged and exaggerated, and students were dismissed while Kaitlyn was cared for. All the while, I stood by the wall in perfect silence. Frozen, like I'd looked straight into the eyes of Medusa herself.

That's when I started to feel scared. Not scared of the

consequences of what I'd just done to Kaitlyn, but terrified of me …

20

Jonathan

I was expecting the house to be empty; it usually was at this time of day. This house had always been too big for three people, especially three who barely acknowledged each other's existence. Still, I couldn't help feeling surprised to find Father sitting in the kitchen; his eyes fixed on whatever he was reading on his laptop.

"What you doing here?" I asked as I headed to the fridge, jarring him back to reality. I downed a whole bottle of water, breathless but still pumped for another jog already.

"Nice way to greet your old man," he said, his eyes not leaving his laptop. "How're things with that girl?"

"She has a name," I said, my irritation apparent enough for him to turn and frown at me. "And it's going okay. Tide's turning already."

"Just be careful with that one, son," he said gravely, scratching the stubble he had started growing. I wasn't entirely sure if this was for a casting or just him not bothering to shave. We never actually spoke about anything acting-related. Even when I was a minor, he left it to Mia or Mother. He never

118

seemed interested.

I lowered the second bottle of water from my lips. What the fuck was he talking about?

"Careful of what?" I asked warily, my guard already up. "Of Tessa? There's nothing to worry about there. She's all good."

"So, her using you to get into a film school does not concern you?" he demanded, adding coolly before I could ask, "Mia tells me these things. All I'm saying is you need to keep your head in the game; ambitious women are brutal. One wrong move, and our reputations could be ruined."

That's rich. Fucking more than rich. And what right did Mia have, telling him about Tessa's stakes in this? So much for things staying between us, I'd actually believed that for a second. Since when had this family shown an interest in who I saw or what I did with them? I'd hardly been set a great example of maintaining a healthy relationship through my parents: they spent their lives pretending the other didn't exist. Instead of rising to his bait, I turned and headed for the stairs.

"Lucky for me, I don't have your taste in women," I said coolly, satisfied by the affronted look he gave me as I went upstairs.

Alone in my room, I flopped down on the bed, and my energy powered down like a battery. I wanted to take another jog one minute, and now I just wanted to sink into this duvet. This room had never felt like my room, even as a kid. All those years working abroad and being in other countries, I'd never put my stamp on this room aside from my clothes, TV and games console – which I hadn't played in so long; PlayStation was onto whatever number it was on now. This looked like a nice guest room, with no character or sign someone had grown up there.

My eyes were on the verge of sleep, but instead I dug my phone out of my pocket and hit the most recent call, meaning to chat to Mia about respecting boundaries when it came to my father. Instead, a much more appealing voice answered.

"Jonathan?"

Any temptation to rant at my agent was erased from my brain when I heard that shaky voice. I sat up, instantly concerned when it sounded like she was crying and trying to hide it.

"Hey, what's wrong?" I asked softly, and my stomach dropped at the silence. Silence except for the sharp intakes of breaths. "Tess, talk to me. What happened?"

"I messed up!" Tessa sobbed, the floodgates opening. "I really, really messed up, and now I don't know what I'm supposed—" She broke off, and I thought the line had gone dead. Instead, she continued in barely a whisper, "I have to go. Sorry."

"Tess, wait," I said, but I was now talking to nothing. I tried calling back, but it went straight to voicemail. I ignored any sane part of me and hurried downstairs and out of the house. One destination, one person on my mind.

* * *

To be safe, I parked and chained my bike in the nearby Iceland car park, choosing to walk the short distance from supermarket to campus. I had no idea where to even start or if Tessa would want me here, but I couldn't just do nothing after hearing how distressed she sounded.

I made my way to the student accommodation building,

trying to look as casual as possible with sunglasses on in autumn. I felt as conspicuous as Tessa in that fucking green hat, but thankfully no one noticed me as I walked up to the sliding doors. And walked right into the glass, smacking my head in the process.

"Fuck!" I hissed to myself, realising too late that there was a card scanner to open the doors. Of course there fucking was; they'd hardly let anyone in. By some small mercy, no one was sat at reception to see my idiocy, but that also meant I had no one to let me in. Brilliant.

A student with braids was practically running through reception inside, swiping her card and colliding into me as she rushed out. For a person with such a willowy frame, the force of her made me stagger and my glasses slid off my soon-to-be bruised nose.

"Move!" the girl barked, her glare turning to recognition. "Shit. You're Jonathan Adeola."

It was a statement, not a question and I hastily made to walk past her before the doors shut. But she grabbed my arm with surprising force.

"I'm not doing autographs!" I snapped, surprised at the look of incredulity as she stepped back. She looked at me like I was a complete prick. To be fair, I'd sounded like one.

"Do I look like someone who wants your autograph?" she asked dryly, giving me a look that said she was completely unimpressed with what she saw. I gritted my teeth when the doors slid shut behind her, leaving me stuck outside. Again.

"No, sorry," I said briskly, choosing to ignore the fact she should be apologising to me for nearly knocking me over. "I'm actually looking for someone."

"Tessa?" she said and her expression lost that bitchy sneer, shifting into genuine concern. Something on my face made her nod, confirming something in her mind. "I'd thought as much."

"Where is she?" I asked, not even bothering to hide how worried I was.

"Up at campus, I was just heading there now. She got into a fight."

"Is she hurt?"

"You kidding?" She raised her eyebrows, but remained serious as she explained, "Tessa's fine, but she's with the dean and course lecturers. If this goes bad, she could be kicked out. Especially if that bitch who started it gets her way."

I turned to head up to the campus building, not even entirely sure what I was going to do or say. Tessa's friend pulled me back, making me feel like a petulant child with the glare she was giving me. I pulled my arm out of her grasp, really trying to keep calm in front of this infuriating woman.

"She's in enough shit without you marching in there white-knighting her!" she pointed out evenly, cutting me off before I could speak. "What's that actually going to achieve? All you'll do is make a scene."

"What am I supposed to do then?" I demanded, genuinely at a loss and frustrated that she was right. She seemed to be weighing the pros and cons of something and sighed.

"Fuck's sake, I'm going to regret this," she said to herself as she turned on her heels and swiped the scanner. She turned back to glare at me, annoyed I was still where I was. "Come on then. And put those stupid glasses back on!"

Oh, right. I did as I was ordered. She had me sign in as her cousin. I caught a glimpse of her name – Ivy Daniels – next to my fake one, Timothy. I didn't know if that was genuine or if she was finding ways to be petty, but I followed her through reception and into the elevator.

We didn't speak to each other and I barely had time to take in my surroundings of bland university accommodation walls before we were getting out and Ivy pulled me along with her, pressing a fob to where a key lock would be. I followed her inside, still fighting the urge to go find Tessa myself. The flat was unremarkable, as in you had to go down a short corridor before going into a hybrid of a living room and kitchen. Instead of leading me down there, Ivy shoved me through a random door.

With a start, I realised I was in Tessa's room. No question about that. Whether it was the books lining the shelves or the DVDs – who actually owned DVDs any more? – this room had a weirdly familiar vibe to it. It was very Tessa. In a digital age, I wasn't surprised Tessa preferred to have physical copies.

"Wait here and don't come out unless it's me or Tessa," Ivy warned. "I'll be back in a bit."

"What if I need the toilet?" I blurted stupidly, feeling more stupid when Ivy shoved the door next to me open and I saw a mini en suite, complete with shower and toilet. Oh. I turned to her and said genuinely, "Thanks for this."

Ivy's expression softened ever so slightly, but she merely shrugged off my words and closed the door. I heard her rushed footsteps and the front door slammed, leaving me alone. I sat down on Tessa's purple duvet, surveying the small room that looked and felt more like a home than my ridiculously massive house ever had.

My eyes fell on a picture on her bedside table – four brunette people smiling on what looked like a beach on a cloudy day, one of them a slightly younger Tessa. I picked it up and scanned the faces. Tessa had her arms around a smaller girl I assumed was her sister, probably a few years younger than her and definitely going through a goth phase. A woman who was definitely her mother was behind the girls – she looked pale and tired, but was somehow still smiling with her arm wrapped around Tessa's shoulders. And what was clearly Tessa's older brother – they had the same green eyes, but his hair was shorter and he had the build of a rugby player – was taking the picture with his extended arm and grinning perfect white teeth as he leaned in closer to his family.

They all looked happy, even though they had chosen a bizarre day to go to the beach and were wearing thick coats. Better than happy, they looked as though they actually liked each other. I couldn't help but notice the absence of a father. There were no pictures of Tessa's dad around this room. It was like he didn't exist. Or maybe that's how Tessa preferred to keep it. I put the picture back and took my time looking around, reading the backs of battered paperbacks and DVDs, all of which were either independent or foreign films. So Tessa clearly wasn't a fan of mainstream films and judging by the wear and tear of *Jane Eyre*, all seven *Harry Potter* books and *Flowers in the Attic,* those were her most-read books. I was surprised to see the *Awaken* trilogy, all hardbacks, on her shelf. I flipped them open. Two were signed by the author herself. She'd never brought this up with me, not once. Even when she knew who I was and the project I was attached to. Was she worried I'd ruin a beloved series she was a fan of? Somehow, critics seemed less important – as long as Tessa liked the first film, I'd have achieved something. Especially if this was going to be my first and last …

I felt like I was getting such an intimate glance into her life, but I only had more questions than answers. Why did Tessa Granger still feel like a mystery?

21

Tessa

My hand really, really hurt. Somehow it was easier to focus on that pain and not the whirlpool of emotions flooding through my head. I'd been sitting outside Dean Patel's office for ages, with nothing but my throbbing, bandaged hand for company. The waiting was the worst, knowing that the four people in there were deciding my fate. Although, to be honest, I was certain how this would end.

I'd lunged at Kaitlyn like I was Bertha in *Jane Eyre*, except I managed to get to her before anyone could stop me. I must have looked like a complete and total psycho; that's what I felt like. The anger that had fuelled me earlier was long gone. A quiet chill of dread had taken its place. Even if Carla had walked in and heard the way Kaitlyn was speaking to me before I tried to leave, no one – not even me – could justify that I had gone ballistic and possibly broken her nose, judging by her shrill screaming.

How could I have been so stupid? How could I have let this happen?

Tears filled my eyes as the reality of this situation sank in.

I was going to be expelled, and if by some miracle I wasn't, I was bound to lose my scholarship and I'd have to drop out anyway. I was about to lose everything just because I couldn't grit my teeth and ignore some snarky bitch. One moment, one mistake would be the deciding factor for my future. I was going to be a failure, but I would be a failure with everyone watching. All those dreams, everything I'd wanted now felt like nothing more than a fairy tale. Had I been stupid to actually think I had a shot at being the first in my family to graduate university? I must've been.

My phone started ringing in my bag; I pulled it out to stare at it. Jonathan's name illuminated the screen. I wasn't sure whether I just needed to hear a voice after so long sat in silence or because I knew it'd be his voice, but I answered.

"Jonathan?"

I hated how broken my voice sounded. For a moment, my throat tightened and I had to fight back the urge to burst into tears. He seemed to hear something in my voice, or maybe it was because this was twice now he'd heard me crying in less than a whole day. I didn't care at this point. I was done pretending everything was okay when it was not.

"Hey, what's wrong?" he asked softly. The tears I'd been holding back broke free, and I tried to breathe through the panic and dread. "Tess, talk to me. What happened?"

"I messed up!" I sobbed, running a hand through my hair and trying to calm down. "I really, really messed up, and now I don't know what I'm supposed—"

I stopped as Amanda popped her head out of Patel's office, I hastily wiped my eyes, but it was clear I'd been crying. She gave me a sympathetic look, but that disappointment was evident in her dark eyes.

127

"We're ready for you now," she said, stepping aside to let me into the office. I tried to compose myself. Deep breath. Just breathe.

"I have to go. Sorry," I said quickly into the phone and hung up, switching it off before shoving it back into my pocket. I got up, grabbed my bag and followed Amanda inside. The door closing behind me had an uncomfortable finality about it, to me anyway.

I'd never been to the head teacher's office. Never, not once. Not in primary school, secondary school, probably not in nursery. Yet being inside the dean's office was more daunting than even I expected. I sank into the seat opposite Dean Patel's desk, uncomfortably aware of the eyes of the other lecturers who stood behind Dean Patel's chair. While Lawrence had that laid-back granddad approachability, Carla had a steeliness about her that was intimidating at the best of times, and that's without hearing her speak with that strong Russian accent.

Amanda chose the seat next to me, which felt like a little show of support. It didn't matter, though. I was basically toast. Burned-to-a-crisp-and-the-kitchen-currently-ablaze toast.

Dean Patel surveyed me over her glasses. Her brown skin showed the first signs of age, and her jet-black hair rocked a few strands of grey. She was a picture of disappointment. My stomach squirmed, and I fought the tears threatening to escape my already red eyes.

"I'm sorry," I uttered, throwing pride and courtesy to the wind as the four academics looked disconcerted by my outburst. "There's no excuse for it, and I know that, but I was provoked. I know that's not how it looked, but I—"

"Ms Granger," Dean Patel said, muting my word-vomit with just my name, "I hoped our meeting today would be under

128

different circumstances, but you must understand the severity of your actions."

"I do!" I said earnestly, berating myself silently when her raised eyebrow said she was not finished. "Sorry ..."

"This is so unlike you," Lawrence said gravely.

"Which is saying something, isn't it?" Amanda said, surprisingly angry. "Look at Tessa's record compared to Kaitlyn's. Both girls – young women – are totally different students."

"That is neither here nor there," Dean Patel admonished curtly. "Tessa assaulted another student on campus. It's a miracle the girl does not want to press charges and involve the police."

What? I'd have thought Kaitlyn would love a chance to tarnish my reputation – with a busted nose as evidence too. This was hardly reassuring. It felt more like a threat she could dangle over my head indefinitely. My stomach felt queasy, like I might throw up or something. I took a steady breath, feigning calm and not showing I was having a tiny panic attack inside.

"I spoke to every one of my students, and from what I heard myself," Carla said clearly, "Kaitlyn's language and the way she spoke to Tessa was in pure malice. There are twenty students, all with the exact same story. I agree, her behaviour was wrong, but they were repercussions of what transpired before."

Dean Patel thought on this. I dared not breathe as my future quite literally hung in the balance. Lawrence's sternness softened ever so slightly, but pity replaced it.

"Maybe we should take into consideration Tessa's family situation ..." he said cautiously as if testing the words out loud for the first time. I noticed he deliberately avoided my look of confusion.

"I'm sorry?" I asked, perplexed, as both Lawrence and Carla exchanged a look. What would my family have to do with any of this?

"I heard the comment Kaitlyn made about your mother," Carla said, sounding more sympathetic than I'd ever heard her, and for some reason, I hated it. "And if you had not charged at her like a bull, I was on the verge of kicking her out of the lecture hall myself."

"I know. It was stupid …" I said quietly, my voice getting some strength back as I continued, "but my mum has nothing to do with this. I should have just walked away."

"You do know we take mental health very seriously at this university," Lawrence said, so kindly it bordered on downright patronising.

"I don't have mental health issues!" I said, shocked, angered by where this was heading. I hastily corrected myself. "I mean, there's no shame in it, and I'd say if there were something I needed help with. But that's not what this is. I think I'd know."

"Exactly. I mean, we offer support for students who have dealt with mental health struggles within the family," Lawrence said firmly, his eyes giving me the most pitying look I'd ever received. "We are aware of your mother's hospitalisation several years ago and …"

His voice became muffled. A stillness settled over me that had me frozen in place. Tears pooled in my eyes and overflowed, the trail they left on my cheeks warming my skin. I didn't want a get-out-of-jail card just because *that* had happened. I'd spent years trying not to revisit those memories, forcing that dark time out of my mind. Sometimes it worked, and sometimes that night was nothing more than a nightmare I'd rather forget. I couldn't, though, and I was reminded of it whenever I showed any kind of emotion.

But Kaitlyn's words had ignited some pain inside me I thought I'd buried. It was still there, waiting in the darkest parts of myself. I couldn't let that define me, though. I wouldn't. Like a dam breaking, memories and images of that night came flooding back.

The noise from downstairs was deafening. They were arguing again. This time was different, but I couldn't pinpoint why. Usually, they died down after a shouting match, but not this time. They'd peaked. Ryan was out with mates, and Aunt May had taken Vee for the weekend, leaving me to deal with the chaos. I'd stayed in my room all night, knowing better than to intervene,

I tried everything to distract myself, and I mean everything. Sitting down at my laptop and writing, reading any book I could lay my hands on and even blasting music through headphones to drown it out. Nothing could drown out how I was feeling. Not on the inside. I hated this, this feeling of powerlessness, of having to sit and wait for the bomb to go off and then keep my fingers crossed there would be no casualties.

Did a part of them enjoy this? This unpredictability that was now their marriage? It had such a routine I could almost script it. Mum would cry and scream she was finished with him. And Dad would leave in a dramatic, slamming-of-the-door exit. And the next day, all would be forgotten but not forgiven. Words were never exchanged, and apologies were never given. It's like they ripped an entire chapter out of a book, and we just had to skim past it. Like it never happened. Then the all-consuming silence in the aftermath was the worst part because that meant waiting. Waiting.

Something smashed downstairs. I resisted the urge to leave my room. My thumbnail dug into the exposed skin of my wrist. The jarred scars had healed, but digging at the soft skin gave a slight sense of relief. The pain was distracting; the physical pain was manageable. The ache inside hurt way more. I needed to find some sense of control.

I shoved those memories away, resisting the sudden temptation I had to run a fingernail over that same wrist. I pulled my sleeve over it, hiding the pink scars from view. No, I wasn't fourteen any more. I didn't need to do that, it wouldn't help, and it never did. That girl who felt so scared and powerless had grown up. What happened that night didn't break her. It didn't break me.

"…which is why—"

"No," I choked out, finding my voice again. "I don't want any pity. I don't want to lose my scholarship either, but if the only thing stopping you from expelling me is—"

"Who said anything about expulsion?" Dean Patel asked, her brow furrowed, and I was dumbstruck into silence. "You aren't being expelled. Honestly, you are lucky you have the majority of your peers backing up your version of events, which is why we are giving you a warning. But this cannot happen again, and I will not be so lenient next time. You're lucky I'm choosing to leave this off your record and not reporting it to Student Finance. Given all the circumstances, we don't need any bad press. Do you understand?"

Words failed me, so I nodded weakly. An overwhelming sense of relief hit me so hard I was in danger of bursting into tears again. A ghost of a smile dared itself to make an appearance on my lips.

"Will you be having the conversation with Ms Danvers?" Amanda glared at the dean, her eyes narrowed into slits. "Because there are a few choice words I'd like to give that student myself."

"Of course," Dean Patel said curtly, turning back to me again with a serious demeanour. "But we aren't done here yet. Teresa, we need to speak with you about your entanglement with this actor. The university faculty has been made aware of your situation, but you must remember we can only do so much. While we will do anything in our power to keep this a safe space for your last months with us, I would like to remind you that your actions reflect on us, and I do not want a repeat performance of today. We won't tolerate any doubt on this university's integrity, especially through the actions of one student. Which is why I expect nothing but the best from you."

The underlying warning was clear, but I gulped and forced somewhat of a smile. Although I still had my place and my scholarship, she'd just made it abundantly obvious I wasn't out of the woods yet. A chill settled in my stomach as I realised I was on fragile ice here, and one wrong move could see everything around me shatter. No one said it plainly, but – like Mrs Robinson with Jon – this woman would gladly watch me drown before letting her beloved university sink if I wasn't absolutely without fault …

22

Tessa

As soon as I walked out of the campus building, the night air hit me with a rush of wind and I let out a harsh breath. I didn't make it far before my body craved rest, exhausted like I'd just swum for my life. I slumped against the wall, sliding down until my butt found the hard pavement. I hugged my knees to my chest, not caring who saw me and instead I focused on calming my breathing. Tears streamed down my cheeks, but I didn't care.

Breathe in through the nose, out through the mouth. Deep breaths, find your centre. Focus on the here and now, not what you can't control.

I'd scoffed at that advice a guidance counsellor had given me as a teenager. Now, it was the only thing keeping me from completely shattering in on myself. That had been close. Too close. I was on a thin tightrope, and now I knew some people were just waiting for me to fall.

I felt a gentle touch on my shoulder.

"Tessa?"

Ivy's brown eyes came into view. She was crouched in front

of me, her face level with mine, and her harsh breathing told me that she had probably run here.

"What the fuck happened?" she demanded. Her next words took me by surprise. "Did those fuckers kick you out? They better not have! If they took the side of that cunt who paid her way onto this course and not you, they're mad! It's fucking discrimination. You were being emotionally abused. Anyone with half a brain could see she was asking for it!"

"Ivy—"

"No, no," Ivy ranted, getting to her feet and looking ready to go to war. "I'm not having this. You're one of the best writers here, and if they—"

"I'm not being chucked out."

"...actually think they can ... wait, what?"

"I'm staying."

Ivy stared for a beat, looking as if I'd cast a petrifying spell on her. Then before I had time to brace myself, she pulled me to my feet and crushed me into a hug. There were a handful of people I felt comfortable expressing this level of affection to, hence why I reluctantly returned the embrace.

"Sorry," I mumbled awkwardly, rushing on when Ivy raised a sceptical eyebrow. "I didn't want to worry you. Or anyone."

"Can you stop apologising for other people's fuck ups?" Ivy dismissed my words, took my arm and started leading me back to our flat, *Wizard of Oz* style. "Anyway, you got a delivery back home."

"Delivery?" My curiosity heightened when Ivy refused to elaborate and gave me nothing but a smug grin. It felt nice that I could still refer to Whitmore as home. Even if it was only for a few more months. The last three years here *had* felt like home, especially with Ivy. Guilt took root in my stomach as I

135

realised I had totally neglected Ivy in all this Jonathan drama and whatever was brewing between us. I didn't want our friendship to become one-sided – she'd been a great support system, but I had no idea what had been going on with her these last few weeks.

"Sorry," I blurted so suddenly that Ivy looked startled. I started over more calmly. "I haven't been a good friend. So much has been going on, and I'm sorry that I haven't been there for you. You know how much I appreciate you, yeah?"

"Fuck. Don't go all mushy on me." She laughed but then sobered. "I should be the one apologising. All this shit that's been happening, and it was me who gave you the stupid idea to go along with the non-gay beard plan."

"You didn't make me do anything. I chose to go along with it."

"Only because I talked you into it—"

"No, it's on me. I was thinking about just getting into the NFTS when this started …" I told her firmly and then hesitantly admitted for the first time aloud, "But I wasn't expecting it to get more complicated with Jon."

"Complicated?"

"Real," I mumbled, feeling myself blush as I rushed on. "I might be reading too much into it, but he's not what I thought he was …"

"You like each other?"

"Yeah, but that wasn't part of the plan. None of this was."

Ivy stayed quiet as we headed into the student accommodation, making our way through reception and into the lift. She took a deep breath and said in a rush, "I started seeing someone. A girl. Melody Lang. She's on the classical music course. I don't know what this means, whether I'm bisexual

136

or gay. I don't know, but I wanted to let you know. But I also don't want to make this a big deal or a thing ... so, yeah ..."

She waited with bated breath for my reaction, but I had none. I just felt happy for her. I knew who Melody was, of course: a pretty Asian girl with a strong Scottish accent who played the violin beautifully at the Student Union and probably one of the sweetest people ever. She deserved someone as amazing as Ivy.

"Does she make you happy?" I asked, and Ivy nodded, her eyes glistening. "Then that's all that matters. Screw the label. Just be happy."

"Yeah, I know ..." Ivy looked lost for words, which was definitely a first. "Thanks."

It was my turn to give a spur-of-the-moment hug, and Ivy looked surprisingly tearful as she hugged me back. She may not like the mushy stuff, but it comes with the best friend territory.

I opened the flat door and was confused when she didn't follow.

"I have a thing with Mel," Ivy said, a glint of mischief in her eyes returning. "Everyone else is out. Your delivery is in your bedroom, enjoy!"

With a smirk, she slammed the door shut in my face. The darkened hallway and the silence from the living room told me the others were out too. Before I could really consider whether I had a package scheduled today, I let myself into my bedroom, and my jaw hit the floor,

Jonathan was sitting on my bed, his legs stretched out, and his back slumped comfortably into my pillows. He was idly turning the page of a book – one of my books, *My Sweet Audrina* by V.C. Andrews – and he looked perfectly content.

Like this was some everyday occurrence.

"What are you doing here?" I whispered in bewilderment, even though whispering was totally unnecessary. His smile immediately set my heart aflutter; that annoying and gorgeous smile set off a Guy Fawkes fireworks display in my chest.

"Hello to you too," he said, sliding off the bed and crossing the room in two strong strides. He pulled me into his arms and I let myself be held, cautiously returning the embrace. For a moment, I let my other senses guide me. The sound of his breathing, the feel of his arms wrapped around my waist, our bodies pressed together, his lips lightly touching my hair.

While my heartbeat was erratic, I could feel his against my chest and under his shirt. Slow, calm and steady. I breathed in his scent and my body responded to his. I relaxed. He made me feel grounded.

"I wanted to see you," he said so gently it felt like a caress. And for once I didn't question it. I just believed him.

23

Jonathan

I'm not sure how long we stood like that, but I just knew the minute I saw her that I wanted to hold her. I wanted to bring that smile back, and I wanted to make whatever had caused her to break down on the phone go away. This protectiveness was new for me – I'd rarely let myself get emotionally attached to a woman before, and the times I had, they'd fucked me over in one way or another. Not Tessa, though; I'd have run here if I'd had no choice and she needed me.

"Thank you," Tessa breathed and made to pull back, but I kept my arms around her waist. She reluctantly smiled and loosely hung her arms around my neck. "Okay. Hugging. Is this our thing now? Are we the hugging type?"

"We're more than that," I said softly, covering up how vulnerable that statement made me feel with a falsely confident grin. I felt her bandaged hand rub against my neck and I let go of her waist to take it in mine. Though the room was lit only by her dim bedside lamp, I could see the sore, red skin visible around the edges of the bandage, and I could only imagine how much her hand was hurting underneath.

Fuck, this hand was something I'd expect to see on a bloke after a proper fight. This wasn't some catty-girl fight, but somehow I wasn't surprised.

"It looks worse than it is," Tessa said casually, but I smelled the bullshit from a mile away, and she laughed. "Okay, yeah, it does hurt. But if you think this is bad, you should see the other girl!"

"Oh, I don't doubt it." I chuckled, secretly turned on by the defiant look in her eyes. "You going all *Fight Club* on me now, Tess?"

"I'll try not to," she admitted quietly, and I pulled her close to me again, wanting her to say more. Instead, she shook her head and forced a grin. "I didn't get kicked out. So that's something."

"That's good," I said. I wanted more information, but wasn't sure how hard to press. "So, what happened?"

"I don't want to talk about it." She sighed, but then her eyes locked on mine as if realising something for the first time. "Why did you come all the way down here?"

"You were crying." It sounded ridiculous out loud, but that was the god's honest truth. She cast her eyes down, unable to meet mine all of a sudden. I touched her chin, and instead of looking at me, she gently pushed me away and walked into the room. She brushed her hair behind her ears, pacing in the tiny space.

"Tessa …"

"Don't, okay? Sometimes it's a bit too easy to forget."

"Forget what?"

"That this is all pretending, that you and I aren't actually—"

"I've never pretended with you, Tessa."

She stopped her pacing and turned slowly to face me. I

could see her mind racing, trying to think of an alternative meaning to what I'd just said. There was none. Whatever this was between us, it was real. There was no need to act or force anything that resembled feelings. It was completely genuine. Although that scared me, I'd rather have my heart stamped on than pretend I wasn't feeling what she was.

"What do you mean?" she said, so quietly I almost didn't hear her. I moved closer and our eyes locked.

"You know what I mean," I told her. She put a hand on my chest as if to hold me back. It stayed there, and she cautiously met my eyes. "And if we're being honest, you feel the same. Right?"

"I think so," Tessa said, her body tensing when I took her waist in my hands. My thumb danced over the exposed back between her shirt and jeans. Her skin felt so soft it ignited memories of that night. This wasn't a momentary lapse in judgement, but I held myself perfectly still as her lips found mine.

The moment my tongue felt hers, a hunger erupted inside me. I craved her; my hands wanted to roam every curve of her body. I wanted to trace every inch of skin with my mouth and memorise every gasp and moan of pleasure that escaped her lips. I backed her against the door, and we laughed between kisses as her head bumped against the wood. I tried to apologise, but that mouth of hers against mine made me forget to breathe. Her fingers tugged at my shirt impatiently, and I willingly lifted my arms, realising I'd do whatever she wanted tonight.

Her eyes drank my body in hungrily, and I couldn't help the smirk as her hands trailed down, her touch sending a wave of sensation through my body. Her hands found my jeans, but I stopped her. I knew she could feel exactly the effect she was having on me, and it killed me to press pause, even for a moment.

"Is the door locked?" I breathed against her ear, not fancying one of her nosey flatmates finding us in a compromising position or two. She answered by turning and locking the door, silencing any more questions.

"Now it is. Get undressed," she demanded with a pout. I chuckled, my lips finding her throat, and whatever else she might have said was lost in a moan. She pressed herself against me harder, and my mouth responded to her pleas for me not to stop. I realised if I wasn't careful, my lips were in danger of leaving a love bite.

"You first," I breathed against her lips, and she shuddered, meeting my lips with the same desire I had burning inside me. I was insane to think last night's stolen kiss was heaven. It was Eden compared to this.

My fingers found her blouse's buttons, slowly undoing them and sliding the shirt off her shoulders. She was so sexy, I had to stop for a moment and admire her. She looked a bit shy with my eyes devouring her in that purple bra, but my lips soon erased any insecurities. From her mouth to her throat, down her chest, over her breasts … I tasted every bit of her as I lowered myself in front of her. I noticed her knees were shaking as my hands found her waist, slowly unzipping her jeans.

"Jon …" she moaned as I pulled down her jeans. I looked up at her, marvelling at this beautiful woman standing above me. Every curve of her was utter perfection. My fingers traced the waistline of her underwear – the same colour as her bra – and her hips moved involuntarily to my touch, wanting more.

"Tell me what you want, Tess," I told her, but her only response was a sigh of frustration and longing as my lips kissed the inside of her thigh. I knew exactly what she wanted, but I wanted to hear her say it. "You don't have to be shy with me, baby."

"I want … Oh god!" she breathed as my fingers slid under her knickers, and she bucked into my touch, closing her eyes. "You. I want you. Please, Jonathan … Jonathan …"

The way she gasped my name had me almost undone. Within seconds, her knickers were around her ankles, and my lips set off entirely new – and more intense – moans of pleasure as my tongue tasted her and made her wetter.

"Woah!" Tessa gasped, holding my head in place as my tongue found the spot that was making her moan my name over and over again. I wanted her – the hardness in my jeans was proof enough of that – but the pleasure I was giving her was arousing me in ways I hadn't felt with anyone else.

Although my brain, and the subsequent blood supply, was focused on the here and now, I was dimly aware of the door to the flat opening and closing outside. I dismissed those concerns, telling myself the room door was locked. Tessa pulled at my arms, and I obeyed her touch, retracing my tracks as I kissed up her body, and she pulled me to her lips again.

Someone was rummaging around the kitchen, humming loudly and out of tune. Should we be quiet? Should we press pause? My body strongly protested, but I braced my hands on either side of her head and used the door as a source of willpower to pull back for air.

"Someone's here," I said, but she kissed me again, and the willpower I had summoned was soon turning to dust. It was hardly there to begin with. Her hands moved from my neck, down my chest and to my waist. I gasped as her fingers undid my jeans and her hand started to stroke my hardened dick in a tortuously slow rhythm. It was my turn to moan as Tessa took charge, now being the one totally in control.

"Just ignore them," she reassured me as she pulled down my jeans and took me back into her grasp. "That feel good?"

"You fucking kidding? Yes!" I breathed incredulously, silencing Tessa's triumphant giggle with a kiss. She almost didn't notice my hand moving back down her body. Two could play at that game. She gasped against my lips as she felt my fingers find her sweet spot again, and her head fell back on the door. Harder than she clearly intended. Whoever was in the kitchen stopped their humming. Fuck.

"Ow!" Tessa whispered. We both grinned but were instantly distracted again. My lips found the soft rounded skin of her breasts, her arched back giving me easy access to the clasp of her bra.

The loud knock on the door scared the shit out of both of us. Tessa's hand flew to my mouth. I was in half a mind to tell whoever was on the other side of that door to fuck off. Maybe she could sense that. If we just stayed quiet, then perhaps …

"Tessie!" a woman's voice called. Tessa's eyes widened in utter horror. "Are you in there?"

Tessa hastily shoved me away, taking me by such surprise that – with the force of her push and the fact my jeans and boxers were around my ankles – I stumbled and landed flat on my arse. Jesus Christ, who decided bedroom floors should be carpeted? I was almost certain my left butt cheek would end up with carpet burn tomorrow.

"Oh my god, I'm so sorry!" Tessa whispered, crouching down to help me and my bruised ego up. The knocking became a bit more frantic, probably due to my arse making another loud thud in here. "Yeah! I'm coming, Mum!"

The blood immediately evacuated a particular area of my body, giving the most effective cold shower ever with one terrifying word. Holy shit, Tessa's mother was on the other side of that door.

24

Jonathan

"Everything alright in there, love?"

"Yeah!" Tessa said way too breezily, both of us trying to frantically dress as quietly as possible. I winced as I caught myself in the zipper of my jeans, biting my lip to stop the hiss of pain escaping my lips.

"Shush!" Tessa whispered, even though I hadn't made a sound. Instead of pointing that out, I hunted for my T-shirt and found it had been flung to the other side of her bed. I climbed across and shoved it over my head, postponing the plans I'd had for this mattress for now. I couldn't fight the grin as Tessa rushed about like she was cleaning up a crime scene.

She hastily buttoned up her shirt, not noticing she was doing it up haphazardly. But she found her jeans and underwear and hurriedly pulled them up, doing an adorable little hop as she hoisted both up and fastened them.

"Tessie, why is the door locked?"

"I was … napping!" Tessa lied, and she whacked my arm as I tried to cover up a snort of laughter. She shoved me towards the bathroom door, reprimanding my snigger with, "Stop being so childish, just hide in there and keep quiet."

"Yeah, because that's real mature," I pointed out as she pushed me gently through the door. My grin grew when she reluctantly smiled. I leaned over, and before she could ask, I quickly sorted her buttons and winked at her relieved sigh. She hadn't noticed.

"Thanks," she begrudgingly admitted. "I'll be quick."

"You better," I said and pulled her in for a kiss. More knocking made her pull away and close the door on me reluctantly. I listened as she made her way to the bedroom door and opened it.

"Hi, Mum! How did you get in here?"

"The little ginger you live with buzzed me in. She was downstairs with some sort of LGBTQ club. What does the Q stand for? I can't keep up. Anyway, she said you were up here."

"Oh! Yeah, I was. I mean, I am. Obviously. I was just a bit tired after studying. Just fancied a bit of alone time, you know?"

Stop talking so chipper. I wanted to warn her. She sounded like a chipmunk with a guilty conscience. I'd bet good money her face was flushed right now. I chuckled at the thought.

"Are you feeling okay?" Tessa's mum asked, and I could imagine she had Tessa wrapped in a tight hug, but her tone suddenly turned sharp. "What happened to your hand?"

Oh shit. That woman didn't waste her time with small talk. Based on the picture on Tessa's bedside table, her mother was the physical embodiment of what Tessa could look like in thirty years The most prominent contrast between them was that her mother had hazel eyes – although you had to look

147

closer at the photo to see it.. Tessa had clearly inherited those eyes from her absent dad.

"It's nothing …" Tessa shrugged it off. "Do you want a coffee?"

"Yes, I'm not stopping long. I'm seeing a show in the West End in a bit and just thought I'd … Tessa, do you have someone else here?"

My stomach dropped, and for a mad moment I imagined she had overheard what I'd been doing to her daughter mere moments ago. Tessa forced a laugh, but I could already tell that would have little effect in swaying her shrewdly observant mother.

"Why?" Tessa asked nonchalantly, cleverly avoiding the question with one of her own. I waited, barely daring to breathe, and a part of me was half expecting this woman to storm into this tiny bathroom and attempt to murder me for deflowering her precious daughter. No, she thought I was already her boyfriend – but thinking something and seeing something are two different things.

"Whose jacket is that?"

Ah fuck. I remembered with sudden horror that I'd left my jacket slung over the desk chair, like an absolute idiot. Even if Tessa could think of a lie that would explain a man's leather jacket left in her seemingly empty room, the delay in opening the door and her flushed cheeks would fill in the blanks. I rushed to the toilet and flushed it, knowing the sound would catch their attention. No turning back now.

I ran the tap, leaned over the cabinet and found a bottle of mouthwash. Under the noise of the running water and flushed toilet, I rinsed my mouth of the taste of Tessa. I spat out the blue liquid and rinsed again with water. With much

JONATHAN

fresher breath, I caught sight of myself in the mirror. I forced
myself not to dwell on the nervous whirlpool in my stomach.
Instead, I took a deep breath and put on the winning smile I'd
mastered after years of practice.

"Babe, we are never ordering from that curry house again!"
I said as I headed out, feigning a perfect look of polite surprise
at the sight of Mrs Granger. "Oh. Hello. I'm Jonathan, Tessa's
boyfriend."

Mrs Granger did an actual double take, her eyes widening
in shock. She looked much healthier than her picture coun-
terpart, but she seemed utterly star-struck right now. This
response was expected; the general public genuinely thought
I lived inside a TV screen. Then they would lose their shit and
act like they had entered *The Twilight Zone* if they caught sight
of me in real life.

"Oh! Hi, Jonathan, Jonathan Adeola! Wow. I'm Tessa's
mother, Grace. Such a pleasure to finally meet you! We've
heard so much about you!" she gushed, shaking my hand so
vigorously she almost forgot what I'd said. "What? Oh! Tessa
knows I'm terrible with Indians – not the people, the food. It
goes right through me. Like a waterfall!"

"Mum, please stop," Tessa begged. Her face reddened even
more when she caught my eye. Grace seemed to believe that
story without question – despite the lack of smell coming from
the bathroom. Tessa still looked mortified as we headed into
the living area for tea, but surely letting her mother believe
her "boyfriend" had a bad case of diarrhoea was better than
the alternative? Even I couldn't make a great impression with
the in-laws if they walked in on me eating out their daughter.

Half my mind was listening to Grace and answering whatever she said, but I couldn't stop my eyes following Tessa

around the kitchen. I was captivated by her: the way she reached up to the top cabinet to grab mugs and revealed the skin of her lower back; the way she bit her lip as she was thinking about something. Everything she did made me want her even more. She glanced in my direction and we shared a secret smile, both knowing what the other was thinking. This woman was going to be the death of me, but I pulled my eyes away and reminded myself to stay present.

The contrast between Grace and Tessa became more and more apparent. While Grace was a clear talker, feeling the need to fill any pause in the conversation, Tessa was the quiet observer and looked content with however a situation played out. When she handed us our drinks, she sat next to me and I wrapped my arm loosely around the back of the small sofa we had to ourselves. I became acutely aware of our knees pressed together and the way Tessa's body responded to the lazy lines I traced down her arm. My smile faltered when I reached her wrist. The skin felt different. I looked down and spotted the pink scars, longer and darker than her otherwise smooth skin.

I entwined my fingers through hers, still looking at the scars. They were thin, about the size of a fingernail, and although they all looked old – some were more faded than others – they were all similar. Did Tessa self-harm as a kid? My stomach lurched at the thought, hating the idea of someone making her depressed or angry enough to resort to that. I wanted to ask her, but now wouldn't be a good time. She seemed to sense my eyes on her wrist. Her chin trembled and she tried to pull away but I squeezed her fingers between mine. Grace's phone pinged and I used the distraction to press my lips lightly against Tessa's head.

Nothing you could do or say could scare me off. I wanted to reassure her aloud, because this in no way changed my feelings for her. I didn't know how much Grace knew about Tessa's scars or even if she knew their origins, but now wasn't the time. Instead, I held Tessa's hand and tried to keep everything as normal as possible. As much as I wanted to ask, I tried to respect her privacy. I felt her body relax against my body, and I knew at this moment all I wanted to do was keep her safe from the media, from my mother, and from whatever demons had haunted her past. She met my eyes, and the way she smiled at me, I realised I was a goner. I was falling for her. Entirely and utterly falling for her.

"Jonathan, you know Tessa writes?" Grace prattled, startling us both again out of our intimate staring contest. "She's very good, apparently. The first in the family to go to university, in fact. But she never lets any of us read what she writes!"

"Oh, she's amazing," I said without thinking, smiling at Tessa's blush. "I absolutely love reading her scripts. She never knows how to accept praise. I think it's her inner perfectionist."

Tessa's face flushed even more deeply at the wide-eyed stare Grace was giving her. Had no one in her family read her scripts? Did one of them actually know what her writing was like and how much joy it brought her?

"She lets you read her short stories?" Grace asked. She frowned when I nodded. "Really?"

"Screenplays," Tessa corrected, and Grace merely shrugged dismissively. "And he's only read one."

"A really good one," I added, and Tessa sighed, clearly torn between pride and embarrassment. Grace paused at this, spotting something as she looked from Tessa to me and back again. Whatever she saw, it made her smile. A smile tinged with sadness, but still a smile.

"So, tell me about those films you're starring in," Grace said, her eyes going fleetingly to her daughter's. "Tessa loved those *Awaken* books as a girl. We lined up for hours for the midnight release of the last one. She cried for a week when she finished it."

"That so?" I asked coyly and grinned wider at Tessa's grimace of discomfort. She elbowed me hard enough to cut off my laugh, clearly fighting the urge to smile.

"It was the end of an era!" Tessa defended stubbornly. "It was on the same level as reading the end of *Harry Potter and the Deathly Hallows*. I was emotionally invested in those characters."

"Well, hopefully I can live up to those high expectations," I said softly, becoming so lost in those green eyes that I almost forgot the woman who birthed her was sitting a few feet away. The film was months away from release, and the chances of me starring in the rest still hung in the balance.

* * *

Grace's fleeting visit lasted four cups of tea, and she seemed reluctant to go, but even she knew she'd have the stage doors slammed in her face if she didn't leave on time. She gave hugs all around, but her happy-go-lucky attitude sobered as I walked her to the door.

"Make sure you take care of her," she said as Tessa went to find her coat. Those words seemed to have a much deeper meaning, and I nodded.

"I will," I told her, but she still looked wary, her eyes scrutinising me harshly, and I was determined not to break eye contact. She was more intimidating than she let on.

"I'm serious. If I find out you've hurt her in any way or put her in danger, you'll have me to deal with."

"It won't come to that."

"It better not," Grace said, hesitating as if a troubling thought came to her. "Tessa doesn't trust people easily; she's always been a bit of a loner. But after what happened with her dad—"

"Found it!"

Tessa came round the corner, not noticing how fast Grace's expression shifted from serious to happy. Fuck, she'd give Oscar-winning actresses a run for their money. She gave a last heartfelt goodbye and hug to her daughter and left in a rush after checking her watch.

"She's going to miss the first act," I pointed out as Tessa closed the distance between us and wrapped her arms around my neck. My hands caught her waist, pulling her closer. "So, did I pass the boyfriend test?"

"I think so," she said, her smile curving into something more mischievous and so fucking sexy. "But there are still parts of your performance that need reviewing."

"That so?" I said against her lips, lightly grazing them with my own. "Why don't we go pick up where we left off?"

Tessa smiled wryly as her lips found mine again. With all of her flatmates out, I fully intended to take her back in that room and get a five-star rating. I responded enthusiastically to her kiss, barely coming up for air.

My phone started ringing in my back pocket. I groaned as I heard the Imperial March and reluctantly pulled it out. Mia rang me on this phone when it was work-related. Usually, that meant it was serious.

I showed Tessa the screen, and she snorted at the ringtone

choice, still keeping her arms wrapped around me.

"Yeah?" I answered, not bothering with courtesy and getting to the point. "What's going on?"

"Are you with Tessa?" she asked abruptly, and I put the phone on loudspeaker, holding the phone between us.

"Hi," Tessa said brightly, and I heard Mia's sigh, unsurprised.

"Hello," Mia said less enthusiastically, "alright, I'm going to keep this short and to the point. Jonathan, both productions are still on the fence about you. The interview is being moved up. This is either make or break for you, so you two need to act up a fucking storm. Virginia, the *Awaken* director definitely wants you and Willow back for the sequel, and we need this interview to sway the producers."

"That's good, isn't it?" Tessa asked, her optimistic smile looking so adorable that I almost missed what Mia said.

"Yes," Mia said cautiously, "but it all depends on how you two play up to the camera. Can you make it look authentic?"

"I reckon so," I said casually, aware of how my left arm was still wrapped around Tessa's waist, and my mind flashed to how gorgeous she looked in her darkened bedroom.

"And I finally got a hold of Samuel Harrison," Mia continued, and my interest piqued. "He's still not convinced, but he warmed to the idea of letting you audition once I told him you were workshopping an independent feature with a postgraduate student at the National Film and Television School."

"That's not exactly true," I pointed out, laughing at Tessa's look of disbelief. "Those details are a bit exaggerated."

"Just a bit," Tessa added, still stunned.

"Those exaggerated details caught his interest," Mia reminded me. "But neither of these productions will touch you if you and Tessa can't sell the love story of the decade. It needs to look real."

It was real. That was the problem. The whole world would be watching for a slip-up, but I feared this interview could actually reveal something more vulnerable about me. When this was a mutually beneficial arrangement, it was risk-free, but now …

Now this person I wanted to keep for my own was also the only salvation for my career, making her a target. Would I even be able to keep my promise to Grace?

"We'll have it covered," Tessa reassured Mia when it became clear I was miles away. I mumbled an agreement and said goodbye. As I hung up, I knew Mia was suspicious of the current nature of my relationship with Tessa. Fuck, I wasn't looking forward to that conversation.

"You okay?"

Tessa's hands held my face, and I met her eyes. How did I even begin to tell her what was going on in my head? She seemed to sense some of it because she kissed me gently on the lips. It calmed some of my nerves.

"Yeah." I sighed, reluctantly letting the rational side of my brain kick in. "I should probably go."

"Probably," Tessa agreed quietly, her eyes suddenly shy as she hesitated. "Unless …"

"Unless?"

"Unless you want to stay here tonight," she offered. "With me?"

The answer came to my lips immediately. We were treading into dangerously intimate waters that my PR team, agent and even my narcissistic mother would lose their shit over. Still, it didn't stop me gazing into her eyes and responding in a whisper, "Yeah, I do …"

25

Tessa

Those three little words made my heart feel like a trapeze artist. I didn't even know what really made me say it, but I knew I didn't want him to go. Whatever was happening here, I didn't want it to stop – nor did he, it seemed. We slipped back into my room and I soon found myself back in his arms, this darkened room like our own secret hideaway from the world. His kisses were slower, softer this time, and I craved every bit of his touch.

"Maybe we should take this a bit slower," he breathed as my hands slid under his shirt, feeling his perfectly sculptured abs that would put Eros to shame. "What if you get another visitor?"

I sighed, knowing that was a perfectly logical concern and knowing my four noisy housemates could turn up any second. It didn't stop me from remembering the way his lips and touch set my senses on fire, nor the way he looked when I did the same to him. He made me feel confident, seen, and – above all – desirable. I wanted this gorgeous man, but a tiny part of me didn't want to rush this either.

"Yeah, maybe you're right," I agreed somewhat reluctantly, but his lips on my neck again made any pouting impossible.

"I'm always right," he grinned that cocky smile, surprising me even further when he began to unbutton my blouse again. "But it doesn't mean we can't have fun in other ways, Tess."

We didn't have sex. There was a lot of kissing and touching, plenty of that. I wanted to memorise every detail as I undressed him, taking note of the way the fabric of his T-shirt strained against his biceps and chest. The way his breathing changed when I tugged the shirt over his head and my hands traced his naked torso. How his full lips tasted against mine, and the way he gazed at me like I was some rare artefact or mythical treasure. No one had ever looked at me the way he was right now.

Down to our underwear again, we lay down. The single bed wasn't built for two people – especially when one of them had Jonathan's build – but I wasn't complaining, especially when he pulled me into his arms. His heartbeat against mine was soothing, it was better than any John Williams music score.

"You're so beautiful," he said between kisses. And the way he was looking at me made me believe him.

I sighed as his lips trailed down my chest and stomach; I took his face in my hands and stroked his cheek, feeling the stubble that was starting to grow. His dark eyes drank me in as he kissed my palm. I froze as I felt his lips against my scars, slowly moving up my arm. I pulled away instinctively, feeling suddenly cold.

"What's wrong?" he asked softly, moving up the bed and lying next to me with such a look of concern I had to look away. "Tess?"

"Nothing," I mumbled. Not having the space to turn away I

158

instead opted for the eyes cast down at my duvet option. "I just … I don't like people looking at or touching them …"

"Your scars?" Jonathan said, propping himself up on his elbow to see me better. "It's nothing to be ashamed of."

"Isn't it?" I asked and met his eyes in the darkness, seeing nothing but reassurance in his gaze. I paused, staring up at the ceiling, and I felt his eyes on me. "It started when I was younger, about fourteen. My dad. He was a right nasty piece of work, a real misogynistic git. It wasn't obvious abuse; he preferred to hurt you with his words. Especially when he had a drink. I really think a part of him enjoyed making us all miserable, like he enjoyed the power trip it gave him. He was like some Dementor, just sucking any hope or happiness out of the place."

I laughed to myself. It sounded as hollow as it felt. I kept my eyes on the ceiling, acutely aware of Jon's hand on my thigh. A reassuring pressure, his fingers moving in soothing circles.

I turned to face him, relieved when I felt his arms snake around my waist. I met his eyes, taking a steadying breath. It was one thing to talk to a therapist about this, but someone in my personal life – yes, Jonathan fit into that category now – was a much more daunting experience. It felt like laying your heart bare in all its bloody glory and hoping that person didn't flee in disgust.

"When their arguments got really bad, that's when the scratching started …." I said softly into the darkness. "It was getting back a sense of control, in a way. I couldn't control how I felt or what was happening, but I could control that. Physical pain was easier to manage than emotional stuff. It wasn't really control, though; I was just hurting myself more. Pathetic, huh?"

"No," he said, a hint of anger in his voice. "The only person who should feel ashamed is your dad for making you feel that way. Do you know what I see with these scars? Someone who went through a dark time, and yet she's still here. You're strong, baby. These just prove that."

I tasted tears and realised I was actually crying, but I pulled him closer and kissed him breathlessly. His touch soothed the whirlpool of anxiety and panic in my head. He didn't run. He was still here. He looked at me, those dark eyes suddenly more vulnerable than I'd ever seen them.

"Promise me something, Tessa," he said, his voice breaking when he said my name. "If you ever feel that way, you call me. I don't care what day or time it is – I don't care – and I'll be there. I mean it."

"I haven't done it in years," I assured him, my smile not wavering, even with the serious look in his eyes. "I mean it. It's been so long I think my mum, brother and sister have genuinely forgotten how bad it got. Seriously."

"And I'm being serious," Jonathan said firmly. "Please, Tessa. Promise me you'll tell me if things get that bad again. You can trust me."

"I know," I said softly, realising in this moment how much it was true. "I promise. Okay?"

His response came in a kiss. Not hungry or passionate. But so gentle and fragile, it was like he was worried I might shatter in his fingertips. I wrapped my arms around him, our bodies pressed together so tightly, and it had nothing to do with the tiny mattress. Later that night, I fell asleep against his chest. His heartbeat was my own personal lullaby; his fingers stroking my hair was the last thing I felt as I drifted into sleep.

"Tessa?"

"Hmm?"

I didn't catch what he said … I barely had time even to register the soft words he breathed into my hair because I was soon engulfed in sleep.

* * *

When I woke up, it was still dark and I was still wrapped in Jonathan's arms. He was lightly snoring into my hair. I took him in, smiling at the totally innocent way he slept. It was like seeing him born anew, with every fear and worry he'd ever had washed away. I eased out from under his arms and scooted out of my bed. He rolled over, his massive physique appreciating time away from the little human. He looked so peaceful. His presence was starting to affect me.

Pulling on his discarded T-shirt, I sat at my desk. With the scent of him on my skin, the laptop light illuminated my face as I logged into my NFTS account. The little clock on the screen told me it was 03:22, but I had an unexplained need to write this now. I typed well into the early hours of the morning, the words flowing from my brain into my application. I was confident with my answers, reading through each section and only tweaking minor grammatical mistakes. I was authentic, I was myself, and I was professional. With that and the twenty-page sample attached, my finger hovered over the button to submit.

No going back. I hit the button, and my application vanished, the screen now informing me it was going through the selection process. I stared at the pink line, outlining where my application could go next: Interview and Outcome. Those two words had terrified me a month ago, but now I was calm.

Whether it was this impromptu writing session or everything that had happened with Jonathan, I was finally okay with the application.

I was a good writer, and I'd done the best I could to articulate that to the review board. That's all I could do. I switched off the laptop, listening to the hum dying down, and I climbed back into bed. Jonathan's arms entwined around me even in his sleep, and my head rested against his slowly rising and falling chest. I wanted to savour these hours of calm I had with him. Because neither of us knew what storm awaited us …

The house was quiet. Really, really quiet. Except for Mum. She was crying loudly. The noise sounded like a wounded animal. Her wails came in long, gasping breaths as she wept from the depths of her soul. I was too numb to move. While she expressed her emotions for the world to see and hear, I kept everything bottled up. My life was playing out like a bad re-run, every line of dialogue and action predictable now. I was just so, so tired. The pain in my arm and the darkness of my tiny bedroom were the only indications of how much time had passed. Tears had dried on my cheeks, and the red line on my arm had been scratched raw, so raw the skin had broken. I listened in the darkness for any sign Dad had returned. He hadn't.

I tried calling Ryan, but he had his phone switched off. I tried messaging some of his mates I thought he was with. I was left on Read – it wasn't an emergency if Ryan's annoying little sister was messaging them. Aunt May was worse. Even with my abridged version of what had transpired, still her response was curt over the phone. "Someone needs to be there for your mum?"

What about me? Who was supposed to be there for me? Dad wasn't, Mum couldn't, Ryan didn't want to, and Vee was too young to really know what was going on. She was shielded from the worst of the fighting. I envied that she still had that innocence, and then hated myself for thinking that way. My wrist really hurt. The already sensitive skin was on fire; my nail had opened up some old wounds in more ways than one. Tears clouded my vision and for one strange moment, I wanted to cry like Mum was right now ... would that make me feel better? Really? I doubted it.

"Tessie?" Mum called, her voice sounding faint even though she was shouting, "Tessie?"

I cautiously rose from my perch on the bed, my throbbing wrist hurting at the slightest movement as I opened the door and stepped into the hallway. I was led by muscle memory rather than conscious thought or any emotion: no anger, sadness, or fear. I just had an overwhelming desire to sleep. As in curl into a ball and sleep forever. Like Sleeping Beauty, except everyone I knew would probably be totally fine leaving me to an eternal slumber for infinity.

As I descended the stairs, I heard it. The thud. And the whimpering gasps for air. The sudden fear that surged through me awakened me from my daze, spurring my legs to run downstairs and into the kitchen.

"Mum!"

My blood turned to ice at the sight before me. She was on the floor, her body convulsing in short fits. Her eyes fluttered open and close as if she was drifting in and out of consciousness. Her head lolled about, her mouth twitching wordlessly. Only groans and short gulps for air escaped her lips.

I ran for the house phone, realising I had left my phone upstairs. It was one of those cordless ones, which none of us ever used any more. It was only reserved for cold callers these days. I dialled 999 and ran back to Mum, who was still in a similar state but seemed aware I was there. Her hand jerked towards me; whether it was to soothe me or ask for help, I had no idea. Doing the first logical thing that came to mind, I put her in the recovery position. Her body still jerked and convulsed, harder than before. Mum whimpered something that resembled a sob, tears escaping her eyes, but I stroked her hair and tried to soothe her.

Breathe. Just breathe. Fear had me gripped in a chokehold. Even taking a breath was difficult. I wasn't sure where the sobs were now coming from, Mum or me.

"It's okay, it's okay, it's okay," I said over and over again, crying myself, and I almost sobbed with relief as the operator finally answered. "Hi! I need an ambulance. It's my mum. She's—"

My eyes snapped open. The persistent tune of my alarm rang in my ears. I groaned as I buried my face in the pillow, not entirely certain whether my fingers hit "off" or "snooze" on my phone's screen. It took me a moment to shake off that vivid dream, so vivid it had almost convinced me I was back on that kitchen floor six years ago. I rolled over in bed, my fingers finding nothing but air and the mattress. I opened my eyes. Jonathan was gone.

Early dawn was creeping through the blinds, but this small bed somehow felt emptier without him. Strange how much this room, this bed and even myself felt different in his absence. I rolled over, catching sight of a folded piece of paper on my bedside table: *Tessa.*

I grabbed it and unfolded it, my smile growing as I read the small note in Jonathan's neat handwriting:

> *I didn't want to wake you, but I thought it'd be safer if I made a move before your flatmates woke up. Although I'd much rather be making you breakfast in bed right now. Last night was amazing; it's definitely made my*

top five list – you've already claimed two of the spots.
I'll call you later today. Have a good day, beautiful.
J x
(P.S. my shirt looks better on you.)

I was smiling like an absolute idiot, but I couldn't help it. I put the note back on the bedside table, sinking back into the pillows. Jonathan's sweet note almost shook away the memories of that night … almost. Even he couldn't make that night go away …

26

Jonathan

Thank fuck this jacket had a functional zip. It was bad enough to be driving through an almost freezing London, without adding being caught shirtless to the list. I had no idea how I managed to pull myself from Tessa's arms. It was so tempting to stay where I was. But I finally did something rational, the cons outweighing the pros. It was barely daybreak when I pulled up outside the house. Mia's car was waiting where Mother's usually parked.

Oh shit.

I drove into the garage, deciding to use the side door to get inside. The hallway was deserted and dimly lit, but I heard murmuring voices in the living room. I crept through the hall, deciding I needed a T-shirt and possibly a shower before confronting whatever awaited me in there. I took the steps two at a time, treading as lightly as possible …

"You have two minutes." Mia's voice cut the silence in the hall like a knife. "Then we want an explanation."

My stomach plummeted, but then I was quickly filled with indignation. I was a fully grown man. Who was my agent to

166

try and make me feel like a disobedient teenager? I tried not to dwell on the fact that, if I was honest, Mia had the most right to berate my behaviour. Whether it was safeguarding me on shoots as a child actor, reading through lines with me and overseeing every production that my mother or father was too busy to travel for – Mia Robinson had more parental authority than my biological parents.

I took longer than two minutes, taking my sweet time in the shower and being more selective over my shirt and jeans than normal. Once I'd got my fill of pettiness and had summoned up the nerve to face the music, I headed downstairs. I found Mia perched on the sofa with Father. I was startled by the sight of her – no suit and no hair pulled back into a ridiculously tight bun. Her greying blonde hair hung to her shoulders, and she wore what I'd imagine an English professor's attire to be: jeans and an unflattering cardigan. She looked so ordinary. It was jarring to see her in clothes designed for comfort. I smiled weakly as I sat opposite her; her grimace looked like she was sucking on a lemon.

"Morning," I said, trying to break the glacier that had developed between us. "Where's the fire?"

"Don't play dumb." Father grunted and looked at me with something resembling disappointment. "It doesn't suit you. I just thought you were smarter than this."

"Still smarter than you, am I right?" I shot back, knowing that was below the belt, and I met Mia's gaze instead. "Can we cut the pretence? Just ask me the question you're dying to ask me."

"Fine," Mia said, "are you sleeping with Tessa?"

"Define sleep?" I asked, knowing I was pushing them both to the brink. "I mean, we've had sex, yes. But last night, we

167

only slept together, so that's a loaded question."

"Jonathan," Father said, losing the perfect composure he prided himself on for the briefest moment. I caught Mia resting her hand on his forearm. A small gesture, but it seemed to calm him. That was weird. He huffed and got to his feet. "You deal with him. I can't right now."

He stalked out in an appropriately dramatic fashion. I deliberately waited for his footsteps to fade upstairs and into his study before turning to Mia. If she was going to call me out on my behaviour, then it was only fair I called her out on her bullshit too.

"That was uncalled for," Mia started, but I cut her off.

"No, what's uncalled for is you sharing intimate and private details about my life when we had an agreement specifically about that. Anything involving my career or Tessa stays between us. This is the second time you've broken that promise," I said firmly, clearly taking her by surprise. "That NDA agreement applied to my father, not just my mother. That man has shown no interest in my career prospects. I don't need him giving sly digs about my relationships. And you know I specifically asked you not to let them read that fucking file weeks ago, and yet it's clear they have! Trust works both ways."

Mia nodded. It seemed quite literally a hard pill to swallow. She took a beat, mustering up the courage to say whatever her response was going to be.

"Yes, you're right," she said with great difficulty. "That was wrong of me, and I'm sorry, but your father does care. I assure you he does."

"That's not the point," I retorted, then hesitated before adding in a firmer voice. "Which is why I want our agreement to be official. I want a written and signed contract assuring that whatever transpires from now on remains in the strictest confidence between the client and agent. There are no private little chats with either of my parents and if you have any concerns, you speak directly to me and only me. Is that understood?"

I could see from her wide-eyed expression that this hurt her; it pained me to see that, let alone say those words aloud. But what she needed to understand was that her actions had caused this. She'd gone behind my back twice now, instead of voicing her concerns about Tessa to me privately. To my father of all people. I mean, why him? Mia had probably done the worst thing she could. She'd instilled that confidence in me to be independent of my parents. Yet, she'd hurt me more than I could say by betraying that trust we had built over the years.

As depressing as it sounded, this steely middle-aged woman who currently looked like a librarian was the closest person I'd had to a friend. Seriously, I'd hardly had the time to develop genuine friendships, moving from various countries, on too many film sets to remember a name and only having a random string of forgettable tutors and child actors with me for an hour a day. Mia had always been a constant.

"I see," Mia said faintly, clearing her throat. "I understand your concerns and why you have them, but I promise I have your best interests at heart. If that is what puts your mind at ease, I'll write up a contract for us both to sign."

"Good."

"But we have to talk about Tessa," she persisted, regaining some of her professionalism. "I don't agree with you getting involved in an entanglement with that girl."

BETWEEN THE LINES

"Entanglement? You make it sound sordid."

"You do realise that you engaging in this type of relationship is dangerous? For both of you," she said through tight lips. She was clearly restraining herself. "Tessa is a sweet girl, but she is not the sort of person that can cope with this lifestyle."

"What? An actual human being?" I shot back. I took a deep breath. "I like her. Now that I've spent time with her, she's more than just a cover."

Mia hesitated. The sympathetic look was somehow more uncomfortable to face than her scolding. "I understand why you like her, but she has issues. Issues that, if we're being truthful, you do not have the emotional maturity to cope with."

My spine strengthened. Anger bubbled just below the surface as I realised she was dead serious. I suspected what she was unsubtly hinting at and my mind's eye flashed with the image of Tessa's scars. If she thought that little of me, then she didn't know me as well as I thought she did. Unless ...

"You read more of that file?" I demanded. Her silence was all the confirmation I needed. "You're unbelievable, you know that? All this talk about protecting Tessa and me, but you knowingly dug into her past for any dirt you could find!"

"Your father insisted—"

"So what?"

I hadn't meant to shout, but it wasn't easy to take a breath to calm myself. I closed my eyes for a beat, not wanting to ask but knowing I had to.

"Without the specifics, just tell me," I said evenly, meeting Mia's reluctant gaze. "What do you, Mother and Father keep hinting at? What the fuck could Tessa have done that's so awful?"

"Nothing," Mia admitted, clearly thumbing through the file

170

in her head and choosing how to give this answer carefully. "But she had a difficult upbringing; her mother spent some time in hospital when she was fourteen, and Tessa had numerous counselling sessions after that hospitalisation."

"That's it?" I demanded.

"No," Mia snapped, irritated by my reaction. "Her mental health could make her fragile, and if someone like her father discovers this is – *was* – a ruse, that could make us all vulnerable."

I caught the cynicism on the word *was*, but neither of us commented on it. Instead, I thought about what she had said. Tessa had gone through a dark period as a teenager – I didn't need Mia to tell me that, but if her dad resurfaced with this media attention … that could have dire repercussions. Not just for my career but for her. It was funny that my agent and parents genuinely believed that file was some form of protection. Fucking idiots. It was a violation and had no purpose but to satisfy their morbid curiosity.

"He's not in Tessa's life, any more," I told Mia, who looked surprised. What do you know, something that wasn't in her file. "But I want that file gone, understand? Digital or physical, I want them gone."

"I can get rid of the digital file," Mia said. "But I don't have the physical one …"

"Who does?"

The answer was written all over her face. Within seconds, I was dialling and waiting with bated breath as the phone rang … and rang. I put the phone on loudspeaker as she answered – the sounds of a cocktail mixer or after-party was audible in the background. So much had been going on, I'd completely forgotten Mother was doing the festival circuit. I hadn't even considered what time zone she was in. It didn't matter.

"Bonjour," Mother's voice sang, and she hiccuped. I could almost hear the dreamy smile induced by whatever she was drinking. "Darling, I am just busy right now …"

Her voice trailed off as if she was holding the phone away from herself or moving into a corridor. The noises of whatever function she was at dulled to a low hum, the raucous laughter and the drunken aristocrats barely audible now.

"Whatever this is, can't it wait?"

"No," I stated firmly and then launched into my demands for all copies of the file on Tessa to be destroyed. I did not want to hear another word about it. Whatever they had read was to be forgotten, and above all Tessa must never know that Mia went digging up her past. To her credit, Mother stayed quiet. So quiet that when I stopped speaking, I thought she had either hung up, or the line had gone dead. Instead, she sighed. A long, disappointed sigh, like she had been snubbed for an award at the last minute. Like her expectations hadn't been met.

"Well, you never cease to amaze me …"

"What?" I asked, perplexed by her shift of tone.

"Of all the people you had to fall for," she said gravely, the alcohol making her words more drawn out than they needed to be. "It had to be *la fille brisée*, didn't it?"

"Don't talk about her like that!" I retorted, her words filling me with the same disgust I would have felt if she had gone up to Tessa and spat in her face. *It had to be the broken girl.* Mother was many things, but I had never heard her be this cruel and spiteful, especially towards someone she'd never even met.

"Surprisingly, your conquests aren't on my list of priorities." Mother dismissed me, sobering herself up with a callous chuckle. "All I expect from you is to clear up the mess you've made by the time I get back to London. I'll dispose of the file upon my return, that's if you haven't become bored to death of her by then."

"What's that supposed to mean?"

"If this interview is a success, any interest you have in this girl will evaporate. She will have served her purpose, and with her not having the intellect or lifestyle you are accustomed to, you will move on to the next naïve nameless girl." Mother was so matter-of-fact, it hurt more than if she'd shouted at me. She genuinely believed Tessa was a phase. Worse than that – she thought I was so vapid and shallow that I'd drop her the first chance I got.

"But," she carried on, her monologue becoming a verbal onslaught of judgement and damnation, "if you decide to keep your little plaything around, be wary. Some skeletons should stay in the wardrobe, son. You'd run a mile if you read what we have; mark my words."

"That's not true," I said, but my voice shook. I couldn't know for sure if that was due to anger or uncertainty.

27

Tessa

I sometimes felt like I was living two lives, a bit like Gwyneth Paltrow in *Sliding Doors*. One moment, one action or conversation and your life veered off in a totally new direction that you never imagined yourself going down. Yet here I was, trying to juggle the two. On a positive note, the *Innocence* cast reading was going better than expected. I had found a good group of actors and cast them in various roles; some were doubling up on the more minor characters. I initially worried about Jonathan's schedule, but it was Sarah's that had hit an initial hiccup in my plans. Days after I offered her the role, she had been cast as the lead in an upcoming TV series which sounded eerily similar to mine. Still, hers centred around a transgender teenager who finds love and the confidence to embrace her identity on holiday with her conservative family.

It was a dream gig for Sarah to be working in Venice, of all places, for six months and playing a character that resonated with her on a personal level, but she rang me up in tears when she broke the news. Shockingly, she still loved my script and hated the idea she was letting me down.

"We'll make it work," I assured her, not sure who I was reassuring here. "But if you need to, I totally get it if you have to step away to focus on this series."

"No, no!" Sarah said in a rush, her voice hoarse from the crying. "I definitely still want to be a part of this."

"Really?" I asked, unable to stop the nervous laugh escaping my mouth. "You've just been cast in a whole TV show as the lead, which sounds amazing. I can't even afford to pay you guys properly, so if you think this is beneath you—"

"It's not," Sarah said sincerely. "Really, you are probably one of the few writers I've worked with who saw me for a role that wasn't specifically about being trans. You wrote this great female lead, and honestly I was honoured you thought I could play her. So if we can make it work and it helps you to get onto that postgraduate course, I'm still in."

That meant more than I could even put into words. It really did. It was true, I hadn't thought for one second about the fact Sarah was transgender when she read for the part. She was amazing and literally brought my character to life effortlessly. If I had the money and could actually put my script into production, I would legitimately want the cast I had found to be in the actual film. I couldn't deny the relief I felt that Sarah still wanted to read for Georgina, but we had to work out the logistics of it all. With everyone's schedules, our rehearsals were confined to Zoom. The plus side of having a primarily middle-aged cast of actors who specialised in theatre, no one knew or cared who Jonathan was. Even Sarah – who clearly recognised him, judging by her surprised look when everyone got on Zoom – stayed totally professional and friendly.

My nerves had calmed about the reading since I'd submitted my application to the National Film and Television School early. It was like an elephant had taken its foot off my chest, and I was able to take a breath. Yes, I was still nervous about the outcome – but nowhere near the way I'd felt before I sent it in. I kept my head down because I had more eyes on me than I was used to. Under Mrs Robinson's orders, I reactivated my social media accounts and kept them private. She thought it would look staged if I remained a social media ghost.

The settings made me feel a bit more secure, but Kaitlyn had found smaller ways to enact revenge for my sucker-punching her. The message requests had veered from fangirls asking about Jonathan in every way possible – from the nice to the downright creepy and into the utterly horrible – to nameless accounts (that ended in several numbers) spamming me and calling me the vilest things imaginable. They weren't brave enough to post anything publicly, but it didn't take a genius to figure out it was Macbeth's trinity of witches. I just had to learn to ignore that annoying notification bell whenever an unknown tried to message me.

Then there was Jonathan. Not to sound like Ross from *Friends*, but I had no idea where this was going. This was definitely more than the agreement and way more than friendship, but neither of us had ventured to bring up what the label was. Did we need to, though? Were we just friends with benefits? No, you didn't have the conversations we had with a fuck buddy. I'd revealed some of my darkest secrets, and he was still here. But we hadn't had sex again since that first drunken night. We'd slept in the same bed every other night and did things of a sexual nature, but he didn't push for anything more. Yet the intimacy we were exploring in those stolen hours made me want much more …

It was also the time we spent outside of the bedroom that

was making me fall for him – the sweet, wry cockiness that no magazine photo could capture. He'd pulled a surprise even I wasn't expecting. We had been drip-feeding the media with shots of us out at London bars and restaurants, with the right amount of PDA to look natural – except the smiles, small touches of hands, and laughs were genuine. When Jonathan was asked to attend a book conference in London with his co-star and the author, it was a promising sign. I had an internalised fangirl meltdown when we walked into Waterstones at the heart of Piccadilly and I was introduced to Yoon.

I tried to keep my cool as Yoon walked over to greet us. She looked totally at home in the high-ceilinged, cathedral-like store among shelves of so many books it gave real *Beauty and the Beast* nostalgia. Before I'd discovered my love of cinema, the joy that came from walking through a quiet bookstore and flicking through brand new books was the highlight of my childhood. Nothing could ever beat that sweet, almond-like fragrance you get from the pages of an unread novel.

"Ah, this is the famous Tessa." Yoon beamed, shaking my hand – totally oblivious to the fact I was opening my mouth like a floundering fish on dry land – and she took a second to study my face. "Have we met before?"

"Yeah!" I said, a bit too loudly, and cleared my throat. "I mean, yes. I went to one of your signings when I was twelve."

Her eyes widened in surprise, her grin growing wider. "Oh! I remember you. You strolled up to my table with such confidence when you told me you wanted to be a writer. Not many girls are so certain of what they want to be, especially at that age. Are you still writing?"

"Yes, I am," I said, grateful that Jonathan had threaded

his fingers through my free hand. I was overwhelmed, not dreaming she would remember one plucky and awkward kid from the next. "I'm graduating with a degree in screenwriting in a few months."

"Stop being modest," Jonathan said softly to me. His smile broadened as he said to Yoon, "She's bound to get a first, based on her writing."

"Is that so?" Yoon smiled, her inky eyes dancing between us as if she'd spotted something we hadn't. "Well, you should be proud of your girlfriend, Jon."

"I already am," Jonathan said, not bothering to correct her on the nature of our relationship and sending my heartbeat racing. I watched as Jonathan talked so animatedly about this film with Yoon and Willow. He genuinely listened to the fans' questions, with his bright smile and straightforward personality. I stood in the back, feeling my cheeks flush whenever he caught my eye and the smile he gave me made me feel as if we were the only two people in this room.

I hung back as he and Willow signed books for the fans afterwards. The level of fandom ranged from shy to downright sobbing with joy. It was a shame there wasn't such a media buzz in these moments, but there was nothing to spin here. At the end of the event, Jonathan led me through the aisles of books, finding a secluded area among the classics.

"Got you something," he said with a boyish grin, pulling a book from the inside of his jacket. I instantly recognised the battered hardback of *Awaken*'s final book *Lost*. I gave him a sceptical look as I took it. He was still grinning. The book looked the same as it did on my shelf in my university bedroom – the pages browned, and the cover's once blue design had faded over the years to a light and unflattering green. Definite water damage and completely unremarkable.

"Why did you take this from my room?" I asked, reluctantly smiling at his grin of anticipation. "Okay, what is the purpose of this theft?"

He gave a low growl of exasperation. "Just open it!" he whispered. I obliged, flipping to the title page, and my eyes took in the fresh cursive note written inside:

> *Tessa,*
>   *I'm glad you took my advice to keep writing. The world deserves to see your stories – on page and screen!*
>   *A.K. Yoon.*

"I saw that was the only one you didn't have signed," Jonathan said cautiously, wary since I hadn't reacted to this gift at all. "I just figured you deserved a completed set …"

"Thank you," I said, and because I couldn't think of anything else to say, I kissed him, and hoped it would convey my feelings better than any words could. The year I was meant to go to the book signing was the December that Mum was admitted to hospital. With everything going on, standing in line for a scribble in a book I'd read a million times seemed stupid. No, it seemed childish. I grew up that winter. Some may say a bit too fast. Yet here was this boy, pleased that he'd made me smile over something so simple and having no idea what this actually meant. This silly, thoughtful gift on a whim was more precious than he could imagine.

His lips responded to my touch, and I could almost forget the origins of this courtship. Almost. I wanted to live forever inside those secluded moments when it was just us. That wasn't possible, though; there was no use pretending. This could all come crashing down around us. Everything hinged on this impending show appearance. But was I actually ready for the aftermath of the interview? What would happen when we stopped playing pretend to the outside world? I didn't have long to find out.

* * *

The phone vibrating on my bedside table woke me. It was still dark outside, and I still felt exhausted, like I had only got an hour of sleep. The screen illuminated my face with blinding intensity. I didn't keep my eyes open long enough to see the caller or the time. Instead, I blearily flopped down onto the pillow, holding the phone to my ear, already on the verge of sleep.

"Hello?" I yawned, rubbing the sleep out of my eyes.

"Be downstairs in ten," the sharp tone of Mrs Robinson caused my eyes to snap open with a start. "Don't be too picky about what you wear. Hair and make-up will want to take a look at you,"

The interview. It was today. Holy shit balls! I checked the time on my phone and groaned inwardly – it was nearly five a.m. Wow, Mrs Robinson didn't mess about.

"Okay!" I said quickly, hanging up before she could say anything else. The fear of that interview had chased away any fantasies of sleep. I was wide awake now. I practically fell out of bed. Even though she'd told me not to worry, I deliberately avoided anything too comfy – or baggy – and decided to go with the only decent jeans I owned and threw a denim jacket over a purple long sleeve Henley. My shoe collection was uninspired and mainly consisted of converse trainers that were non-negotiable with comfort.

I made my way through the silent flat, envying how my flatmates were able to sleep uninterrupted and without a giant waiting to take them to a London studio. The building was eerily quiet, which would have been creepy any other morning. It was a relief now. The newly appointed security guard gave me a nod of a greeting in reception. I dared a glance around as I walked out into the chilly dawn air. The campus grounds were almost still, just a few students stumbling home to their respective flats, one singing a pitchy rendition of "Sweet Caroline".

Mrs Robinson leaned against a sleek black car, looking like a powerhouse boss out of a Shonda Rhimes political thriller. I suppressed the powerful urge to gulp in front of her. Her eyes scanned my attire up and down, giving barely a nod as she gestured for me to get in. I chose the backseat, deciding our relationship was nowhere near me sitting shotgun. Disappointment dwelt in my gut for a second when I saw Jonathan wasn't in the car. I sensed Mrs Robinson's eyes reading me like a book as I pulled on my seatbelt.

"He's already at the studio," she answered, pulling out of park and making her way out of the campus.

"Oh, okay ..." I said brightly, my nerves audible in my voice, and I forced myself to clear my dry throat. "Are we okay to be driving without backup or security or something?"

Mrs Robinson chuckled, which I'm not sure was supposed to be reassuring or patronising. Maybe both. I wasn't trying to set the Women's Rights movement back a century, but we were two women, and mainly male paparazzi put us at a clear disadvantage if we're looking at numbers and physical strength alone.

"We thought it would be best if you both arrived separately and early," Mia explained, turning into the early morning traffic with ease. "And I also thought this would give us a chance to talk. Just us girls."

Oh. Her using the term "just us girls" gave me the same feeling of discomfort as when my grandmother decided she would give me the sex talk. Instead of the usual birds and the bees cringe-fest, Gran chose to use the pencil case metaphor. An original one-woman monologue of how we felt very proud and protective over our pencil case and wouldn't give pencils away to anyone as girls. Well, our womanhood should be treated exactly the same, and we should never give such a precious gift away to just anyone. Yep, I'd wanted to curl up and die during that conversation. I hoped this would not be a repeat …

"Girl talk?" I asked, a tiny nervous laugh escaping my lips before I could stop it. "I'd have thought you'd be prepping me not to make an idiot of myself in front of the world today."

"I think both you and Jonathan are prepped enough," Robinson said, her eyes fixed on the road ahead. "You've handled the media attention better than even I expected."

Wow. A compliment I didn't entirely deserve; the only good thing I'd done was to keep my head down. The university and Jonathan's PR team had kept me surprisingly safe during these crazy times. Tabloids tried to do stories on my family, but they were so dull in their ordinariness that they were quickly scrapped. Ryan was a minor-league ruby player – the fact he was gay made an uneventful splash in the press – and Vee was still a minor who, aside from having a mouth that would scare off the most brutal journalist in England, also had nothing newsworthy. The same went for Mum and even my elusive

182

father, which surprised me. The truth was, it was pure luck that no skeletons had stumbled out. We were utterly unique in our dysfunctional mundaneness.

"I've just kept my head down like you said," I assured her, but her hesitation made me pause, and I decided not to drag this out. "I'm guessing this is about Jonathan and me, yeah?"

"Yes," Robinson said briskly, relieved I had sped up the small talk. "I don't need to know the details. It is none of my business after all …"

I didn't bother to correct her. She was right, but I waited as she tried to sum up her point into actual words.

"It's clear Jonathan does care about you," Robinson said with something sounding like pity, "but I wouldn't be doing my job if I didn't warn you. Having a relationship under the spotlight is not as easy as we've made it look. We've carefully staged the narrative around you both, but we can't always offer that protection. Even the strongest relationships have been torn to pieces. Your lives aren't your own. They belong to the public. You will belong to the public, and no matter how much he cares for you, his career will always come first."

"I …" I started, but no words came out. Why was she dropping this on me now? Now, when I had to convince the world I was in love with Jonathan. A massive flaw in that plan was that there was no acting required. I was falling for him. Not the actor or the media heart-throb, the sweet and carefree Jonathan I saw behind closed doors. Did she see that too? Was she trying to soften the blow because he didn't feel the same way? I found my voice with difficulty, almost overcome with an urge to be sick. I sounded way calmer than I felt as I said evenly, "You're right. This really is none of your business."

"I just don't want to see either of you get hurt," Robinson

concluded, sensing I was not going to entertain this topic further. "That's all, believe me."

I didn't know what to believe any more. I just needed to get through today, that was all …

28

Jonathan

My stomach was in knots.

I sat in the green room, which was not actually green at all. Green rooms never were. I didn't go near the finger food they had set out. Instead, I was completely restless. I hadn't had time to go to the gym or even a run that morning, so I was there with all that energy and desperate for a release. I'd sensed something was up the minute I saw Tessa trailing behind Mia in the reception, her expression wiping the grin off my face completely.

"Hey," I said after they signed in, concerned by the withdrawn look on Tessa's face. "What's the matter?"

"Nothing," Tessa said simply, not caring I could see it was a bald-faced lie. My alarm bells started ringing when I reached for her hand and she flinched away the moment our skin touched, as if I had burned her.

"Tessa—"

"Let's just get this over with, okay?" she brushed me off, dutifully following the runner assigned to her. As soon as the elevator doors had closed on her, I turned to Mia furiously.

"What did you say?" I demanded, and she immediately held her hands up in surrender, not even attempting to deny she'd fucked up.

"I simply told her some home truths," she said vaguely, then continued in a defeated voice as it was clear that answer wasn't good enough. "That the two of you pursuing an actual relationship was unwise, in the long run."

"What?" The word was quieter than I'd expected as disbelief momentarily clouded my anger. "What gives you the right to say that?"

"I'm just looking out for you, Jonathan."

I held up my hand, silencing whatever she was going to say. Of all the days, it had to be this one. I sensed the receptionist's eager stare on us. I shot her a look, and her eyes darted back to her computer screen. I was determined not to have a repeat of the Yana Marcus shit show. This was make or break, and I needed this to go well.

Instead of losing it, I bit down on the words I wanted to hurl at her and followed my runner to hair and make-up. Today wasn't the day to lose my shit, not again. I plastered a smile on my face and kept any conversation brief but polite. Someone from the wardrobe department popped his head in as I was getting a last-minute touch-up from the tattooed make-up artist – she kept it simple, actually admitting, "You don't really need it." However, I wasn't sure if she was referring to my skincare routine paying off or making a sly comment about black skin. Either way, I just nodded. Not today, not today. Thankfully, Mia was preoccupied with calls in the hallway – so we didn't have to try and be courteous around strangers. I was still annoyed at her interference.

"Very nice," the slim wardrobe guy approved in an indistinguishable accent that was clearly not his own, his haughty demeanour quite off-putting. "I think O is right. We'll keep it natural with these two!"

"Natural?" I said, perplexed, as he nodded and actually stroked the fluff on his chin that he was trying to pass off as a goatee.

"Yes, O wants the viewers to see the real Jessa!" Wardrobe Guy gushed, his authentic accent slipping in, which now seemed to be Geordie. "O wants the audience to see the couple behind the curtain. No smoke and mirrors, just authenticity."

My stomach plummeted at that … was Ochuole trying to catch us out? This morning I had been on cloud nine, utterly confident in my relationship with Tessa. There was no official label on it, but it was mutual. Now I had no idea what was going on in Tessa's head. We'd been put in different green rooms, and I couldn't stand this, the not knowing. Fuck this. I needed to talk to her now.

I turned and headed for the door, but my runner had become my personal shadow, and the door swung open before my fingers touched the handle. It was like she was hovering on the other side.

"Can I get you anything?" the dark-haired woman asked in a rush, clearly surprised I was on the verge of walking out. "We're actually about to head down to set soon. In like, five minutes. Actually, four."

"I need to speak to my girlfriend," I said, the title coming out with unnerving ease … yet it sounded pretty nice. I desperately searched my memory for this girl's name to appeal to her. "Please … Steph, this is important."

Thankfully, she didn't look offended – so I got that right at least. Steph bit her lip, clearly weighing up the pros and cons. I breathed an actual sigh when she reluctantly nodded, flicking through the papers on her clipboard.

"She's in room twelve."

"Where's that?"

"Across the hall."

Seriously? I was mere fucking feet away from her, and this conversation was essentially pointless … great. I gave her a fake smile of gratitude and walked past, acknowledging her panicked warning that I only had a few minutes. I was out the door before she got cold feet and decided to shadow me. I crossed the hall as quickly and casually as I could and slipped into Tessa's green room without drawing the attention of the many crew members fixated on their various jobs.

Her eyes widened in surprise as I closed the door softly behind me, a miniature sandwich halfway to her lips. Unlike me, Tessa had made a dent in the food provided. I gave a fleeting smile, hoping my face was masking the swirl of nerves in my gut.

"I wanted to see you," I stated, thinking it was pretty apparent by my presence alone. Clearly not. I couldn't help chuckling as Tessa glanced at the sandwich and ate it whole. She gave a defensive glare, quickly chewing with her mouth clamped shut while still trying to give an indignant look.

"I didn't have breakfast, don't judge me," she said after she swallowed, smiling sheepishly when it was clear as day I wasn't. A worrying thought obviously crossed her mind as I walked closer and crouched down in front of her. "Has something happened?"

"You tell me," I said softly, relieved when she let me entwine my fingers through hers. I met her green eyes. Her hand in mine gave me the confidence to say, "I heard about your conversation with Mia."

"Oh."

"Yeah, oh."

She hesitated, her eyes cast down and focused on our hands. She took a moment to gather her thoughts. The silence was torture, but I didn't want to push her. This was most definitely the worst time to have this conversation, but it needed to happen. There was no way we could go out on that set if we weren't a united front and on the same page.

"If what she said made you think I don't have feelings for you," I said, my stomach squirming when her eyes widened at that – cards were on the table now. "She's wrong. I do, Tessa. It has nothing to do with all this. It's you. Everything I've said before, it's all true."

"I know," her voice was soft, but she met my eyes with such openness. "I feel the same, but what happens after all this? When we aren't in the spotlight any more? Or we have to prioritise what really matters?"

"Well, you have made the A-list for my priorities." I half-grinned and when her mouth formed a tiny smile, a glimmer of hope dared to make itself known. "I'm not going to pretend like I have all the answers or act like I know what will happen, so let's just focus on right now. You and me."

"Yeah. Sounds good. I'm sorry, I'm just freaking out about all this and Mia – Mrs Robinson – didn't help much," Tessa rushed on, looking embarrassed now. "It's just last-minute nerves! I swear. I'm not going to bail on you if that's what you're also worried about. I promised, and I'm going through with this. It's just—"

Her tirade only stopped when I pressed my lips to hers; a soft gasp was the only noise that escaped her mouth now. Her face was flushed for an entirely different reason as she pulled back, her hands cupping my face as she grinned shyly. The softness of her fingers caressing my cheek was torturously gentle, like she was holding something precious. I was half-tempted to close my eyes and completely allow my senses to memorise the feel of her skin against mine. Fuck, I needed to get a grip. What was I, a fucking cat? If anyone was going to make me putty at their touch, it was Tessa Granger.

"Okay," Tessa said, leaning forward to kiss my lips again lightly. "Oh, and you've definitely made my exclusive list too."

"Oh yeah?" I said wryly, but the frantic knocking on the door shattered the moment. We both turned to frown at the sound. You'd think the building was about to burn to the ground, given the urgency with which this person was rapping their knuckles on the wood.

"YOU NEED TO BE HEADING DOWN TO THE STUDIO, LIKE NOW!" Steph's voice was muffled through the thick door. The doorknob stayed very still … maybe she was terrified of the thought of seeing my bare arse and some sexual antics on a couch many celebrities have sat on before us. I laughed at the idea. I took Tessa's hand and we headed out. Steph looked visibly relieved by how quickly we stepped into the hallway, scanning our unruffled hair and neat clothes with intense scrutiny. Yep, she'd definitely thought we were fucking.

"Your agent is waiting for you on the set," Steph said, adopting a shaky professionalism that she'd lacked all day. Maybe the fear of a scandalous sex scene had boosted her confidence, now that she'd been proven wrong. "If you'll both follow me this way, please. Thank you."

We followed her through different corridors, the hectic

behind-the-scenes of a live show going on around us. All I was focused on was how good it felt to have Tessa's warm hand in mine. We caught each other's eyes and grinned like little kids, both relishing this tiny moment of privacy before cameras and the world analysed every word we said for the next hour. Fuck, my nerves were kicking in now.

"Are you ready for this?" I asked her in a voice for her ears alone as Steph rushed off for someone to mic us up. I noticed the sound operator digging out a shotgun mic and lavalier mic for each of us. Wow, this studio was on point and clearly had the cash to splash. The best set-up for an interview was actually one of each of those microphones – that way, you had quality backup audio recorded. Tessa gave a squeeze of my hand in response, a reluctant smile playing on her lips.

"God no!" she whispered, but then smirked as she added, "But we're doing it anyway. So fuck it, come what way."

29

Tessa

My stomach was in knots.

Could the sound guys pick up on my erratic heartbeat, or did the cinematographers spot the sweat setting up camp on my skin? God, I hoped not. It was embarrassing enough that Jonathan's fingers were threaded through mine, but he didn't seem fazed by holding my clammy hand in his. He squeezed it tighter and gave me a reassuring grin, setting off an entirely new set of butterflies in my stomach. We were sitting on the massive sofa of the lavish *O Show*; four cameras pointed at us from various angles and frames as crew members rushed about for final preparations. We were going live in five minutes.

From all my years of studying media, I knew the mechanics of a production in theory perfectly. It was another thing actually to see it play out in front of your eyes. So many people just think of the presenter or interviewees on this type of show and never realise an entire crew-army are behind the scenes hard at work. All of them were efficiently focused on their crucial role on set. It was kind of impressive.

The set made me feel a bit sick, though – it reminded me of a cranky old lady's living room, complete with shelves of nameless books that were purely decorative. The literature-themed decor was overwhelming in person and lacked any subtlety, making it abundantly clear who the demographic for this show was. People like me.

Ochuole made her way on set with a few minutes to spare, going over the script with a stage manager trailing behind her, nodding frantically. Her confident strides into the room had me in awe. She had a presence that would give Miranda Priestly a run for her money. She greeted us politely enough but clearly had other things on her mind.

"Pleasure to see you, Jonathan." Ochuole beamed a brilliant set of white teeth. Her accent had the tiniest hint of a Southern twang. Her eyes landed on me. "And here's the lady causing all the buzz. Try not to look so nervous; just relax."

Ha. Easier said than done, but I forced a feeble chuckle as she sat opposite us. Everyone was doing last-minute touch-ups, it was like watching the running of a ship, and before I had time to think about what to say or do, those dreaded words came.

"And we're on in, five … four …" the stage manager announced. His voice made me start, then his fingers signalled the countdown as the show's theme tune was audible from the control room. The red LIVE light came to life, that small cue telling us thousands were watching us.

"Welcome back to *The O Show*." Ochuole beamed at the camera focused on her, already knowing where to look. Her smile was welcoming, like the viewers watching were beloved visitors coming into her actual home. "I'm pleased to say I'm joined by Jonathan Adeola, who is due to star in the fantasy series *Awaken* that's set to release in cinemas this December, alongside his partner, Tessa Granger. These two have been causing quite a stir, on and off the screen. They're here for a tell-all interview. But before that, let's take a look at a teaser of Jonathan's upcoming release."

The screen behind us lit up, showing a snippet of the film – the actress playing the heroine Rae storms into the armoury, stopping dead when she sees Jonathan's character during a training session, both actors shirtless with their muscular physiques on full display. Okay, so this film was big on the Female Gaze. The slow-motion shots and the close-ups of his tight muscles as he dances around his opponent with ease distract from any tension that could develop between the characters. Swords clash in a detailed, choreographed routine, Jonathan's Kai ultimately getting the upper hand. He catches the eye of Rae, a smirk that looks somewhat similar to his own curving lips.

"Enjoying the view?" Kai asks cockily, and Rae seems to snap out of whatever trance she was in, now glaring at him.

"Professor Braun wants to see you," Rae informs him curtly, turning to leave and shooting him another glare over her shoulder. "She's not happy with you."

"When is she ever?"

I found myself fighting the urge to cringe at this dialogue. Where was the subtlety? The back-and-forth banter? The scene ended on a jarring note. Rae stumbles, and a series of flashes reveal distorted spoilers for a potential second and third film before she collapses. Somehow Jonathan manages to run across a training field in time to catch her while still looking heroic and brooding.

Wow …

I remembered to put on a broad smile and clap along with the crew. Everyone looked ecstatic. Except for Jonathan. I caught his eye and realised he looked just as confused as I felt. Maybe even a bit disappointed. I got the sense this was his first time seeing that scene. He forced a grin as O drew his attention back to her.

"Great stuff, Jonathan!" O beamed and looked to the crew, all of them adding to that statement with another cheer. "I'm sure this one is going to be a hit with the ladies – and some of the men too!"

He laughed. It sounded disingenuous to my ears, but that disarming smile was enough to fool anyone who didn't know him.

"Now, before we discuss that more, we need to discuss the elephant in the room," Ochuole said gravely. "Can we talk about the Yana Marcus interview?"

"Yeah, of course," Jon said half-heartedly, and it was my turn to squeeze his hand reassuringly, giving him a smile to match.

30

Jonathan

I'd known this was coming, but my stomach still dropped to what felt like the Earth's core. I took a deep breath and nodded. It was my time to put this to bed. That scene preview had utterly thrown me. Where had the fuck had those close-ups come from? Two months I'd spent training to do all the film's fight sequences – I'd got it down so well, my stuntman wasn't required for those scenes at all – and all I had to show for it was fake sweat dripping over my biceps, chest and even a weird fixation on my fucking nipples! I'd been promised any nudity would be tasteful, but now a film I was proud of looked like a cheap vanity project.

I could worry about that later – or Mia could when she called up the director, Edythe, and reminded her of the terms of my fucking contract. Right now, I needed to make sure the world heard once and for all about that dreaded Yana Marcus interview. I met O's eyes with genuine sincerity. No acting required.

"I'm not proud of it," I admitted truthfully, focusing on how soft Tessa's hand felt in mine. I cleared my throat. "I'm really not. I've prided myself on always being a professional. I mean, look at my parents – it's in my blood to tell stories in one way or another. I admit I lost my temper, but I also couldn't just sit back while my co-star and I were subjected to homophobic and racist bigotry. It doesn't excuse my behaviour, I know."

"Anyone who saw that interview could see you both were clearly distressed," O said seriously, her facial expression still empathetic. "I'm all for finding a story, but emotionally manipulating an interview to gain a reaction is not how journalism works. Especially when her only criticisms were discriminative."

"Still, I shouldn't have lost my temper and shouted. Even though what she said was hurtful, I'd like to apologise to Yana for that," I said, and was relieved when O smiled. "That's why I'm glad to have had Tessa during this time. She's been amazing."

Out of the corner of my eye, I noticed a pink flush colouring Tessa's cheeks and my grin broadened. O's eyes swivelled to Tessa, her brown eyes training themselves on Tessa's green ones.

"He's just being modest," Tessa brushed off, smiling despite herself. "He's the amazing one. He's too much of a gentleman to say otherwise, but knowing when you're in the wrong says more about his character than Yana Marcus."

"Quite right," O agreed. "Can I just say, I think you've found a keeper with her. And honestly, I'm amazed how you two managed to keep your relationship out of the public eye for so long. How did you meet? We're all dying to know!"

31

Tessa

As a writer, you learn one thing very quickly from readers – or in my case, viewers. No one wants reality. They want the fairy tale. Regardless of what the media looks for or moviegoers say, they want that escapism and to delve into the romantic notions of make-believe. So, I told Ochuole exactly what she wanted to hear.

Robinson assured me not to sound too scripted, to leave enough space for people to fill in the tiny gaps. I couldn't help my imagination conjuring the fantasy world I was claiming to be fact – where I was sitting on my bench reading and caught the eye of a handsome stranger. Trying to sell the idea of Jonathan and I losing ourselves in a conversation wasn't a lie, except that it had happened in Leicester Square and not the Botanic Gardens.

As I told the story of our first meeting on a random spring day, I blushed at the omission. I'd had no idea who Jonathan really was, which was true. My mum once jokingly said that telling a lie is much easier when there's a truth at its heart. Jonathan's reassuring grins and the pressure of his hand in mine made the tightness in my chest loosen with each word. Instead, I could almost imagine Jon and me on that bench, the frozen dæmons entwined behind us. I was selling the fairy tale, but I really wished it was my reality at times. I caught Ochuole leaning closer, totally engaged in what I was saying.

"What book was it?" Ochuole asked, adding by my expression, "The book. What was it you were reading?"

"*My Sweet Audrina*," Jonathan said easily, just as I was about to say *Amber Spyglass*. My stomach plummeted as I realised that was a detail that we could have messed up on, but Jonathan flowed effortlessly onwards. "She sold me on Virginia Andrews' prose style. I had to read it for myself. I quickly learned Gothic horror has really inspired Tessa's writing and was totally blown away."

My mind flashed back to Jonathan lounging on my bed, reading my battered copy. Did he have that plan in his head from then? I kept the smile on my face, nodding like this detail was not anything new to me.

"That's sweet," Ochuole said genuinely, looking between us. "Well, you managed to keep your budding romance private till these photos hit the tabloids."

The screen beside us brought up a slide of snapshots I'd wished I'd never see myself. That blurred night was finally given some clarity, showing Jonathan and I entwined on the dance floor in that Soho club. That red dress, our lips inches apart as we danced to a song neither of us could remember. We'd deliberately avoided the hype of these pictures with both of us removing ourselves from the internet, plus Mum's reaction was enough.

For the first time, my staged smile slipped. I wasn't prepared for this.

"What inspired that night out?" Ochuole asked, but I really didn't have an answer.

32

Jonathan

Don't react. I shot Mia a warning look. She looked ready to charge onto the set and drag us both off this couch. The irony! Where was that urgency last time? I squeezed Tessa's cold fingers in my hand, giving a wide grin to the interviewer and taking hold of the narrative.

"It was spur-of-the-moment," I said casually, holding O's attention. "We were taking advantage of our last free night. We'd spent the whole summer together in a bubble, but I knew she'd be busy with her last year of university, and I had projects in the works. So we just wanted to have a night on the town."

"Were you worried about the press attention that coming out publicly with Tessa would bring?" O asked tentatively, not knowing how much she had hit the nail on the head. "Was there any concern about that?"

"Yeah," I said honestly and, without looking at Tessa, I did something I swore I'd never do in an interview. I told the fucking truth. "I was scared. I still am. What I've found with Tessa has been something I honestly thought I wouldn't be able to find. It sounds mad, but she makes me feel normal. She calls me out on my ... stupid moments, and she's so funny. I didn't think you could be so physically and emotionally attracted to someone, but we just clicked. I mean, I wouldn't have blamed her if she'd done a runner when this started. It's a lot to take, being with someone who grew up in the industry."

"I'm not that easily scared off," Tessa said softly, and I turned to her, her green eyes making me honestly forget we were being watched by so many people. For a shining and ridiculous moment, it really felt like we were alone.

"I know." I smiled, not sure why I felt a bit sad at acknowledging that. I knew it was true, and her faith in me felt foreign and somehow completely natural. "That's why I love you."

33

Tessa

My brain and mouth froze entirely, like I was a film stuck on buffering. Never had someone said those words to me – apart from people to whom I was directly related. I'd never dated anyone I even wanted to say those words to. I had everyone held at arm's length. I hardly had the best example of a romantic relationship from my parents, so I kept myself buried in fictional love stories and refused to be that vulnerable in real life. Now here was this boy, saying words that no one had told me, and my heart slammed against my ribcage at the feelings it set off inside me – all in front of thousands of viewers.

Was he being serious, or was this part of his career-saving plan? No, I knew from the sincerity in his brown eyes that he was being genuine. No one is that good an actor. He loved me … he loved me, and I loved him too, which was insane because we barely knew each other. And yet …

Those words were both miraculous and petrifying at the same time. I wanted to say it back, because I did – I loved him, body, mind and soul. But feeling it and telling are two completely different things. Those words had the power to break you … I'd seen it first-hand.

So I suddenly understood the absolute terror that making an epic and totally vulnerable declaration like Julia Roberts' character in *Notting Hill* would have caused. Because trust me, I was feeling it. This girl sat next to a boy who was too terrified to ask her just to love him, but she did it anyway. "I love you too …"

34

Jonathan

Fuck. Tears pooled in my eyes, even though I was smiling like an idiot. I wanted to hear her say those words again and again, but I pulled myself back to the present. I met O's eyes and knew she had captured this moment as TV gold dust. It wouldn't have been my ideal place to tell Tessa I loved her for the first time, but since when had any of this been ideal?

"I can see the love here," O said wryly, probably already calculating the retweets and views this interview was going to get her. Although this was a better choice of an interviewer, I wasn't fooled – she knew what made good telly. It was just a bonus I was making this work in my favour. I dared a glance at Mia, who looked visibly relieved as the interview continued without a hiccup. It had gone perfectly, if I said so myself. Tessa was brilliant and a hit with Ochuole, and for someone who'd never been interviewed on live TV she had that instant likeability about her.

"So what are we expecting from you next?" O asked, the question tinged with a hint of finality. "Aside from the next films in this series, any other roles you want to tackle?"

"Loads," I half-laughed, my stomach finally loosening its knots. "I'm looking to branch out. But we'll have to wait and see."

Ochuole thanked us both for coming, and with an announcement of what was coming next – "Can influencers make good authors?" – the red lights switching off signalled the commercial break. When we finally heard the stage manager yell, "Cut!" we were ushered off set with rushed goodbyes to Ochuole.

With my fingers threaded through Tessa's, my chest swelled with pride when I caught sight of Mia's beaming face waiting for us in the much quieter corridor. She looked close to tears as she surprised both of us by pulling us into tight hugs. Even Tessa looked lost for words, but smiled nonetheless.

"You were bloody marvellous!" Mia gushed, and then, as if remembering where we were, she composed herself. "I'll be calling Edythe. The cut of that scene was not the one we approved. If she pulls another stunt like this, I'll have her for breach of your final cut contract. Honestly, that scene looked ridiculous."

"She's probably trying to sell the Female Gaze appeal," Tessa said, her cheeks turning pink when I caught her eye. "Shut up. It's a feminist theory term representing the gaze of the female spectator, character or director. Still, I don't think replicating a male gaze sexualisation of the guys helps the fight for equality."

"Quite," Mia agreed, already scrolling through her phone for the number. She excused herself, leaving Tess and me alone. Feeling emboldened and on a confidence high, I pulled Tessa to me and kissed her on the lips. My arms encircled her waist, unable to conceal the goofy grin I had plastered on my face.

"I can't thank you enough for this," I said softly, even though we were alone. "Even if this doesn't work—"

"Don't think like that, Jon."

"If it doesn't," I continued, "I'm glad I had you in my corner. Not many people have had my back like you have. Even under these crazy circumstances."

"We are all fools in love," Tessa said wryly, laughing softly on the last word. "Although, I doubt Jane Austen had this in mind when she wrote that."

"Are you saying I'm your Darcy?" I asked cockily, not thinking Tessa had a period kink. "Didn't think you had a thing for Colin Firth?"

"I don't. I never liked the BBC adaptation either. Matthew Macfadyen was a much better Darcy," Tessa admitted like it was something controversial to say aloud. Then her voice lowered to a shy whisper as she mused almost to herself, "Although … you'd look better in a wet Regency shirt."

Her eyes widened in horror at the admission; her embarrassment only intensified when I raised an eyebrow flirtatiously. Maybe I could look into some Regency castings, especially with the diverse productions nowadays – the idea was appealing, mainly to see the look of mortification I could already visualise on Tessa face's if she saw me go Mr Darcy on her. As if sensing where my thoughts were heading, she gave me a flustered look of annoyance as she turned and headed towards our dressing rooms with me beside her. She tutted as if she could read my dirty mind. My wry grin just confirmed it, which naturally made her cheeks flush even pinker.

When we'd grabbed the rest of our stuff, a new nameless intern escorted us to the reception. The quiet corridors were a surprising welcome, but my good mood dampened when Mia came into view, looking worried and livid. Behind her, I could see why. The glass doors revealed a mob of paparazzi. Their cameras were already flashing blinding lights at us. Fuck, I thought we'd have more time than this. Mia had planned the schedule to avoid a tabloid frenzy.

"Christ …" Tessa breathed as Mia joined us. "Is there another exit?"

"Car's already outside," Mia said reluctantly, and I caught that grimace again. "We'll make this quick. You'll be fine."

"Absolutely," I lied, although I could tell she wasn't reassured. I didn't blame her. We had no security detail, no backup plan. As if sensing our predicament, a burly security guard made his way over to us.

"Could you give us a hand?" I gestured at the journalists, whose muffled shouts and questions were audible despite being separated by glass. I wondered why they hadn't triggered the sensors to open the door, but the receptionist from earlier was sitting stoically in her seat. She shot a glare at the security guard – as if she was the one being targeted. He nodded, his thick neck barely moving, and before I could talk myself out of it, I followed the massive suit and my fragile-looking agent with my hand holding Tessa's sweaty one. As soon as the sensors were turned back on, the glass doors slid open, and the noise and lights were apocalyptic.

"Jonathan, are you really in love with Tessa Granger?"

"Is this not a bit too convenient?"

"What do you say about Yana Marcus's latest Twitter thread? Is this a publicity stunt?"

"Do you ever worry about your moment having passed as an actor?"

"Do you think this film is your final role?"

208

"Tessa! Tessa, how much are they paying you?"

Fuck. Off. I ignored all the questions. My eyes focused on the muscular back ahead of me. The questions became more inappropriate and obscene. What should have been a few minutes' walk felt like aeons. One scruffy face came uncomfortably close, shoving a microphone underneath Tessa's nose.

"Ms Granger, how does it feel? Being a celebrity's beard?" the bearded reporter sneered as his eyes swivelled in my direction. "Seriously? Do you expect people to buy that little performance?"

The heavy shoved the reporter away before I could, which was lucky because a sleek black limo came into view. As Mia ducked to open the back door, my fingers slipped out of Tessa's grasp. Before I could turn and let her in first, the heavy took my arm and shoved me inside. My face collided with new leather seats, and before I could pull myself properly into a sitting position, the back door slammed.

"Drive, now," Mother's voice said icily as I sat up and saw her sitting ahead of me. I turned, frantic, as I realised Tessa wasn't in the car. Both Tessa and Mia had vanished from view. Fear flooded me as the car began moving away from the studio. Even the journalists knew to move out of the way, the driver keeping a steady pace as the journalists decided to chase instead of block.

"Wait, where's Tessa?" I dived for the door, hearing the click as I shoved against it. The blinding flashes at the window burned my eyes. "Open the fucking door! Oi! Stop the car!"

"Do not swear at me! Honestly, the girl will be fine." Mother snapped, glaring at me like I was a petulant child throwing a tantrum as I shoved against the door and even kicked it.

She sat back in her seat, already becoming bored of my very valid reaction. "So dramatic. You know you get that from your father, don't you? Have a glass of Scotch, darling. Calm down."

"Yeah, because that's your answer for everything!" I shouted at her, bile rising in my throat. Something else had caught the paparazzi's attention. They were running – actually running – after what looked like a dark-haired figure. Tessa! She was being chased by those fuckers! Where was Mia? How the fuck had this career move descended into chaos? Did Mother expect me to sit here while my girlfriend was hounded like a dog?

"Fuck this, let me out!" I demanded, still beating the shit out of the door. My rage only intensified when Mother merely poured herself a glass of Scotch. I lunged forward and slapped the glass out of her perfectly manicured hand. The dark liquid soaked into the carpet, surrounded by shattered glass. Her hand remained frozen in mid-air, still cupped as though holding the now broken glass. Her eyes narrowed into slits, and without warning, she slapped me across the face. My cheek stung and my eyes burned. I had no idea whether it was because of anger, pain or hurt. I was not going to cry in front of her; I never had before – like fuck was I going to start now. The limo gradually sped up, leading into the heart of London and away from the only two people I wanted to be with. If the driver heard the commotion, they deliberately chose to ignore it.

"Do not ever do that again." Mother's voice was barely a whisper and yet it was filled with contempt. "You're fortunate that you played your part perfectly, but do not push me. You always were *un enfant émotif*."

"I'm not being emotional," I retorted, but she scoffed as she poured herself another glass. "And it's not a performance. I meant every word."

"Yes, but this infatuation with the commoner is becoming quite tedious." Mother sighed, giving a warning look as she sipped the Scotch. When it became clear I wasn't planning on knocking another drink out of her hand, she continued. "Mark my words. This will end in heartbreak, which is why you should break this off before you become attached. Alas, you've never taken your mother's advice, have you? But I have bigger things to worry about than your latest plaything and that imbecilic representation of yours. Much more important things. Like your future."

"Since when did you care?"

If that offended or hurt her, she had the best fucking poker face on the planet. Instead, she passed a folder over. I cautiously took it. A screenplay was inside. Perfectly neat and professionally held together with "Prodigal Son by Samuel Harrison" printed on the title page. I was stunned to be holding the complete draft of the film I was desperate to read, but here it was. Inside the envelope, I found actual audition scenes. As I flicked through the pages, I found a final note on the last audition page:

> J,
>
> *Get the tapes to me by Friday, and we can talk when I land in London.*
> *Samuel.*

"What? How did you even know about this?" I asked, almost wary of its authenticity, mainly because I hadn't spoken to her about this. "Harrison didn't even want me to audition; how come he changed his mind?"

"Jonathan, I thought I'd taught you better. It's not about your talent. It's your connections that'll get you what you want. Fortunately, you have a mother with the right connections." Mother's smugness was sickening; she laughed dryly at my expression. "Mia mentioned to your father her devastation over not being able to secure you an audition. At her own failure more like. As luck would have it, I met Harrison at the Venice Film Festival, and your name came up. His interest was piqued when I assured him of your enthusiasm for the role. What? Did you really think Mia could get you an audition with an Iris-award-winning director when you're the only name casting on her books?"

That was harsh, but Mother seemed unperturbed by her ridicule of Mia and instead gestured at the script. "I took the liberty of proofreading it. It's a good choice, I must admit. More mature, which is what you need. There are a few love scenes, but Harrison is a tasteful director and totally professional—"

My phone rang, reminding me – with a start of guilt – of Tessa. I hastily answered, not even checking the ID.

"Tessa—"

"She's safe," Mia's breathless voice answered instead, and my stomach leapt, only to drop with the following four words. "She's with her dad."

35

Tessa

Everything happened so fast, I barely had time to process it. Before I could follow Jon into the car, the on-loan security guard slammed the door behind him. The limo sped away, and suddenly I was the centre of attention and staring after the speeding vehicle with a face that must have had my dumbfounded emotions written all over it. Flashes of lights blinded my vision. I held up a hand, as if that was enough. Mia was shouting angrily at the gormless security guard, but I couldn't understand what she was saying. What felt like physical walls were closing in on me. I shoved past whatever journalist was in front of me, forcing my way out of the sea of bodies.

Just. Keep. Moving.

The flashes of cameras fuelled me to move faster, but my breathing had changed. My chest felt like Devil's Snare had wrapped itself around my lungs in an agonising grip, each breath a painful effort to force air into them. The terror of succumbing to a panic attack or being crushed by savage gossip vultures had me breaking into a run as soon as I saw an opening onto the street beyond.

I didn't look back at them; I knew they were following me. I didn't look back at the retreating limo; Jonathan wasn't going to save me. Was I naïve to think he could? That didn't matter, not now. I ran through unfamiliar London streets, having no idea where I was or where I was heading. I only realised I was in Shaftesbury Avenue when I very narrowly dodged a group of animated tourists in the theatre district. My feet hit the pavement hard as a cramp took what felt like permanent residence in my side. Theatres, okay. That meant crowds that I could hopefully lose these creeps in. Many had given up the ghost, but I could still hear some reporters persisting in their pursuit.

"TESSA! We just wanna talk!"

"Why did Jonathan leave without you?"

"Trouble in paradise?"

Fuck. Off.

I wanted to scream far worse at them, but forcing air into my lungs and not falling flat on my face was more of a priority. A familiar sight had caught my eye – the Apollo Victoria Theatre. I remembered seeing *Wicked* there for the first time with Mum when I was sixteen, and sure enough the emerald poster of Elphaba smirking as Glinda whispered something in her ear greeted me through the wide-open theatre doors. I took the stairs three at a time, relieved when I found the green-carpeted foyer crowded with theatre buffs and musical fanatics. It must be the interval.

I gasped for air, leaning against a pillar as my legs trembled with shock and sheer exhaustion. Now that I'd stopped running, I could really register how my clothes clung to my sweaty skin and the pain my muscles were in, having carried me this far. My heart sank when I turned to look towards the large double doors and spotted the reporters craning their necks from the street beyond. Maybe there were celebrities here, or safety for the cast was taken more seriously, because they didn't have the nerve to push past the security who stopped them from coming inside.

Not taking any chances, and before anyone demanded a ticket I didn't have, I hurried into the nearest bathroom. It took a second for my eyes to adjust to the sudden colour change. It was like seeing the *Wizard of Oz* in reverse. Whereas the foyer was bright in its green glory, the toilets had a grey staleness with even darker tiles lining the walls. I leaned on the sink for support, running the cold tap and splashing water on my face. I took a breath and caught sight of myself in the mirror.

The girl staring back at me looked nothing like the cool girl who'd sat next to her famous boyfriend on national TV. Sweat had caused the little make-up I had on to smudge and run down my face; the effect made me look like I had been ugly crying. I washed the last remnants of mascara and lipstick off my face, partly for the relief of fresh water cooling my skin. The pale face that peered back at me looked exhausted, with dark circles under my eyes and a blank expression. Exactly how I felt inside. Could this be how Cinderella felt after midnight? In a second, she went from a spectacle to behold to the unremarkable girl running for her life. The magic was well and truly gone, and there was no Prince Charming. It was just an illusion.

I felt my throat closing up, but I forced myself to keep my emotions in check. No, I wasn't going to cry. I wasn't a damsel who needed saving. I'd just proved that. But it hurt that I had been left to fend for myself – especially after telling him I loved him on live TV, like an idiot.

A cubicle door swung open, and a woman with auburn hair and looking way too smartly dressed for a trip to a matinee show made her way towards the sinks. She smiled at me. I barely twitched my mouth in return.

"Enjoying the show?" the woman asked. I nodded, noticing her rubbing hand sanitiser into her hands despite having just vigorously washed them with soap. "Nikki Handcock is doing a superb job, don't you think?"

"Oh, absolutely," I lied, forcing a disingenuous grin. I leaned over the tap and gulped a mouthful of water, my throat as dry as sandpaper. I felt better, but my legs were still like jelly. The woman frowned and tilted her head at me as I dabbed my mouth with a paper towel. She was polite enough not to ask why I looked like I'd walked solo across the Sahara Desert, I noticed for the first time.

"I still can't believe one of my clients is starring in a West End show," the redhead gushed as if I knew this detail, and maybe she sensed my confusion because she hastily added, "Oh, I represent Nikki. This is her first time officially playing Elphaba. She's been the understudy for the past year – I kind of feel like a proud parent, which is bizarre. I'm Rebecca Thomas. From Unique Talent agency, heard of us?"

"Sorry, no, I haven't."

"Shame, you're quite pretty. Do you—?"

"I DON'T GIVE A FUCK ABOUT YOUR SHOW!" a broad-Scottish, female voice roared outside the door. "I'M LOOK-ING FOR SOMEONE!" The voice was coming gradually closer.

Terror gripped me as I turned and bolted into the nearest

cubicle, locking the door on the politely concerned agent. I clambered up onto the toilet seat just as the door burst open. I heard the heels of Rebecca Thomas turned to the female as another set of shoes clattered in.

"I said you can't just barge in without a ticket." The hassled-sounding male usher seemed petrified of being in the women's bathroom.

"I told you, I'm just looking for someone for an interview," the Scottish reporter snapped at him, then turned to the agent. "You! You see a little white girl? Brunette, about twenty or so."

"That narrows it down," Rebecca said coolly, and I waited with bated breath, praying that my tired legs didn't give up on me now. "Care to be a bit more specific?"

"Don't play me," the reporter sneered, already losing any semblance of manners. "I saw her running in here."

"Well, if the young lady was running, she obviously doesn't want to speak with anyone," Rebecca shot back. "And judging by your people skills, I can't blame her."

"Ma'am!" The usher yelped as the cubicle next to mine had its door kicked in. My heart jumped into my throat. I'd never been more aware of my breathing and the thumping of my erratic heartbeat. "Security!"

"I'm going!" the reporter snapped. I could imagine the scathing look she must have been giving Rebecca – as I had no idea what the journalist looked like, I'd mentally cast her terrifying fierceness as a hybrid of Pam Ferris' most petrifying roles (Agatha Trunchbull from *Matilda* meets *Harry Potter*'s Aunt Marge), with a Lorraine Kelly twang.

As the bathroom door swung hard against the wall and bounced back into place, the silence sent shivers up my spine. With a shaky sigh of relief, I sank onto the toilet seat and had the weirdest sensation to crack up laughing or burst into tears. I ran a hand over my sweaty brow, taking slow and deep breaths to keep hysteria at bay. It was the soft knock that ironically startled a small cry from my lips, and I pressed a hand to my mouth, hating the tears that broke free.

"Are you okay?" Rebecca asked softly, probably guessing I was precisely the opposite. The silence that followed prompted her to add, "She's gone. I promise."

"Oh great!" a high voice responded, which sounded nothing like me. And then, remembering she'd asked a question, I added through choked tears, "Yep, yes. I'm fine. Absolutely."

The bald-faced lies sounded feeble and totally pathetic, which is why I wasn't shocked to see Rebecca there to greet me as I unlocked the cubicle door. Wordlessly, she handed me some tissue and I hastily dabbed at my eyes, which gave me the excuse not to elaborate on what had just occurred.

"First time? With the press?" Rebecca asked the statement like a question, and I shook my head, avoiding her sympathetic gaze. "Tell you what, why don't you join my fiancé and me in the bar? Just until the interval ends, hopefully, she'll have given up by then, if she's lurking outside. Then we can chat or not, although my soon-to-be husband is a bit of a talker anyway."

She laughed at that, and I found myself chuckling along with her, even though I'd found nothing she'd said at all funny. Feeling suddenly like a child desperate to be looked after and have an adult take control, I followed the redhead out of the bathroom and into the theatre's bar. She was probably a decade older than me, but she walked with a confidence I'd only seen in the likes of Mrs Robinson and even Ivy. That self-assurance and indifference to anyone except those who mattered – I'd never had that. Was it something about London? I mean, there were times like this where I was reminded just how small and sheltered my world had been before moving here.

No, whatever my upbringing was … sheltered was definitely not one way to describe it. The emerald bar had the same grandeur as the foyer. Unlike any community theatre back home, the Apollo Victoria Theatre embraced the historical architect while also paying homage to their show's mise en scène. Obviously I had been too young to drink in here at sixteen – and I'd spent almost the entirety of the interval reading the programme and relaying all the facts on the cast, crew and even the building to Mum. Now I could appreciate the beauty of the theatre.

Rebecca led me to a dark-haired man sitting at the bar. I could only see the back of his thinning hair which was more grey than dark brown. Rebecca had already begun introducing us, before he even saw her approaching. "Matthew, we have a plus-one joining us. The poor girl's been through an ordeal in the loo. Long story – oh, what's your name, sweetheart?"

I stopped dead in my tracks when the man turned to greet me, his smile vanishing as soon as we recognised each other. Our identical green eyes took each other in. We both looked drastically different compared with our last meeting six years ago. Dad, or Matthew – that parental name sounded wrong, even in my own head – had aged horribly. His face had wrinkled before its time, and despite the expensive clothes and having lost weight, he had the air of Del Boy. Matthew Granger always had a habit of reinventing himself to be more important or sophisticated than he ever was. A class act, but it was just arrogance. I had the sudden impulse to turn and run, but my feet were rooted to the dark green carpet.

"Teresa?" Matthew breathed, his brow furrowed in disbelief and confusion. Was he still imagining me as the teenager in our too-small living room, glaring at him through bloodshot eyes as he told Ryan, Vee and me that he was leaving for America after everything he put Mum through? By the blanched look on his face, I knew he was visualising that scene himself. Guilt or shame flickered in his eyes, but I felt neither. No, I just felt anger simmering just below my calm façade.

"Oh god!" Rebecca gasped, looking back-and-forth between us in shock. "I didn't know … Oh my god, hi!"

Before I knew it, I was being hugged by my future step-mother. With my arms pressed to my sides by her embrace, we stood there uncomfortably as I neither accepted nor rejected this act of affection. She pulled back apologetically, and I caught the jerk of the head she shot at Matthew in my direction. He stumbled off his stool, sheepishly raising his arms as he advanced towards me.

Oh, hell no!

I stuck my hand out instinctively and the movement stopped him in his tracks so fast you'd think I'd drawn a sword or wand on him instead. His eyes darted between my face and hand. He actually had the nerve to laugh. It was a hoarse laugh and barely met his eyes. That smile faltered when my hand didn't waver, and he awkwardly shook it. Did he expect me to hug him? My expression remained stony as I pulled my hand from his.

Rebecca hovered between us like a terrified referee. "Teresa, it's lovely to meet you finally," she gushed, and I watched as the bad-arse woman shrank before my eyes, morphing into a doting wife as she stepped beside Matthew and linked her arm through his. "Your dad's told me so much about you. I can't believe how beautiful you are! And clever – the first in the family to go to university! Amazing! What are you studying again?"

"Poetry."

"Screenwriting," I corrected him bluntly, glaring at the obvious glance of disquiet he gave Rebecca. He really had no idea who I was. Not one clue.

"Right, how are your little scripts going?"

Little scripts? That hurt more than it should have, which only made me angrier as I stood opposite this pathetic man. In two words, he'd made my life's ambitions and all of my achievements sound like a childish hobby. His cruel dismissal was condescending and I was sure he knew it, but I bit my tongue and refused to show how much that question stung. Instead, I realised something that made my stomach drop. He'd never read anything I'd ever written, or even knew what I wanted to do as a career. So how did he know I was studying writing? I'd long suspected that Vee or Ryan was relaying details back to our dad. This just confirmed it. Surprisingly, it hurt to know for certain one or both of my siblings had disregarded my wishes to keep him out of my life.

I held my head high. And with a confidence I didn't feel, I responded coldly with, "Actually really good, I've applied to the National Film and Television School for my master's."

"That a good school, is it?"

"Babe, it's one of the best," Rebecca pointed out, glancing my way with an apologetic grimace. "That's brilliant, Teresa. Hope you get in."

"Thanks, and it's Tessa, actually," I corrected, noticing the cynical snort Matthew tried to hide. "What?"

221

"I suppose it's better than Tessie or whatever the fuck Grace used to call you," Matthew smirked, and I had a strong urge to punch that smug look off his face. My knuckles were still healing from the last time I lost control in a public space, so I resisted taking a swing at him. Instead, I was saved from answering his condescending comment by my phone buzzing in my bag. I hadn't thought to check it; making my escape had been my main priority.

I unlocked my phone and was greeted by a string of messages and missed calls from the last person I'd expected.

MRS R: Where are you, Teresa?

MRS R: Tell me where you are, and I'll come and get you. Just let me know you're okay.

MRS R: Call me when you get this. I'm driving around trying to find you!

MRS R: This is getting ridiculous! Teresa, answer your phone!

Even as I was scrolling through, I spotted the three moving dots as Mrs R was undoubtedly writing another panic-stricken message. I hastily wrote back a response before she could send yet another message:

ME: I'm okay. Sorry, I was a bit busy being chased. I'm at the Apollo Victoria with—

I hesitated for the tiniest second before reluctantly typing:

ME: —my dad

I hit send and watched the three dots vanish. Barely a minute went by before the phone buzzed with another message from Jonathan's uncompromising agent.

MRS R: Stay where you are. I'm on my way. Be there in five.

I felt an incredible feeling of affection towards Robinson,

who, despite her straight-up control freak persona, was genuinely concerned for me at this moment. I chose to ignore the concerned messages from Jonathan, and locked my phone. It may have been unfair or childish, but I didn't want to speak to Jon right then. A rational part of me knew he'd never intentionally abandon me to the wolves, but that feeling of desertion was still fresh in my mind. I wanted to speak to him when I had my emotions in check.

"Everything okay?"

I met Rebecca's anxious eyes and gave a brief nod but didn't return her smile this time. I'd rather stand outside on the freezing cold pavement than continue with this farce. Weirdly, having Robinson appear on my phone screen had reminded me of who I was. I wasn't a little girl in need of shepherding around. I was a grown fucking woman, and I didn't need to stand here and speak with the man who hadn't bothered with me in years.

"I have to go," I said shortly. Then, a bit more kindly, I said to Rebecca, "It was nice to meet you."

"You too, Tess," Rebecca said genuinely, looking disappointed that this reunion had not blossomed a renewed father-and-daughter bond. "We'd love to have you at the wedding. Vee and Ryan are coming. It wouldn't be right, not having the whole family there."

"I'll think about it," I said but secretly was categorically against being in a room with this man ever again. Another sting hit me when Rebecca confirmed both my brother and sister were going. Neither had even mentioned we were about to have a much younger stepmother. I was struggling with the feelings this stirred inside me. As much as I didn't want to speak about my dad, I felt my siblings were indifferent to how news such as this would affect me.

"Boyfriend?" Matthew asked, his mask slipping as the question sounded more like an insult. "Surprised he doesn't want to come and meet your old man. Not very considerate, is it?"

"Why would he?" I demanded, glaring at him now. "You haven't talked to me in six years. Not even a birthday card. Do you actually think I'm looking for your approval? It's none of your business who I see or what I do with them."

"It is when my daughter's on the news with one of his sort! Spreading your legs for a fucking posh prick. And a darkie. Do you have no self-respect?" Matthew snapped, each poisonous word feeling like a slap. Tears filled my eyes, but that only fuelled his cruelty. "Look at you, trying to act better than me and pretending you haven't just been a media whore this whole time!"

"Matthew!"

People were staring now at us, and an uneasy hush descended over the bar. All eyes were on us, and Rebecca stared at my dad in stunned silence. He started, but the genie was out of the lamp. Everyone had seen a side of him I had known for years, but this was the first time it had been aimed at me with such spite. Tears welled in my eyes, but a change had washed over me.

At this moment, I truly accepted I didn't have a father.

At this moment, I knew with startling clarity that if this man died I wouldn't cry a single tear over him.

At this moment, I felt nothing but contempt for him …

"Actually," I said with a cracked voice. I cleared my suddenly tight throat. "I think I'll pass on the invitation. Because I don't think I could stomach being in the same room as you. Don't ever speak to me again. I don't even want to see you again, after this. You haven't been – nor have you ever wanted to – be my dad. And the feeling is mutual. I don't care what relationship you have with Ryan or Vee, but keep me out of it. I'm done with you. I have been since I was fourteen. I'm not Mum. I won't put up with your bullshit or end up in the hospital like her."

"Hospital?" Rebecca asked, turning on Matthew with fear momentarily clouding her anger. "What did you do?"

"Nothing! Why are you making it sound worse than it was?" Matthew rounded on me furiously and then started pleading with Rebecca. "It was stress, that's all. We were going through a messy divorce. You know that. The woman just doesn't want me to be happy, and see, she's poisoned Tessa against me!"

"I have a mind of my own," I shot back, and as I turned to go, I gave Rebecca one last bit of advice. "Google psychogenic non-epileptic seizures. Oh, and good luck."

I walked out of the bar then, leaving the happy couple in the chaos of raised voices, pleads and lies. The cold air hit me as I rushed through the double doors and stumbled down the steps. Clouds now overshadowed London, and a light rain drizzled on my hair. I looked around for a sign of Robinson, desperate to be taken away from here, and him, as fast as possible.

"Oi!"

Before I had time to turn, a hand gripped my wrist and spun me, and I was face to face with Matthew. I cried out in pain as his nails dug into my wrist. The hatred he had for me in this moment was terrifying. He looked at me like I was a disgusting bug he was dying to squeeze the life out of.

"You can't stand me being happy, can you?" he hissed viciously, not loosening his hold on me despite how hard I tried to pull away. I was scared now, and painfully aware of how much stronger he was than me. "You are a spiteful little bitch, just like your mother!"

"Get off me!" I shouted, desperate for someone to notice what was going on. A passer-by saw but immediately averted their eyes and hurried on. They'd rather claim ignorance than face the risks involved with helping. Or just watch a nightmarish scene from afar, disconnected from it somehow. "I didn't say anything that wasn't true, even you know that!"

"Bet you loved stirring, didn't you?" he sneered as my shoes suddenly found the edge of the kerb. One wrong move and I'd fall into the oncoming traffic. "You just can't let the past stay in the past."

"What? Go along with your revisionist history?" I demanded, glaring through tears at the cruel man I once thought I'd never hate as much as I did now. "I'm not pretending, especially to keep you lot happy. So, let me go, or I swear—"

"Why, what are you going to do?" Matthew sneered, but his eyes widened in surprise when I stamped hard on his foot, and with his wince of pain I pulled free of his slackened grasp. He lunged at me again as I dashed to cross the street. He seized my elbow and turned me back towards the theatre. "No you don't, Teresa! Now you're going to go back in there and apologise for what you said, and tell Rebecca you'd love to be a bridesmaid. And then, you'll keep your mouth shut and smile. You understand?"

"You're insane! Get off!"

"I've had enough of this. You're not ruining what I've got going with Rebecca! Now go back in there and—"

"Excuse me!" a more assertive voice shouted, and we both spotted Robinson storming over. Her steely gaze was like an electric shock as Matthew let go of my arm, and I stumbled to her. "If you touch her again, you will regret it."

"That so?"

"Yes, and that's not an empty threat. If you put one finger on her again, I will destroy any feeble respect you have for yourself. That's something I'm quite good at."

Robinson caught me, and it was only then that I realised how unsteady I felt on my feet. I was shaken and secretly thankful that Robinson was stronger than she looked. With a look of total indifference, she guided me back to her car. As I climbed into the back seat, I was dimly aware of Matthew shouting. The words were distorted as if I was hearing them underwater. Robinson ordered me to put my seatbelt on, that I heard. It got caught twice, but I eventually buckled it in. As the car started and drove away, I saw Rebecca storming out of the theatre and confronting Matthew. Did she see? Did she hear what he said?

Truthfully, I didn't care. My wrist throbbed painfully, and I absentmindedly rubbed it, noticing it was the one with the scars. My skin had reddened from where his hand had been, a brand new mark to overshadow the old ones. All of which were caused by him in one way or another.

"Are you okay?" Robinson asked softly. Her genuine concern had somehow started to break through the fog in my brain. "Do you want me to call Jonathan?"

"No!" I said quickly, answering both questions frantically. And with that, I began to cry. Robinson drove me back to campus without speaking as I sobbed my heart out till I was hiccupping into silence, which neither of us broke.

* * *

I wasn't sure if it was the crying, running or escaping the clutches of my abusive father but I felt drained as I made my way up to my flat. Had I even said goodbye to Mrs Robinson? I couldn't even remember …

Feeling like a ghost, I made my way through the thankfully empty flat to my darkened bedroom. My phone was ringing; the screen illuminated my face. Ryan calling, Jonathan calling, Ivy calling, Vee calling, Mum calling – all their names becoming a long list of missed call notifications. I don't know how long I watched the screen, but the screen's light eventually faded to black. I switched it off, comforted by the silence that followed. I took off my shoes and dumped my jacket on the floor, only to curl up on my bed and stare at the wall opposite. Spines of books and DVD cases blurred in front of me as silent tears made familiar tracks down my cheeks.

I didn't know how much time had passed, but my pillowcase was damp when I heard a soft knock at my door.

"Tess?" Ivy called gently. Of course, it was her. She knocked again, but I didn't have the energy to answer.

"Maybe she's gone out?" a soft voice said reassuringly. Was that Melody? I'd only met my best friend's girlfriend twice, but it was possible.

"The receptionist said she came up here, and she hasn't signed out," Ivy said, her concern rising as she knocked on the door. "Tess, we know you're in there. You okay?"

"Fine," my voice came out hollow but clear, and the knocking stopped. "I'm just tired …"

"How'd the interview go?"

"Great, really great …"

Silence. Neither of them believed me, but they stayed in the hallway. I was thankful for that, at least. I didn't want to see their worried expressions or hear their words of comfort. All I wanted was to lie here and be left alone. That was all.

"Okay," said Melody, and I could sense she was getting the hint, "well, we're out here if you want some company. We'll just be watching a movie, and you're welcome to join us. More the merrier …"

I said nothing, but eventually their footsteps retreated into the living space. The quietness I had needed was broken with the muffled sounds of whatever film was playing in the other room. Climbing under the duvet, I closed my eyes and craved the sweet escapism of sleep. I just wanted that brief reprieve from the dark thoughts which I prayed wouldn't slide into my subconscious …

36

Jonathan

I didn't hear anything from Tessa for the rest of the day. Not a single word. Her phone was off, and if it weren't for Mia's assurance that she'd taken her home, I'd be headed there myself. My unanswered calls and unread messages sent a clear message – she needed to be left alone, and I'd happily give that to her. I just needed to know she was okay. We'd had a generally favourable response from our interview, but the aftermath had given gossip columns some material to twist into their own narrative. It didn't have the same impact as Yana Marcus's shit storm. She'd gone on a Twitter rant, but even her followers had pointed out that the press threat was a dangerous situation for us – confirmed by the photos of me being shoved about and of Tessa being chased through the West End that were currently circling the socials. A hard dose of reality for the cynics, but my stomach churned when I saw how terrified Tessa was while I was locked in a fucking limo.

Like she was dropping off a parcel, Mother had dropped me home, handed over my audition folder and promptly ordered me to film my audition ASAP before demanding her driver take her to Soho. I'd had a strong suspicion she was headed to Soho House for drinks – an exclusive for industry professionals and A-list celebrities. Father was on set, filming a new detective drama for the BBC, and the house was again unoccupied when I stepped inside. When I was a kid, I sometimes felt like I was living in a doll's house – often wandering the massive rooms with only tutors, nannies and Mia for company. Most days, the quietness of the house was only broken by whatever TV show I was watching or the chattering of a random employee paid to care for me. Any other day, I'd have welcomed this familiar stillness, but not today. Mia wanted to speak in person, which only added to my anxiety. I sat at the kitchen table and read through my sides for what felt like hours as I waited for Mia to arrive. As soon as she did, I jumped up and bombarded her with questions.

She assured me that Tessa was fine as I followed her into the kitchen, but I wouldn't drop the subject. If her dad was there – a piece of shit whose abuse had pushed her to self-harm – it was not good. I didn't trust that man as far as I could throw him.

"He's not a nice man," Mia reluctantly admitted, and I could see anger simmering behind her eyes. "She was shaken, but I think she was otherwise unharmed."

"That's not all, is it?" I asked urgently, and Mia's hesitation said a thousand words. My fingers clenched. I tried to stay calm. "Tell me what happened. All of it."

"By the time I arrived, I saw her running out of the theatre. Her father caught up with her. He was furious, and ..."

"And what? Did he hit her?" My voice sounded calm, but in my head I was already punching the faceless man into a bloody heap. I flexed my fingers, but my whole body was tense. Maybe Mia sensed this because she beckoned me to sit while she poured us both coffees.

"No, but he did become physical ..." she admitted as she sat opposite me and handed my coffee over. I held the mug tight, giving my cold hands some warmth and something to do other than imagining committing GBH. "He grabbed her arm, and he threatened her. From what I could gather as I got closer, he was angered by something Tessa said to his partner. Although judging by his reaction, I'm certain she wasn't wrong in what she said. Once I made my presence known, his demeanour changed drastically."

"The weasel probably shit himself," I muttered bitterly and made to get up, my undrunk coffee still steaming. "I need to see her."

"That's what *you* need, not her," Mia scolded, and those words alone caused me to sit back down, a pang of shame settling in my stomach. She was right, but hearing it aloud was still tough. "What you need to do is film those sides for Harrison. Your mother worked a miracle getting him to consider you. I'm sorry I couldn't do the same ..."

"That was just luck," I reassured her, smiling when her unease softened. "I know you did everything you could."

"Thank you. I appreciate that." Mia pulled herself together, and before I could say anything else, she added, "Oh, I have some good news. That scene is going to be re-edited, so you won't have to file a lawsuit during the next film."

Well, that was something, at least. I tried to feel relieved, but my enthusiasm for this franchise had deflated the moment they fixated on my body rather than my performance ... I needed a new challenge.

* * *

I felt hot under the studio lights, trying to re-read the lines I had already memorised and not let my other shit ruin this audition. One advantage of living in a gigantic house owned by parents with more money than sense was that one of our spare rooms had been made into an audition studio. The furniture was minimal but chic, like everything else in this house. The filming equipment was state of the art. The only thing it didn't come with was a line reader.

I sat in front of the camera, composing myself as I'd finally settled on an outfit for the character I was reading for. Jordan was a jock and valedictorian, so I'd decided to go for a boy-next-door charm. I'd complemented a red-and-white varsity jacket with dark jeans and a simple T-shirt, with three alternative shirts at the ready for the other scenes. That was the easy part, picking clothes out for a character. However, I was overthinking each line of dialogue. It required acting. Proper acting. These scenes weren't about taking my shirt off or snogging whatever girl or guy I was playing opposite in a ridiculous rainy scene. No camera twerks or thirst traps. Just real shit.

The dialogue flowed effortlessly off the page and, aside from Tessa's student script, I'd seldom had the chance to read for a part like this. I murmured the lines back to myself, finding myself slipping into Jordan's American accent as the words solidified in my memory. I had this. I really had this. I looked up as I heard a soft knock on the door, and met Dad's mahogany eyes. How long had he been standing there? I hadn't been expecting to see him this week, let alone tonight.

"Mia told me the news." Father grinned, acting like it was

common for us to speak across what was his old audition studio. "That's awesome. Great work."

"I didn't do anything," I muttered, my eyes returning to the script and suddenly wishing I was alone again. "Like always, Mum saw a situation and took control without even asking."

"Don't think of it like that. I'm sure he liked the look of you or saw your reel and thought—"

"He didn't, though. He literally got backed into a corner by Mum, and for what?" I let out a sigh of frustration, reluctantly looking up as Dad sat opposite me. "I … I don't want to mess this up. I want them to see I can actually do justice to a serious part."

"You want them to see you as more than just mine and your mother's son?" Dad spoke aloud what I hadn't, but he was on the fucking money. He waited, and when I didn't correct him, he nodded to himself.

"I don't mean that as a bad thing. Really. But sometimes I wonder … do I actually deserve this? Because sometimes it feels like it's just my name or producers wanting a diverse casting that's got me this far …"

"I thought the same at your age, especially after me and your mother got hitched. And that was at a time where I was sometimes the only black cast member on set. But I proved any doubters wrong," Dad said firmly, his eyes blazing with emotion in a way I'd never seen before. "Jon, we may have opened the door, but you need to prove you deserve to be in the fucking room. You're a grown man, and if you want to be taken seriously in your craft, you need to start taking yourself seriously first. Do you think we would have put this much effort in if you weren't talented? Course not, it's all been you. You got this."

Shit, that had made me feel more emotional than expected. It was the closest I'd ever got to having a compliment from him. And even more than that, it was the first time he'd hinted he was proud of me. That acknowledgement meant more than words could say. I cleared my throat and smiled my gratitude. Words sometimes weren't needed in moments like this. Sometimes, the person opposite just knew. His smile assured me as much.

"You got this," he repeated and made to get up. "Want me to get Mia, or you got someone coming round?"

"Actually, would you mind reading for me?" I asked, and when he hesitated, I quickly added, "Don't worry, it was just a thought."

"No, no. I mean, yeah, I'd be happy to. If it's cool?"

"Yeah, course."

I handed him a copy of the scenes as he sat back down. This was new territory for us, but I was almost in awe at his complete professionalism as we started to dissect the script. Before the camera was even recording, we rehearsed different ways to play the scene to add my own spin to Jordan. What was he thinking? How was he feeling? What were his relationships with the other characters?

This was a screenplay we could discuss for hours, and not once did Dad make me feel stupid for voicing my own ideas and suggestions; he actually agreed with me. That was a bit surreal in itself.

As I was counted down to record my first scene, all my worries and fears momentarily faded into the background.

37

Tessa

I was in that weird moment between waking from a deep sleep and slipping back into it, my eyelids heavy and feeling like I hadn't slept at all. Today's events had brought specific memories rushing to the forefront of my thoughts. I didn't fight it this time. I let myself become consumed by the long-buried moments from my past …

Psychogenic non-epileptic seizures. So, like a seizure but triggered by stress instead of lights. I sat in the living room, only half listening to what Aunt May said. She stood in front of the three of us as we sat on the small sofa – little Vee wedged between a stoic Ryan and myself. I'd been unable to engage in a real conversation since Mum and I returned from the hospital. Aunt May was trying to explain our mother's health in a way that wasn't terrifying or upsetting. How could you actually do that? Unlike Ryan and Vee, I didn't need a medical description. I had seen it in real time and had listened to the doctor's diagnosis as I held Mum's fragile fingers in mine. I remembered that night with cinematic clarity, even down to the hard plastic seat I was sitting on at Mum's bedside.

As Mum was physically and emotionally zapped, she kept slipping in and out of consciousness. Whenever she was awake, and her bloodshot eyes found mine, one word was breathed over and over again – sorry ... sorry ... sorry – to the point I actually craved the moments where she was asleep. At least then I could cry without making her feel even more ashamed. It wasn't her fault. I knew that. I didn't blame her but seeing her seizure had broken something inside me. My mum wasn't superhuman. Like anyone, if pushed to her limits ... she'd break. Dad had done this. He'd caused all of this. Just as I was aware of Mum's mortality that night, I was now acutely aware of the monster my father was – someone who had turned my mother into a shell of her former self.

I hated him. I truly, honestly hated him. Watching Mum take shallow breaths in her sleep was one thing I clung to. My one certainty when everything else was a fog of misery and rage. My childhood had ended that night. I'd stayed there till Aunt May showed up. She couldn't meet my gaze as she spoke with Mum's doctor. Guilt was written all over her face whenever she dared a glance at me. Good. I knew she was thinking back to my call where I'd pleaded for her to come and get me, but she hadn't cared or thought I was exaggerating.

Dad didn't come. He didn't even call. Aunt May said weakly that she'd left messages. I didn't know whether that was true or not. Either way, he should have been in a hospital bed, instead of Mum ...

Now, Aunt May was desperate to atone for abandoning her sister in her hour of need. As Mum was on bed rest, May had stepped in as unofficial guardian. She'd sat us all down to explain the situation, which was more for Vee's benefit than Ryan's or my own. We both understood fully what had triggered this, even if my brother didn't want to accept it.

"Will Mummy get better?" Vee asked softly, her eyes shining with

unshed tears as she clung to a cushion on her lap. Her eyes darted around the room as if she was looking for Mum to bound into the room, full of smiles again.

"Of course she will, love!" Aunt May gushed, but Vee buried her face in my side and I wrapped an arm around her small body. May's words were hollow, and she knew it, but neither May nor Ryan met my eyes. Since that night, this had become a regular occurrence, but so had my selective mutism.

"That it then?" Ryan asked, itching to leave the room. He had rugby practice ... so he said, but I knew it wasn't that. He was going to see his boyfriend. The boyfriend no one knew about. Even I wasn't supposed to know, but I'd seen them in town together. They'd looked ridiculously happy, which is why I let him keep his secret. That wasn't my story to tell.

"No ..."

Aunt May definitely avoided my eyes as she turned and walked out of the room. I glanced at Ryan, who shrugged in response. We listened as the front door opened and closed. Murmured voices gradually grew louder. Vee scrambled from under my arm and hurtled into Dad's arms.

"What's he doing here?" I demanded, glaring daggers at May. She looked tempted to shush me, but instead she frowned as I turned on Dad. "Get out! Or are you here to finish her off?"

"Teresa, please!" Aunt May's eyes widened and she flinched as I leapt to my feet. "Sit down, he wants to talk—"

"Like I give a fuck what he wants!" I retorted. A gasp escaped from her lips. In many ways, she looked like Mum – except she acted more like a woman stuck in time, where she believed the toxic patriarchy of this household was normal. Dad was another person who refused to meet my eyes. Maybe he saw the seething hatred I had for him. He tentatively entered the room and sat on an

armchair furthest away from his older children, with Vee clinging to his hand like it was her life jacket in unknown waters.

"Tess, just sit down," Ryan snapped, pulling me back onto the sofa. Maybe he was worried I'd attack our father or something, because – without looking at me – he whispered, "Let's just get this over with. The sooner he talks, the sooner he leaves."

I knew Vee would cling to every word he spoke, her round eyes filling and ultimately overflowing with tears as he avoided looking at any of his children. The conversation had ended in tears, except for me. He was going to America "for a bit", but there was a finality in his voice. He wasn't planning on coming back. When Vee started wailing, I couldn't stand it another minute and hurried out of the room.

Even though I was sitting on the stairs, I could still hear Vee begging her daddy to stay, promising him the moon and the stars, and saying she wouldn't be bad any more. His words did nothing to soothe her, and I could just imagine him untangling himself from her frantic grasp. I watched him head for the front door, not looking back as Vee's pleas turned into sobs. I guessed the only reason Vee wasn't running after him was because Ryan and Aunt May were most likely trying to calm her down.

He met my eyes, looking at me for the first time. Neither of us said anything, and with a fleeting glance at the stairs above me, he turned and closed the door on his former life. Aunt May rushed into the hallway, glancing between the closed door and me.

"What did you say to him?"

"Nothing," I said honestly, but my voice soured as I added, "He just did what he's always done. The only thing he's good at."

"He's still your father, Teresa."

"What? Is that supposed to give him a free pass?" I demanded, but Aunt May avoided meeting my eyes yet again. It was just a

239

word, a genetic connection that was purely biological. If a man could leave his daughter crying on the floor, he didn't deserve that title.

I made to go and check on Vee, but Aunt May moved to block my path at the foot of the stairs, and I cautiously sat back down. My gut screamed at me what this was about, but I waited as she searched for the right words. This woman didn't do well with uncomfortable subjects. She'd rather pour any maternal instincts she had into her six cats and definitely not the niece she'd avoid if she could help it.

"We need to talk," she said in an uneasy tone. And when she couldn't find words that could be deemed sensitive or tactful, she took my arm and pulled up the sleeve. "About this."

My arm was now cleaned and bandaged, concealing the scars and cuts trailing from my elbow to my wrist. During that night at the hospital, a Jamaican nurse had spotted me scratching as I waited in a corridor for any updates on Mum. And when she asked if I was okay, I felt the blood soaking through my sleeve from a fresh cut. I was ushered into an office, where she sat me down and tended to my self-inflicted injuries. She warned me that any of my cuts could have turned septic, and a pang of shame hit me. What if Mum had had to deal with me getting sick? What if these did become infected, and I ended up bedridden ... or worse?

That was enough to shake me out of those dark thoughts and resist the frantic urge to scratch, especially when the doctor explained why Mum had collapsed. But the nurse had told Aunt May, clearly thinking a "responsible adult" should know the details. Of all the people, I wished it wasn't her who knew first.

"I'm not going to do it again."

"You expect me to believe that?" Aunt May scoffed, her eyes narrowing when I held her gaze. "If your mother wasn't recovering, I'd let her deal with this. Lord knows, the woman has enough on her plate."

"Which you've just added to by inviting that bastard back in here! Or did you think that little chat would play out differently?"

"I ... didn't think he was set on leaving ... I just thought he deserved a chance to explain himself before any rash decisions were made. He has a right—"

"Did it cross your mind that he's not what we need?" I demanded, jerking my head to the room above, where Mum was still asleep. "Or what about her? What about what she needs? Or what's right for us lot?"

"No, but as I'm taking care of things around here" – my urge to snort died on her following words – "I've taken it upon myself to inform your head of year about the situation. They're putting you in contact with a counsellor. We all believe, after everything, you need professional help."

"That's your answer, sending me to some doctor? Don't bother, I'm fine."

"Funny, that's what your mother always used to say." Aunt May's condescension had a hint of pity, but she held my gaze as she continued. "Anyway, this is not up for debate. I'm taking you to a therapist the school has recommended. Who knows, maybe this will do you some good. Anything is better than hurting yourself, Teresa."

* * *

I still had Doctor Shah's number. Just in case. I'd hidden it inside one of my books, but I couldn't remember which one. I slid out of bed and switched on the bedside lamp, my eyes adjusting to the orange glow as I headed for the bookcase. My finger trailed the spines, thinking back to when I had been given Doctor Shah's card. I'd used it dismissively as a bookmark, planning to bin it as soon as my mandatory sessions were over. Yet, I couldn't bring myself to do it. Doctor Shah had been one of the few adults in my life who had listened to me. Really listened. There was no pretence with her. She let me vent. And there were definitely a few tears. May was wrong about many things in that time. But not Doctor Shah – I needed that space away from my family. Looking back now, I had been on a dark path, and Doctor Shah had helped steer me away from that.

I flipped through the pages of each book, discarding them more carelessly as I searched for that card. Paranoia made me worry. I must have thrown it away – possibly by accident. But I quickly rationalised I wouldn't have done that. Still, I searched a bit more frantically as each book turned up empty.

Come on, where the hell was it?

A part of me knew I could quickly look her practice and number up online, but then I'd have to switch on my phone or laptop. I wasn't ready to do that just yet. My fingers found *Wuthering Heights*. The worn paperback had a slight dent within the pages. I opened it and found Dr Shah's faded card hidden within. Relief flooded through me. I smiled at the card like I'd rediscovered a long-lost pen pal. My eyes landed on a random passage as I took the card out, noticing the last page I'd been reading years ago in that waiting room:

> *"I cannot continue in this condition! I have to remind myself to breathe – almost to remind my heart to beat!"*

Was this irony or foreshadowing? Whichever it was, I held my breath as I switched on the phone. It had been six years, and it was highly unlikely she'd still have this number. But I also remembered Dr Shah promising me during our final session that she never wrote off a patient, even after they had grown into adulthood. I wondered how many went back to their childhood therapist for her to make that call?

"Hello?"

Oh, I wasn't expecting her to answer, especially at this hour. Shit, what time was it? I checked my phone, which had begun vibrating as unanswered messages came through. Nearly ten. Oh god … I shouldn't have called; I should have –

"Hello?" Dr Shah's voice sounded older, weary at this time of night.

"Hi!" I said hastily, and then, clearing my throat, I spoke in a much calmer voice. "Hi, Dr Shah. It's Tessa, Teresa Granger, in case you don't remember, I—"

"Tessa, of course, I remember!" Instantly, her voice switched from irritation to genuine happiness, which released some of the tension inside me. "It's so lovely to hear from you. How are you? How's university?"

"Both good," I said and faltered. "I'll be back home in a week or so for Christmas, and I was wondering if … if we could meet up, just for a chat?"

"Of course," Dr Shah said. "Is this formal or informal?"

"A bit of both," I admitted, but I didn't elaborate. I think she expected me to because she waited for a minute. If this concerned her, she didn't convey it.

"Let me check my diary tomorrow, and I'll get back to you," she said. "Is this a number I can contact you on?"

After we hung up, I felt considerably calmer, but I knew I had to make other calls. Jonathan had to wait. I had another matter to deal with. I scrolled through the list of missed calls and found her name, certain now that she was the one talking about me behind my back. I hit call and waited for her to answer.

"Hey!" Vee's bright voice answered on the third ring, filled with worry. "Are you okay?"

"Fine," I lied, keeping my voice calm and even. "But we need to talk about Dad – no, let me speak. I love you, but I don't want him to know anything about what's going on with me. Have whatever relationship with him you want, but leave me out of it."

"I didn't mean – I just, he is our dad …"

"Our dad who called me a whore and shouted abuse at me in front of his new Mrs and a bar full of people," I retorted, still sounding calm. Her gasp was audible, and I knew I was shattering her image of him, but I wasn't going to lie to her. "So I'm only going to say this once: I don't want anything to do with him, and I won't be going to his wedding. Me and him are done. Do you understand?"

"Yeah …"

I'm sure she thought I was being selfish or cruel, but I was done putting other people's feelings ahead of mine, when mine were never considered, especially by my family. If that made me selfish, so be it.

38

Jonathan

Three takes of four scenes that were roughly three or four pages each sounds easy, right? Wrong. By the time we'd wrapped, it was well past midnight and I was fucking zapped. If it wasn't the lighting, the camera was temperamental and cutting out when I was halfway through a line. Each re-take, my gnawing frustration only diminished my newfound confidence. Dad seemed to sense this. He wasn't unkind; he was efficient and practical in his responses.

"Take your time with it. Don't say it all in a rush … If you fuck up, keep going, and we can always do another take. The minute a casting director spots you know you've said a line wrong and it's thrown you, it'll put them off. You don't have to be line perfect. Just keep it natural …"

I took on each word of advice, critique, and suggestion without complaint or argument. Tiredness tugged at my eyes, but I kept going until we had three decent takes of each scene. I forwarded them to Mia, deciding I'd prefer she gave it a once-over before sending the final tapes.

"Thanks for this. Again," I said as we headed onto the landing and to our respective rooms. He gave a mild smile, that was it.

"It's all good," he said, but his phone vibrating caught his attention. I watched his face change as he read a text, a flicker of a smile curving his lips. "I gotta go out for a bit. Get your head down, and we'll talk in the morning."

"Oh. Everything okay?" I said, unable to keep the suspicion out of my voice. Especially as it was technically *already* morning. Who'd be blowing up his phone at this time? Only two types of callers pull that stunt – an emergency that absolutely cannot wait … or a midnight tryst. An uncomfortable feeling settled in my stomach, but I tried to ignore that gut reaction.

"Just work." He shrugged me off and headed downstairs instead of into his office. A part of me wanted to ask more but fatigue kept my mouth shut. Whatever he was doing, I knew for certain he was lying. The truth was, I partly wanted to stay ignorant of the personal lives of both my elusive parents.

The house was dark and quiet. Mia had left an hour into our recording session, and Mother hadn't yet returned home. She was probably still mixing with London's elite, unfazed as long as she'd got a drink in her hand. I felt a slight unease when I thought about how she'd take full credit for this role if I were cast. No, Dad was right. I had to prove I deserved to be in the fucking room.

I groggily undressed, flopping down on my bed in my boxers. My face sank into the pillow and I felt my body relax for the first time all day. Still … my arms craved to wrap themselves around Tessa's waist as I fell into a much-needed sleep.

39

Tessa

Walking Whitmore at night was strange. It wasn't like I hadn't walked across campus in the dark before. It was the stillness of the whole place, like the entire university had retreated into the unusual silence of the halls. The sullen security guard who'd replaced a beaming receptionist was the only face to greet me. I showed him my student card as I walked past his desk and his eyes followed me as I headed upstairs.

The library was just as quiet, but I noticed a few students cramming in a late study session at laptops or poring over textbooks. Instead of joining them, I hit the button to call the lift and took it up to the fifth floor. The great thing about the campus library was that students had access to it, day or night. Which was just what I needed tonight.

As suspected, the fifth floor was empty, and I headed over to my unofficial table to set up my laptop. I could have done this at home, but when I'd headed to the kitchen to grab some snacks and caught sight of Ivy and Melody snuggling on the sofa and debating what to watch, I felt like I was intruding. They'd invited me to join their movie night. Still, I had no desire to be a third wheel … or to watch Renée Zellweger's ludicrous courtship with a slutty Hugh Grant (who would be a human resources case in real life) or Colin Firth recreating his Mr Darcy character in more modern attire. Ivy had made me binge the *Bridget Jones's Diary* trilogy one too many times; I'd spotted too many flaws to really enjoy it.

I'd politely declined and told them I needed to work on an upcoming essay, which was true … it also gave me an excellent excuse to just get out. As I plugged my memory stick into the laptop, I pulled up the essay that was due in just a few days. This module dipped a bit into psychology, and my essay centred on the rise of the female warrior archetype. It discussed the portrayal of Hermione Granger in the eight *Harry Potter* films – essentially arguing that by fairy-tale standards, Hermione had more hero characteristics than the actual main character.

As I flipped through the textbooks I was referencing, I heard the lift doors open and close. I didn't look up from the page till I heard a light, almost airy scoff behind me.

"Look what the cat dragged in." Kaitlyn's sickly voice had me jumping in my seat, and I turned slowly to see her standing over me. I was hit with an unnerving sense of déjà vu as she smirked down at me. Any remaining marks from my punches had been hidden under heavy make-up that I could see clearly under the library's lights. This was the first time we'd even acknowledged each other since that day. Our tutors had rearranged our classes to avoid any repeat performances.

"Mind if I sit?" Kaitlyn asked but grabbed a chair and dragged it across the carpet to sit beside me without an invitation. Her smile made me more nervous than her cruel comments. At least then I'd know what to expect. "What are you working on?"

"Homework. I'm just finishing up an essay."

"Oh, I'm surprised you still have time for all this," Kaitlyn said patronisingly, waving vaguely at the computers and bookcases around us. "I'd have thought it was all beneath you. Especially after your little telly debut."

"Well, my education isn't beneath me."

"No, I don't suppose it is …"

I waited, but she didn't say anything more. I gritted my teeth, knowing I was on dangerous ground here. I wasn't fooled by her calm façade. She knew she had me cornered to sit and hear her out, but like a cat and mouse she was enjoying toying with me until she went in for the kill. I decided to beat her to it.

"Kaitlyn, I'm sorry for—"

"No, you're not," she cut in, her smile vanishing as whatever apology I was about to say died on my lips. "Let's not even go there. We both know you thought I was being a cunt. Maybe I was. So you aren't sorry. Two black eyes and my face swollen up like a fucking peach for over a week. Do you think I want an apology?"

No, I didn't. She was right. I wasn't sorry. Neither was she; I could tell that by her nonchalance. I met her eyes, and when I didn't attempt to appease her or plead with her, she laughed to herself. She laughed harder when I frowned in response.

"You're not even going to deny it?"

"No."

"Good, that'll make this a lot simpler. You're going to do me a little favour. Something to call us even."

"What are you talking about?"

Kaitlyn composed herself, and I could tell she was getting to the point now; the real reason she was sitting in an empty library in the dead of night with the person who sucker-punched her weeks ago. She fished in her bag for something, clearly enjoying the suspense. She pulled out a flimsy and crumpled piece of paper and handed it to me.

I read the two lines warily. "Rose Tyler & the Female Companion Complex in "Doctor Who" by Kaitlyn Danvers."

That was it. No essay, no references, no bibliography or filmography. These words took up the entirety of the page.

"What's this?" I asked, expecting her to pull out more pages. And when she didn't, I added cautiously, "Do you want me to proofread your dissertation or something?"

"No!" Kaitlyn chuckled and then sobered, glaring at me through icy blue eyes. "I want you to *write* my dissertation. All of it."

"No way," I said quickly, furious she had the nerve even to think such an insane idea. This was the shit that would lose me my degree and tarnish my name for any other future school. I cast a glance around the area. We were alone. Anger coursed through me when I saw she was dead serious. I pushed the paper back at her like she'd shown me something horrific, rather than a bland title page. How could she expect me to write her entire dissertation when I had my own to write?

"You're not exactly in a position to say no to me," Kaitlyn snapped, but I shoved past her as I packed away my laptop and books. Fuck this. Today was not the day to mess with me. I headed for the elevator and stabbed the down button, determined to get away from this narcissistic bitch. I felt her hand grab my elbow, and I spun instinctively, shoving her away from me with a ferocity neither of us expected. For a split second, I was back on that pavement with my dad glaring down at me. Not now. Now I was glaring into blue eyes instead of green. Still, I was breathing hard with tension that I forced myself to suppress. I held the strap of my laptop bag as Kaitlyn composed herself, but she looked shaken. Even she couldn't hide that.

"Fuck off," I hissed at her, my voice rising with each word. "Today is not the day to mess with me, seriously. Did you honestly think you could walk in here and try to threaten me? You really are as stupid as you look."

"Stupid?" Kaitlyn sneered, but she could see the power play had long since shifted. This was not going as she had planned. "You assaulted me in a hall full of witnesses!"

"Which you provoked! Everyone knows that; why do you think I'm still here?"

"Because the university couldn't handle the bad press." Kaitlyn spotted my hesitation, and like a leech, she jumped on it. "That's it, isn't it? They're shit scared of any media backlash it'll cause. Is that because you're spreading your legs for a celebrity or because you're an actual charity case?"

"Fuck you ..."

"It is!" Kaitlyn cackled, regaining her bitchy persona. "That changes things a bit, doesn't it?"

"It changes nothing," I shot back, relieved when the lift doors opened and I stepped inside. "I'm not getting kicked out of here for plagiarism. You want that dissertation done, fucking write it yourself!"

I pressed the button for the ground floor, savouring the satisfaction I felt at wiping that condescending smirk off Kaitlyn's face. It felt better than punching her, although both had their pros. Her hand struck out, and I jumped back, half expecting her to smack me in the face. No, instead, her hand stopped the doors from fully shutting, and I watched as they slowly reopened, her palm preventing the censors from closing the doors again. Her blue eyes darkened and a cruel sneer curved her lips, which terrified me to my core.

She pulled out her phone and clicked on the screen several times. She shoved it in my face and my stomach turned to ice as I watched a video play out. It was me. Me screaming like a banshee as I landed fist after fist into Kaitlyn's face. The angle was close – too close to be a random student. And I could tell it was one of Kaitlyn's minions on camera. And I could see the fury and pure hatred in my eyes. I stood stunned, watching myself as if I was the villain of a bad TV show. That was how it looked, though. No context, or anything Kaitlyn had said in the moments beforehand. I just looked like someone attacking an innocent bystander.

Only when I'd watched myself being dragged off did the camera turn on the weeping Kaitlyn curled in on the seat. Her tears mixed into the blood coming just as fast from her nose, but she still managed to look dead at the camera. Her wide eyes looked so vulnerable, so unnerved by this assault. She was a brilliant actress.

She pulled the phone away. Her nasty grin was one of victory, but I felt paralysed where I stood. I tried to speak, but no words came out. No wonder Kaitlyn hadn't wanted to report me to the police. Why would she? She had a tape that could destroy my entire life with one press of a button. She'd just been buying her time, waiting for a perfect opportunity to trap me. Now she had.

"Now," Kaitlyn said briskly, finally letting go of the door and stepping back, "I can make this all go away, of course. If you write my dissertation, a dissertation that'll bag me a first,

I'll delete this video and you'll never hear about it again. If you don't, or you tell anyone about this, I'll post it all over the socials. Don't think your boyfriend would like that, would he?"

Was she serious? Like my biggest concern would be what Jonathan thought. God, she really was a fucking idiot. A video like that going public would destroy my life, and that's not an exaggeration. I'd lose any chance of getting into the National Film and Television School. No agency would want to represent me and I'd be forever known as a hysterical and violent psychopath. No one would care what had happened before that camera started filming, or want to hear my side. The video would be the only narrative needed to destroy all my goals and aspirations. I thought about going to Amanda or even Dean Patel but quickly dismissed it. Even if they believed me and intervened, what would stop Kaitlyn from posting it out of spite?

Nothing.

She knew she had all the cards but I gritted my teeth, and resisted the urge to run at her and smash that phone into oblivion.

"How am I supposed to trust you?" I demanded. "What's to stop you posting that after I write you your stupid essay anyway?"

"You're still acting like this is a negotiation." Kaitlyn raised a perfectly curved eyebrow, and just as the doors began to close her voice floated in. "You have until June. Otherwise, you're going to be the next viral hit!"

The doors closed on Kaitlyn and I leaned back against the mirrored wall behind me, my entire body shaking. I pressed my trembling hands against my mouth, not sure if I was suppressing a sob or scream.

* * *

Blindly, I rushed past reception and into the cold night air. The fledgling winter breeze was a shock to my face; my skin felt like it was burning. I pulled out my phone and pressed on one of his many missed calls. I hit call. Swallowing whatever pride or stubbornness I'd clung to, I just knew I needed to be with him tonight. Only when I heard his groggy voice did I realise what time it was. Shit.

"Tess?"

"God, I'm sorry," I said in an apologetic rush, common sense and guilt kicking in a bit too late. "I know it's late, and this is a really stupid time to be returning a call. Shit, I shouldn't have even called. Listen—"

"*I'm* so sorry," Jonathan butted in earnestly, and I clamped my mouth shut. "Baby, I would never have left you like that. I swear to god, I didn't know that would happen. I had no idea my mother was even going to turn up."

"I know … wait, your mum was there?" I said, thinking back to that gigantic limo's tinted windows. There had been not one hint of hesitation; she'd been quite happy to literally leave me in the dust once she had Jonathan. "She doesn't like me much, does she?"

"She doesn't know you."

"That's a yes." I half-laughed and felt the knot in my chest loosening. Just slightly.

"It doesn't matter what she thinks."

"It kind of does. She's film royalty."

"Can we not talk about my mother, please? Don't worry

about her. It's just me here tonight." Jonathan sighed and his voice sounded more relaxed. He was probably lying down. "Why aren't you asleep anyway? You good?"

"No," I admitted. "Can I come over? I can't stay here. Not tonight."

"What happened?" Jonathan's voice lost all signs of sleepiness. His concern made me smile, and I felt even worse for doubting him earlier.

"Nothing life-threatening, but I'd rather not talk over the phone," I said and then hesitated. "Unless you'd rather go back to bed."

"Yeah, but not without you." The tone of his voice sent a shiver coursing through me that had nothing to do with the weather. We both knew the possibilities of what an empty house with no intruders could mean … and if I was being honest, I wanted those possibilities to become a reality.

My phone chimed, and I checked to see Jonathan had sent me an address. His address. I'd never booked an Uber so fast in my life.

40

Jonathan

Twenty minutes felt like an eternity. An actual millennium had passed by the time the doorbell rang and I bounded downstairs, yanking the door open to find Tessa on my doorstep. She was staring up at the house like she was standing on the porch of the White House. Her green eyes were wide and her mouth slightly open, as if trying to find the words to describe her awe. I'd never looked at any of my parents' investments like that. It was just what I was used to.

What would my reaction be, standing on Tessa's doorstep?

As soon as her eyes met mine, I pulled her into the warmth of the house and my arms. I breathed in the scent of her hair as her arms tightened around my back.

"Hey." She chuckled against my chest and tilted her head up to smile at me. "Some day, huh?"

A laugh escaped my lips, but words completely and utterly failed me. I never wanted her to be in that kind of danger again. No more media circus or interviews; I'd never have a repeat of today. I wouldn't be surprised if she wanted to run for the hills.

No – out of everywhere she could've gone, she'd come here. She saw me as her safe space. God knows, she was officially mine now.

My lips found hers and I prayed she understood how much I was worried and how much I fucking loved her. The kiss deepened as her arms encircled my neck, our lips now dancing to a familiar routine. This felt so right. So fucking right. Without thinking, I unzipped her coat and she let me slide it over her shoulders, where it dropped to the floor.

She pulled back, her palm sliding off my neck and resting on my frantically beating heart. Both of us were breathing hard.

"What's going on?" I asked as she looked at me. She really looked at me. There was a desire in her eyes that I'd never seen before. "I heard about what happened with—"

"I don't want to talk about him. I don't want to talk about any of it." She silenced me with another kiss. Her hands slid over my shirt and her touch sent an electric shock through me.

Any rational thoughts were erased from my mind as her lips claimed mine again.

"Everything has been so crazy, except this …" Tessa whispered against my lips, her eyes locking onto mine with such passion it made me speechless. "Except you. I want you. I want you now. We'll deal with whatever drama tomorrow. I just want you to be here. With me."

Fuck.

Tomorrow the world could fucking freeze over, and I'd die smiling. There was no restraint between us now. We went upstairs, going into my darkened bedroom as if we had done this a thousand times before and not just once.

I let her tug my shirt over my head and soon her lips were trailing from mine to my chest. Her hands roamed over each curve and muscle like she wanted to memorise every single detail. I realised with unnerving certainty that I'd let this woman do whatever she wanted. I wanted her to know my body as intimately as I craved hers.

I let out a moan and crushed my lips to hers as we undressed each other with a hunger neither of us could explain.

"Jonathan …" My lips trailed over the gorgeous curve of her neck. I laid her on the bed, both of us in nothing but our underwear. We were entangled, barely daring to come up for air as our hands explored each other fervently.

Fuck. One kiss. One touch. It was not enough. Would never be enough. I wanted this. I wanted her.

Always.

I felt her shiver in my arms and I pulled back, hesitating when she pulled me on top of her.

"You sure this is what you want?" I whispered, searching her eyes for any doubt or hesitation. There was none.

"Yes," she breathed and then paused, looking concerned. "Do you?"

"Course I do," I said between kissing her soft skin, each gasp of pleasure spurring me on as I trailed down her chest and stomach. "I love you, Teresa Granger."

"I …" Tessa moaned as I discarded her underwear and my lips trailed a familiar path, tasting the sensitive skin underneath. "I love you too. Oh god, I love you … Jonathan!"

41

Tessa

I was becoming undone. This man totally consumed me. Any shyness or uncertainty I'd felt within my sexuality was fading away with each tantalising kiss and soft caress.

I'd thought Jonathan was beautiful when we first met, but somehow that word didn't do him justice. With nothing but the moonlight illuminating our naked bodies, I'd never felt more desired. The way his dark eyes drank me in was intoxicating.

I felt him harden against me, and a moan that sounded more like a frantic whisper escaped my lips. God, I wanted him. I didn't want to think or worry about anything else. I just wanted to be loved by this person who made me feel seen.

Who saw me. The real me.

He seemed to sense my thoughts because he leaned over and rummaged through the bedside table. He pulled out a condom and leaned back. He tried to pry it open.

Nothing. He muttered under his breath, even trying to use his teeth. I sat up, amused by his frantic attempts to free the condom from its foiled tomb.

"Need some help with that?" I asked, and his glance at me had us laughing like a couple of teenagers. I held my hand out and he reluctantly dropped the wrapper in my palm.

He snorted when I opened it with ease. He held out his hand, but I held it back, enjoying his frustration as his eyes (and one particular part of his body) were hungry for me.

"What are you doing?" Jonathan's curious smile played on his lips as I took his hands and, despite his Thor-like physique, he let me guide him into where I'd just been sitting. Total trust, without question.

I gave him a gentle nudge against his chest and he lay back onto the pillows of his humongous bed. He bit his lip as I straddled his waist, my hand gently stroking his dick. Hard, wet and sensitive to each stroke.

"Tess …" he begged, closing his eyes and moaning even louder as I continued my exploration of his body. "Fuck! Please, baby …"

I slid the condom on, and gently eased myself onto him, bracing my hands on his strong shoulders.

A moan simultaneously escaped both our lips as I felt him inside me. Holy Mother of Dragons!

"Fuck," I breathed as I began slowly thrusting my hips, getting used to the sensations exploding through my body.

"Yeah, baby, how's that feel?" he breathed against my lips, his fingers unhooking my bra and flinging it across the room.

Like he didn't know! I laughed through frantic gasps, my moans only becoming louder when his hips moved to match mine.

"Tell me, how does it feel?" he smirked as his lips teased my neck and his hands explored my chest. "Because, baby, you feel amazing. So. Fucking. Amazing."

"It feels good!" I practically whimpered, our thrusts becoming just as needing. My lips found his and with desperation our moans were briefly silenced.

"You don't have to hold back with me," Jonathan reassured, his fingers brushing my hair from my face. "It's just us here. Just you and me."

"God," was all I could utter. A wave of pleasure rocketed through my body as Jonathan's hips moved with tortuously precise thrusts.

Before I knew it, he'd flipped us over – now I was the one on the pillows – and my legs encircled his waist. His lips found my neck and I completely let myself go.

This was the most intimate, most exposed I had ever been. But I couldn't hold back the moans and pleas for him. I didn't want him to stop and he seemed more than content to grant that wish.

Nothing was ever going to be enough. I wanted him more than words could say. Every sensation inside me was on fire. I was gasping for air like a drowning woman, yet I was in pure heaven.

That first night was a blur, but this … It was like remembering and discovering those feelings with HD clarity. I wanted to remember every detail, and even then I wanted more. So, so much more.

My legs began to tremble and I gasped against Jonathan's lips as the intense sensation began to rock my body. I was so close and, judging by his breathing, he was too.

"Jonathan …" The word came out as a sigh, my body already anticipating the ecstasy that was coming. His mouth lifted into a wry smile, his hand playing with my nipple. I arched my back, craving both his touch and the feeling of him inside

261

me.

His lips found my exposed neck. I was sure there were going to be love bites on my neck tomorrow. Right now, I didn't care. His tongue traced my skin expertly, homing in on my most sensitive spots.

My nails dug into his back as I felt myself reaching that climax, my body practically begging for the release.

My moans mixed with Jonathan's and I almost missed the words whispered against my lips and skin. They were so gentle. It was like he was praying.

"I love you. I love you so much. Yeah, that's it, baby. You're so beautiful, so fucking beautiful."

The tingling sensation was now building and consuming me, my body moving with his with an animalistic need. I had no control whatsoever over the sensational release that flooded out of me.

I let myself go just as Jonathan did, and we both surrendered to the hot and sweaty ecstasy that burst between us with such intensity I almost couldn't breathe.

This would be the moment for the cringe declaration of love in the movies. Not here though, not in real life.

Tiredness washed over me and I felt nothing but love, encircled in Jonathan's strong arms. I was so at peace I'd almost entirely drifted into a dreamless sleep before Jonathan even pulled the duvet over us.

I didn't want this night to end. I just wanted to love this boy forever …

42

Jonathan

The early morning light crept through the curtains, a golden light breaking through the room. Tessa's dark hair spread out over the pillow. She was lying on her stomach, so perfect, almost like a Greek goddess with her beautiful body outlined in the soft glow.

My fingers lightly traced up her spine, marvelling at the smoothness of her skin. I chuckled as she jerked away from my fingertips, knowing I'd found her ticklish spots.

"Stop it," she warned teasingly and fought a giggle as I continued to trace lazy lines down her spine. She whacked my hand away and I caught it, pulling her onto my chest and silencing whatever comment she was going to make with a kiss.

She pulled back, resting her chin on my chest. She looked thoughtful but smiled as my arms found her waist.

"What you thinking?" I asked, tucking a strand of her hair behind her ear.

"That we'll have to return to reality soon."

"Really? Fuck, was this just a perfect dream? Man, I

should've realised."

"Shut up. You know what I mean."

"Stop worrying." I sighed when she still looked troubled. "We're over the worst of it. Now we can just focus on us. You and me."

"You make it sound so easy," she said, and I shrugged like it was just that simple. It was, in my book.

"Because it is," I said smugly, rolling us over so I held myself above her. She tried to protest but my lips soon had her smart mouth occupied.

We had so much to look forward to. Whatever the future held, I wanted to see it through with her.

* * *

My phone buzzed like it was on crack, one notification after the other. I groggily dragged myself from Tessa's embrace, making sure to ease myself out of bed without waking her.

I padded across the room, finding my crumpled jeans and my phone. I checked my emails, and my stomach lurched.

Harrison had emailed no more than seven hours after receiving my sides. Mia was cc'd into this too, but she hadn't messaged yet. It was still early, so that wasn't a surprise. She'd probably be getting into the office now. I opened the email, reading the short message inside:

> J,
>
> *Great sides. I'd be happy to discuss this project more when I'm in London. Let me know if you're free on the 16th. I think we have something special here.*
>
> *H*

Did I fucking read that right? He liked my audition? He wanted to talk to me? He described my take on his character as *something special*?

I uttered a weird little laugh; it almost didn't sound like me. I wanted to jump in the air and whoop in the fucking nude but I settled for a silent fist pump. I didn't want to wake Tessa, even though I was on cloud nine.

Mia. I needed her to set up this meeting before anything else could dampen this high. As quietly as I could, I found a decent set of clothes and dressed quickly. Tessa didn't even stir.

I pulled on my jacket and headed over to my bed. This was a sight I could get used to, waking up with my beautiful girlfriend every morning. I leaned over and lightly kissed her head. It was a soft kiss, but I swore her lips curved into a smile as she slept on. I reluctantly left, making sure to close the door behind me softly.

I'd text her on the road. No point waking her up after last night. She needed her rest, that I was confident of.

Driving through the early dawn, I was ridiculously happy …

I should've known this was all too good to last …

I strolled past the indifferent receptionist's desk. She barely glanced at me as I signed in. Charming. I took the stairs, still buzzing and grinning like a twat. When I reached Mia's office, something immediately felt off.

There was a commotion inside. I saw her walking past the misted window. Another silhouette followed her. She wasn't alone. Fuck, was my agent having a sex life? And in her office? Scandalous, especially for her.

It was hard to imagine Mia having any kind of life outside

her work. Outside of me, if I was being honest. I felt terrible for that assumption, especially as she'd overseen everything in my childhood, adolescence and even now in my adulthood. She was constantly checking on me, and I'd never thought to ask anything personal about her.

I didn't want to embarrass her, so I made to turn as the muffled voices spoke inside. I'd grab a coffee and take a stroll. That would give her enough time to sneak her mystery bloke out. I laughed under my breath, almost feeling like a kid who'd overheard some juicy gossip. When was I last this unapologetically cheerful? I genuinely couldn't remember, but I loved it.

"Jonathan can't ever know about this."

My blood froze and I stopped in my tracks. I cautiously turned back to the door. Mia sounded worried, really nervous about the prospect of my knowing whatever was going on in that office.

Was she worried I'd report her to her partner for having a love life? Course not! It was none of my business what man or woman she chose to sleep with or date. I didn't want to think of that at all. I especially didn't want to have a conversation about it.

"He hasn't suspected anything. Why should he start now?" a voice asked smugly. A familiar, deep American voice. No … no, no, no, I must be hearing this wrong. It couldn't be him. Not him.

"He's not a child, Michael. Christ, you know I hate lying to him. We can't keep doing this back-and-forth. It's not healthy for him."

"Why should it matter? It's not like you're his mother."

I backed away as Mia's figure stormed towards the door,

but I saw him stop her. Both were closer to the window, their features slightly more defined. Him. It was definitely him.

I wanted to leave, turn around and erase this moment from my brain. I couldn't. My feet were firmly rooted to the spot. Anger coursed through me, the betrayal poisoning any happy memories I had of either of them. They were fucking. Fucking for years and right under my nose. Under Mum's nose. No wonder Mia kept me on. It gave her regular access to quickies with my father.

"I didn't mean that," he said softly. The tenderness in his voice made me feel sick. Sick.

"You're just like her," Mia hissed with surprising emotion. "You just see me as the hired help. Or you think I see that boy as my pay cheque. Nothing more. Don't you?"

Yes. I certainly did now. His silence confirmed he thought the same. Mia pulled out of his arms, walking further into the office. He followed and they both disappeared out of my eyesight. I crept closer, their voices clearer now.

"Don't touch me!"

"Jesus, I said I was sorry. Baby, come here …"

"Thirteen years I've been with him." I heard Mia choke on tears, genuine tears. "I raised him more than you and your precious wife combined. Me! Yes, he's a talented actor, but you know what? I'm the closest thing to a parent he's had. And he might not be biologically mine, but I love him like he's my own. So don't you ever throw that in my face again."

An uneasy silence followed. Although what she'd said was true, that didn't justify her screwing my dad for Lord knows how long. My disgust overshadowed any filial affection I had towards Mia. I knew on some level that my parents' marriage was dead. Why not just get a divorce? Leave. Surely that was better than living a lie or taking on secret lovers. What a fucking joke.

"I'm sorry," Dad said again, and already I'd heard enough of this bullshit. "But don't worry, Jonathan hasn't got a clue. He's a sweet kid, but we both know he's not that bright."

I grabbed the handle and forced the door open. Both my father and my agent jumped in fright. I glared at their guilty expressions and scanned the chaotic state of the usually immaculate office.

My gaze lingered on the scattered papers on the desk, where the most mess seemed to originate. This office used to be my sanctuary, but now that had been ripped away from me. It was tainted, no longer a safe haven. That angered me more than words could say.

"This is cosy, isn't it?" I scorned. Mia couldn't bring herself to look at me. Shame was written all over her face. "Oh, I'm sorry. Do you want me to wait outside while you go for round two?"

"Son …"

"Fuck off," I snapped, cutting across whatever he was about to say. "I'd like to speak to my agent. In private."

"I'm not going anywhere," Dad retorted, looking nowhere near as guilty as Mia. "We're going to discuss this like adults."

"Right, okay," I said, and their brief moment of relief was short-lived. "Let's call Mum, and we can all discuss how you two used me so you could fuck for nearly two decades on the sly. I'm more than happy to do that. Why not?"

That caused Dad to hesitate. He knew I was being dead serious. Finally, he was taking me seriously. He straightened his wrinkled shirt and slipped on his shoes with a glance at Mia. He paused as he headed to the door. The stony silence between us felt like a fourth presence.

"Hear her out, son. Please?"

Drop. Dead.

I waited until the door had closed behind him, that click sounding thunderous in the dead quietness.

"Jonathan …"

"How long has this been going on?"

"A while." Mia didn't elaborate, but she'd already confirmed my suspicions. However long, this had been going on for years.

"Oh," I said and laughed hollowly. Tears stung at the corners of my eyes. "No wonder you kept me on your books this long."

"No!" Mia cried and moved as if she wanted to comfort me. I backed away and she faltered. "No, I kept you on because I've always seen your potential. You're talented. And not because of your parents, but because you have a passion for performing I've never seen before … and I care about you, you know that …"

I didn't know what to believe any more. Everything felt like a lie. Nothing about these people felt genuine. It was just one big dirty secret.

"Right …" was all I could manage to say, my throat feeling dry. I swallowed, avoiding her gaze.

"I'm sorry. I never wanted you to find out like this."

"It doesn't matter," I muttered. And when I turned back, I saw her as nothing more than my agent. This was a professional relationship. I was her job. "Did you see the email from Harrison? He wants to meet me about the part later this month."

"That's fantastic!" Mia looked genuinely happy, despite her red eyes and tear-streaked cheeks. "I'll check the calendar and book it in."

"I'd prefer if Clarke took over this one," I said coldly, hating the pain that flashed across her face like I'd shouted. "I think I'd prefer him to take over everything for me instead. There's a conflict of interest here, so I think it's time that I looked elsewhere for representation."

"That won't be necessary!" Mia rushed, but I shook my head. Yes, it would. The damage had well and truly been done. How could I let her represent me, knowing she was sleeping with my father?

Although neither of us could say it, it was clear as day. There was no coming back from this.

43

Tessa

This bathroom was bigger than my entire university flat! The shower's high-tech was something I'd expect to see in *Blade Runner*, but the water was perfect. Once I figured out how the thing worked.

I was disappointed to wake up and find Jonathan not beside me, but after last night – and the early hours of the morning – I wasn't worried and was beaming like the Cheshire Cat. I seriously felt giddy, like a schoolgirl who'd fallen in love for the first time. Yet this was more than some crush. I was actually in love and loved in return, something I'd never thought possible.

After sleeping with someone in his own house, Jonathan wouldn't sneak out – that was more my style. I rationally assumed it was a work-related emergency. Although I should probably check my phone to know he was okay.

With my hair still damp, I pulled on yesterday's clothes and headed downstairs for the kitchen. That was easier said than done. In the cold light of day I realised how much of a labyrinth this house was.

I'd overlooked the details of the interior of Jonathan's house on my arrival. My mind had been on other things. The decor was exquisite – modern and yet with an air of old money. Like, old aristocrat money.

Rooms that could've housed half my university lay perfectly decorated and undisturbed. Maybe I was too used to having chaos erupting in my house, but I couldn't imagine growing up in a place so grand and yet so silent. There was a beauty to this house, but it also made you feel undeniably lonely within its walls.

What was it like, not to have a house full of noise and life? It weirdly felt like the house was mourning that it had never truly been a home.

I made my way down the staircase – which honestly could have been a real-life replica of the staircase in *Beauty and the Beast* – and found myself back on familiar ground in the large hallway.

My jacket was hanging on the banister and I pulled out my phone. I had several texts from Ivy. I hastily sent an "I'm not dead" text – and read the latest from Jonathan:

JONATHAN: With Mia. I should be back soon. Work stuff.

Huh … that was quite blunt. Did something happen with *Awaken* or something else he was in the running for? I started to type a response, too distracted to hear anything else.

"Miss Teresa?"

I jumped, spinning on my heels to face a middle-aged Latino woman in a maid uniform that looked very practical, not like a bad French Noir movie: long-sleeved black shirt and matching trousers and plain shoes. Her olive skin was lined and etched into a permanent frown. Her black hair – streamed with white – was tied back into a tight bun.

"I … Hi! Yes, I'm sorry, I was just …" I showed her my phone as if that stupidly explained itself. My face burned as she muttered something in Spanish, already exasperated.

"Ophelia wishes that you join her for breakfast," she said, her tone bored as she turned and led me through the massive house.

Crap. Ophelia LeMahieu, an absolute legend in the art of all things cinema, wanted to sit and have breakfast with me … after I'd had sex with her son. Brilliant. What a knockout first impression I was about to make. Why hadn't I dried my hair properly?

Because you thought you had this ridiculously extravagant house to yourself, the logical part of my brain pointed out.

I was led into a finely decorated dining room with a large oak table – far too big for a family of three – taking up the bulk of the room.

Ophelia was sitting at the head of the table, already tucking into her breakfast as she casually read a copy of *Sight & Sound*. Her face was on the cover, which she seemed indifferent to.

She was as beautiful as any photographer had portrayed her. Pale and dark-haired, she had a demanding presence that stunned me into silence.

"Miss Ophelia," the housemaid announced and pushed me further into the room. Ophelia looked up from her magazine, smiling as if I was a regular at their household.

"Teresa, such a pleasure!" She rose and gave me a broad smile. "I was beginning to think you'd been taken ill. You were up there for so long. Come, I've saved you a seat. Thank you, Rita. That'll be all."

She indicated the chair on her right. A full English sat there waiting. It was probably cold by now. Her introduction had uncomfortably put me in mind of Ralph Fiennes' Lord

273

Voldemort, especially when she said, 'I've saved you a seat' with such inviting sweetness that sounded more like a threat.

I went over and, with an apologetic smile, sat beside her. She didn't move to embrace me or shake my hand. Instead, her eyes examined me like I was under a microscope.

"I'm so sorry. I didn't think anyone else was here," I admitted, and she waved me off.

"Clearly." Ophelia sighed. "Although Jonathan has never brought a woman home before. He prefers to keep that side of his life … private."

I tentatively picked up my fork and started eating. Yep. Stone cold. Although I would've heard if she or Rita had called me for breakfast, surely? Rita certainly had no problem making herself heard. She'd probably get on with Mum like a house on fire.

"I didn't mean to intrude," I began, but again she waved this off.

"Don't be ridiculous. It's thanks to you that Jonathan's reputation is saved. This family is forever indebted to you," Ophelia said, her smile slipping as she continued. "Now all that fiasco with Yana Marcus is sorted, we can all return to the way it was. The way things should be. The correct order of things. Do you understand what I'm saying?"

"I'm not sure I do …" I said, but I was pretty sure I did. Back to normal, as in pre-Tessa. She knew I had caught on because her pretence dropped instantly.

"I think you do," she said firmly, her brown eyes that were so much like her son's narrowed in contempt. "This family has an image to uphold. An image I've worked my entire life to build. And I, for one, am not having it ruined by the likes of you. You've played your part. Now, this is the final curtain call."

"The likes of me?" I demanded incredulously, not believing her nerve. "I'm sorry, but what goes on between your son and me is none of your business."

She paused then, contemplating me with interest. Her mouth curved into a pitying smile. "He has played his part, hasn't he?" she mused, laughing softly to herself. "My poor girl, do you not know this was all a performance? You were a one-night stand, nothing more. Do you think he would've looked twice at you if it wasn't for the scandal he was in? No, you'd have been another nameless conquest. He needed to sell a story, and you were the perfect candidate – a girl with no connections or industry links, who the media would either love or hate. You were disposable, but it's fortunate for you that this played out extremely well. Too well, now I see."

I'd only had two mouthfuls of bacon and egg, and I already felt sick; my stomach was churning as bile rose in my throat. I shook my head, words failing me as this woman looked at me with infuriating pity. Like I was a wounded animal that she was putting out of its misery.

"You're lying," was all I could muster the courage to say, but it sounded weak to my ears.

"Am I?" she smirked nastily. As if she was enjoying herself, she stood and left the room. For a childish moment, I hoped that was the end of it. She was lying. She had to be. Jonathan would never be that callous and manipulative. I pushed the freezing breakfast away, all appetite gone. This woman was twisted! No wonder Jonathan never brought anyone here. It was a house of horrors.

Just as I was getting ready to get up and get the hell out of there, Ophelia returned with a brown envelope clasped in her hands.

With a smirk filled with pure venom, she placed it in front of me.

"What's this?" I asked, for some reason not wanting to touch the thick folder. The urge to vomit my pitiful breakfast had been replaced with a fear I didn't want to name.

"You," Ophelia said, standing over me with the confidence of a high priestess. "Jonathan likes to – what is it you British say? Dot his i's and cross his t's."

With trembling hands, I opened the file and pulled out its contents. It was – as she so casually put it – me. In written form. From my birth certificate to my school records and even my medical history. It went on and on, including background checks on each of my immediate family members. Mum, Ryan and even Vee were all here. Nothing was private. The worst part, there were even transcripts of my sessions with Dr Shah. My personal and most intimate details were displayed for the Adeola family to read.

I'd told Jonathan things I'd never told anyone. Ever. Yet he'd already read it in these papers, along with his mum and god knows who else.

Teardrops spattered onto the pages and as much as I tried, I couldn't stop them. I'd never felt so violated. There I was, thinking what Jonathan and I had was real. And all the while he'd been playing me.

He'd even stooped to digging up dirt on my family, all to make sure I was this perfect innocent wallflower to shield him from the media onslaught.

Wow, he was good. He was so good. He'd achieved the impossible. He made me trust him. He made me love him, and he was playing a character all this time. Everything he told me, was that just him improvising on the spot? Did he even think of what this would do to me?

God, we even slept together last night – after he was already in the clear and the media buzz had calmed. What was that? A perk?

I was really crying now, hating that Ophelia so casually stood by and watched. I hated her; both she and her son could rot in hell!

"You see why this little charade has to end, don't you?" Ophelia said evenly as if she hadn't just shattered me into a million pieces. "Because you and I both know that if you hadn't been in that hotel that night, another oblivious girl would be sat in your place. You're no different than the others. No, I take that back. You're more than a pretty face. You're smart. Which is why I have an offer for you."

"I don't want anything from you!" I spat, shoving myself away from the table and barging past her. I couldn't believe I'd felt anything for Jonathan or believed his lies. This house's superficial beauty just hid the occupants' ugliness within.

"What about the National Film and Television School?" Ophelia's voice stopped me in my tracks. I turned to face her, glaring at her smile of satisfaction.

"Excuse me?"

"*Chérie*, do you not think I'd do research of my own?" Ophelia asked. "I heard of your little plan to get the school's attention. A staged reading. A sweet but childish idea. There are only two named casting and a reading that'll probably be held over Zoom. It's a waste of your time. Your writing ability should be the focus, not that display of mediocrity."

"Why do you care?" I demanded, my hands clenched tightly on the folder. It was beginning to crumple in my grip.

"Just so there are no misunderstandings over your place in all this, I'm willing to offer you my assistance." Ophelia smirked. "I have pulled some strings with the board and put myself down as one of your references. Don't fret. I'll do nothing but praise your talents, and it helps strengthen your application by having an industry professional vouching for you."

"Why would you go through the trouble?" I shot back. She looked surprised, like she genuinely expected me to be grateful or something. "Besides, I'd rather earn it on my own merits. Not your bribes."

"I couldn't bribe the school even if I wanted to," Ophelia dismissed my words and then added cruelly. "But wouldn't you prefer to be known as a talented graduate from a prestigious film school and not my son's little whore? You can have all the talent in the world, but reputation is everything. Once that's stained, you can never wash it away from your name."

Her words cut me like a jagged knife, twisting in my gut for good measure. I took a deep breath, forcing myself not to focus on the fact I was breaking apart on the inside. They were all the same – Ophelia, Kaitlyn and Jonathan. Money made people feel invincible. People like me were nothing more than pawns to be thrust into danger and discarded on the battlefield.

"Now, you can finish your breakfast, but I want you to leave this house by the time I get back. And never speak to my son again," Ophelia said coolly, the threat unmistakable in her voice. "Do you think you can manage that?"

Oh, I definitely could. After today, I never wanted to set eyes on this fucked up family again.

Fighting back the tears, I stood still as this woman glided

past me with such indifference I may as well have been part of the furniture. The house was silent once again and I had nothing but my sobs for company. In one swoop, this woman had broken me.

Well done, Jonathan. You just played your best role of a lifetime.

44

Jonathan

I pulled up outside the house, dismounting my bike as Mother stepped out. Despite her glamorous style, I recognised the pale and hungover symptoms she hid underneath her make-up. She was hungover as fuck, but wouldn't let it show.

"Rough night?" I asked, not caring for an answer. My mind was still stuck on the revelations of today.

"No such thing." Mother shrugged and then, catching sight of my expression, turned to face me properly. "What is the matter?"

"I sacked Mia," I said, not wanting to discuss it further. But her reaction surprised me. She stared, unfazed by my agent of eighteen years being cut loose.

"Oh, your father will be disappointed," she said, and I scrutinised her face. No surprise, not even mild curiosity. Why was that? Unless …

"You know?" I asked, and her gaze didn't waver, not once.

"About your father sleeping with your holier-than-thou agent?" she asked, bitterness filling each word. "Of course I knew. Do you think I'm a fool?"

"How can you be so calm?" I demanded in disbelief. "Aren't you angry? They've been lying all this time. How can you be so obtuse?"

"Because it was convenient," she admitted casually. Maybe the fact she was still drunk from the night before was making her so loose-lipped. "While she was attending to your father's needs, and yours, I was free. Free to pursue my career. I wasn't tied down within the constraints of motherhood and marriage. So yes, her sleeping with my husband and looking after you made my life much easier."

"Was I that much of a burden?" I asked, not as hurt as maybe I should've been. I'd long suspected she felt that way, and it felt oddly therapeutic to hear her finally say it.

"You weren't," Mother said. "But love is a fickle thing. Your art must be your true love, no one can afford distractions. Especially not you. Which is why I dealt with your little problem in there."

My eyes followed her head jerk, lingering on the house. Dread filled me as I glared at my elusive mother.

Tessa. No, she wouldn't.

"What the hell did you do?"

"Told her the truth," she said with an air of finality. "It's for the best …"

I didn't hear whatever bullshit excuse or justification she was spewing; I was already running into the house.

* * *

"Tessa!"

No response. Not even Rita bothered to poke her head out of the kitchen. I checked the living room and dining room.

Still nothing. Could she have gone already? No, she couldn't have.

I ran up the stairs, taking them two at a time. My bedroom door stood ajar and I cautiously stepped inside, trying to calm my breathing.

Papers were lying in a circle around her as she methodically read each page, sitting cross-legged on the floor. Her eyes were bloodshot but her face was void of any emotion. Once she finished a page, she put it on a pile. What was she putting them in order of? And how had Mia found so much? Those documents must go back years, detailing every aspect of her life.

Seeing it all laid out before me, it felt wrong. Dirty. A violation in its clinical portrayal of someone's life. It was wrong on every level, and how stupid I was to think a personal folder like that could be so easily forgotten.

I'd believed Mother when she'd said she had destroyed the file. I'd trusted her. And she'd been waiting to use it against Tessa all this time.

No, she wasn't using it against Tessa. She was using it against me. Tessa was just the collateral damage. This was sick. Really fucking sick.

"Tess …"

"Makes for great reading this, doesn't it?"

"Tessa, please listen …"

"You know my sister is in here too?" she asked, glaring up at me through tearful eyes. "I mean, she's fifteen. A minor. Her only crime is her weird obsession with trashy vampire fanfiction, but I suppose you can never be too careful. Am I right?"

"I didn't know that, I swear."

"No?" Tessa's voice rose in anger. She grabbed another pile and flung the pages at me. "What about those? Transcripts from my therapy as a kid. We're going into criminal territory here. Those are meant to be confidential! I trusted you. I told you things I've never told anyone and then I come to find out you already did a background check!"

"I didn't!" I pleaded with her. I moved closer and she clambered to her feet to back away. "I swear, I never read what was in there. I couldn't. I wouldn't do that to you!"

"You expect me to believe that?" she hissed, looking at me with such hatred I couldn't meet her eyes. "I mean, it's one thing to use me to revive your acting career. But why take it this far? Why pretend to have feelings for me? Why have sex with me!"

"Because I was falling for you, because I didn't have to pretend with you!" I swore, closing the distance and taking her shoulders. She tried to shrug me off, only reluctantly meeting my eyes. "I never wanted that background check. I never even knew about it till Mia dug up all that stuff."

"Oh! So it was your handler? And here's me thinking she actually cared about me," she scoffed and brushed past me to put some distance between us. She crossed her arms over her chest and turned to face me, still fuming. "She did try to strong-arm me when we first met, though, so hardly surprising she dug up every little secret of my life. I should've known then. You realise how messed up your family dynamic is, right? It's twisted."

"Are you of all people trying to preach about fucked up family dynamics? You?" I snapped and immediately regretted it as the cruel words lingered in the air between us. Her green eyes flared with anger despite her tears and I instantly tried to backtrack. "I didn't mean that – I swear. I promise you. I told them to get rid of all of this, and I trusted that they had. Everything that happened between us was genuine. It was all me. When my mother said she'd destroyed that file, I had no reason to doubt her …"

Although I realised now that she'd never said it was gone. She just said she'd get rid of it once she landed back in England. And like the idiot I was, I didn't think to check she'd kept her word.

"And you just took her word for it?" Tessa shot back. And when I couldn't answer, she seized a handful of the papers and began tearing them into tiny pieces. She did this over and over again till the room was covered in nothing but shreds of paper. Their words were unreadable now to anyone who'd attempt to read them again.

"I'm such an idiot," she whispered to herself as she stared down at her life in pieces at her feet. "None of this was real. None of it …"

I turned her to face me, cupping her face in both of my hands. She didn't pull away, but her face was full of nothing but hatred. All she saw was my betrayal, my lies and my deceit. She couldn't see me any more. Only an actor, just a liar with class and money.

"It is real, Tess," I said earnestly, leaning closer as she pulled away. "No, no, listen – I fucking love you. I do! Please, I swear to god I never learned anything about you from anyone but you."

"Then why didn't you tell me about this? Why not just tell me what Mia did or even that your mum had an entire Pandora's box dedicated to me?" Her question momentarily stole my voice and her eyes locked on mine. She nodded to herself. "You knew I'd back out the minute I discovered my family had been investigated. I'd have run a mile. You could have me play the perfect girlfriend if I didn't know. You're just as bad as them!"

"I'm not …"

Why didn't I sound confident? Because she was right, in part. I had been scared of what would happen if she knew, so I pretended it hadn't happened. Look where blissful ignorance got me.

"I swear, I never wanted to hurt you," I pleaded with her, but I knew she didn't believe me.

"But you did anyway."

Those four words hurt like a physical punch to the gut. If she was screaming at me or even hitting me, I would see her rage on full display. This, though – her detachment from me – was torture. This ran so deep, she didn't even have the mental strength to lash out.

Her phone chimed a notification and she pulled herself away from me. She checked the screen, her expression blank.

"I've booked an Uber. It's outside," she said shortly, frowning when I caught her eye. "Don't worry, I won't be going to the press. I wouldn't anyway, but your mother made sure of that."

"What's that supposed to mean?" I asked, desperate for Tessa to look at me the way she did only a few hours ago. "What did she say to you? Did she threaten you?"

"Like you care …"

She turned and stormed out, heading downstairs quicker than I expected. I chased after her, catching up as she reached the door. I slammed my palm against the door over her head. Our bodies pressed together. Neither of us moved. Only our slow and shaky breathing broke the silence.

Tessa turned to face me. She didn't push me away or shout. She looked tired, completely broken and defeated.

"Let me go, please ..."

"We can work past this." Tears were pooling in my eyes now. I wasn't trying to reassure her. I was begging her now. Really begging. "I swear I'll never do anything to hurt you like this again. You know this was never staged. I told you that before and I meant it. We love each other. That counts for something. Doesn't it?"

"No," Tessa said with a harsh edge and then everything shattered with her final words. "Because I don't love you any more. Not after this."

My body seemed drained of all strength and I let my arm fall as if it was a ton of bricks. I stepped back, feeling suddenly hollow as her words hit home. I deserved this. I may not have been the author of this chaos ... but I let others take control of it and twist it into something ugly. Now, here was the conclusion. Her eyes stayed on mine. She didn't regret a single word.

"I never want to see you again," she said, choking on her words as she tried to hide the fact she was crying too.

I watched her pull the front door open and slam it behind her, leaving me with nothing but my despair and guilt in her wake.

Everything I'd ever known was built on lies and pretence. Now I'd driven away the one real thing in my life ...

The End... For Now.

About the Author

T.J. Ryan is a Hertfordshire-based Author, Screenwriter, Director, Playwright and Film Reviewer. Having graduated with a First Class in screenwriting in 2018, he has written several scripts for stage and screen.

T.J. Ryan is naturally drawn to writing diverse and complex casts of characters while tackling complicated subject matters with integrity and honesty. His debut novel *Between the Lines* was written during the COVID-19 Pandemic.

For his film work, his directorial debut short film (*Womanhood*) premiered at the Watford Film Festival and was nominated for Best Ensemble Cast at the Prodigy Film Festival in 2019. more recently, one of his feature scripts was a semi-finalist at the SWN Screenplay Competition in 2020.

You can connect with me on:
- https://twitter.com/tjryanwrites
- https://www.facebook.com/tjryanwrites

Printed in Great Britain
by Amazon

20170000R00171